Marrying a Marquess

Widows of Mayfair, Book 3

Christine Donovan

ARE YOU SIGNED UP FOR DRAGONBLADE'S BLOG?

You'll get the latest news and information on exclusive giveaways, exclusive excerpts, coming releases, sales, free books, cover reveals and more.

Check out our complete list of authors, too!

No spam, no junk. That's a promise!

Sign Up Here

www.dragonbladepublishing.com

Dearest Reader;

Thank you for your support of a small press. At Dragonblade Publishing, we strive to bring you the highest quality Historical Romance from some of the best authors in the business. Without your support, there is no 'us', so we sincerely hope you adore these stories and find some new favorite authors along the way.

Happy Reading!

CEO, Dragonblade Publishing

Additional Dragonblade books by Author Christine Donovan

Widows of Mayfair Series

Loving an Earl (Book 1)
Pursuing a Duke (Book 2)
Marrying a Marquess (Book 3)

Dedication

This book is dedicated to my wonderful granddaughters, Olivia Christine, Rory Claire, and Claire Elizabeth. You bring so much joy into my life. Love you to the stars, the moon, and the sun and back!

PROLOGUE

London 1805

"MY MOTHER TOLD me I'm going to marry you when I'm eighteen," Lady Priscilla Amesbury, all of ten years old, tilted her chin in defiance, much like her mother did on occasion. The Earl of Crowley's entire body shuddered. At twenty-four, the thought of marrying some future version of this ten-year-old was inconceivable. At his age, he was the epitome of a rake, and he worked hard to keep his reputation intact.

His nights were spent at his clubs, gambling dens, and private parties full of rakehells and lightskirts. Occasionally, he attended a formal ball or Almack's to appease his mother. Otherwise, he lived for his pleasure only. He did, however, have his standards. He never gambled more than he could afford to lose, and when it came to courtesans, he was very selective.

Feet stomping on the wooden floor of the entry hall pulled him out of his wayward thoughts. "Did you hear what I said?" Lady Priscilla, arms crossed, lips trembling, and pools of tears in her hazel eyes, glared at him.

"I heard every word you said, Priscilla."

"It's Lady Priscilla to you."

He swallowed his chuckle. "Lady Priscilla it is then. I heard what you said. That is still eight years away. Much can happen in that time." He paused and touched his fingertip to her small, pert nose. "You may find a dashing prince to marry and leave me at the altar."

She stomped her booted foot again. "I would never do that to you. I love you, and no prince will change that. I will be your march . . . march . . ."

"Marchioness."

"Yes. That. Mother said I will be that someday when your father is gone."

"Sprite, I'll make a deal with you. If I'm still single at thirty-four and you have no suitors during your first Season, I will marry you if you wish. But anything can happen in those years. You may come to dislike me and prefer someone else. I may marry another lady and have a nursery full of children by then."

"Noooo!" she shrieked, covering her ears with her little hands. "Nooo. Mother said I was to marry you. You can't marry someone else. Motherrrrr!" she screamed as she ran up the stairs to the drawing room.

Nick took that opportunity to slip out the door to his waiting carriage. Several hours at White's was just what he needed to get his mind off his future.

CHAPTER ONE

London 1810

NICK RECEIVED AN invitation to a masquerade ball at the private residence of Mr. and Mrs. Hayward. He wasn't one for masquerades but decided after the day he'd had to send a late reply. The Duchess of Avery, with her daughter, Lady Priscilla, had visited for afternoon tea, and his mother had insisted Nick attend. They had openly discussed his marriage to Lady Priscilla in three years. Three years? That was a lifetime away. Anything could happen during those years. He would not promise or sign any document forming a legal betrothal contract. Both the duchess and his mother were displeased with him.

Lady Priscilla sat quietly and said nothing, which was unlike her. He wondered what she was thinking. At fifteen, he had to admit she was becoming a beautiful young woman. Deep auburn hair framed her classically beautiful face. Large hazel eyes constantly moved around as if every little thing interested her. But would she also become the wife for him?

His carriage pulled up to Hayward House, dressed as a Privateer for the event. He recognized some of the attendees but didn't know many others. He wasn't surprised since he had only a passing acquaintance with Mr. and Mrs. Hayward. After an hour of standing off in a corner sipping sherry, he was approached by a lady dressed as a courtesan, which he thought was quite bold.

"Hello." She curtsied. "I'm Esmeralda, and you are?"

Her voice was soft and seductive, and warmth spread inside his belly. He bowed over her gloved hand, brushing his lips across her delicate fingers. "Captain Burke, at your service." Nick flirted with Esmeralda and she flirted back, seeming to enjoy herself as he drank two glasses of sherry.

"Well, Captain Burke," she said after a while, "there is a small gathering at the home of a friend of mine not far from here. Since this party is quite dull, would you care to accompany me?"

Usually, Nick didn't escort ladies to the homes of people he didn't know, but tonight, he'd had a great deal to drink, including the two sherries with Esmeralda, and was bored out of his mind. "It would be my honor, Esmeralda." He licked his lips. His mouth was suddenly dry as a bone. The room tilted, and his feet refused to move. She wrapped her arm through his, helping him along as they made their way to the entrance and out the door to an unmarked carriage. Once inside, Esmeralda snuggled up against him. The inside of the carriage appeared to be moving in circles around him.

The coach lurched forward, and Nick was nearly unseated, causing him to chuckle. "I must have consumed more sherry than I thought. Please forgive me, my dear, while I rest my eyes."

A few seconds after closing his eyes, he opened them to stop the spinning.

"We have arrived," Esmeralda said softly.

"That was fast. Did I fall asleep?" he asked, as the inside of the carriage still spun in circles.

Esmeralda helped him out of the carriage and inside. She possessed the strength of two gentlemen. They entered the townhouse to laughter and raucous sounds coming from up the stairs. At least, he believed that was where they came from. Esmeralda's arm, wrapped around his waist, led him up the stairs to a drawing room full of people. If he had not been so deep into his cups, making him wonder what was in the sherry, he would have recognized several of the gentlemen present, gentlemen who had questionable reputations amongst the *ton*. As it appeared to him, though, the faces of the room's other occupants were blurry, round orbs without any facial features.

Esmeralda led him to an overstuffed chair and poured him a drink from a sideboard, which he downed in one gulp. He may as well get more foxed because the feel of this place was odd. Even with his impaired vision, he saw the bodies of women and men in various stages of undress. His eyes traveled back to one couple and swore they were both men. Men out in the open? Indeed, he must be seeing things. He closed one eye, trying to focus but to no avail, while his body slumped into the chair. His mouth felt like it was stuffed with cotton, and he licked his lips slowly. The room and all its occupants faded into the background. Had Esmeralda drugged him?

"Captain Burke," she whispered as she straddled his lap. "You have too many clothes on. Let me divest you of your shirt."

Cool air caressed his chest, and he shivered as Esmeralda tossed his shirt onto the floor. In a short span of lucidity, he wrapped his arms around her and kissed her. Their tongues tangled in slow motion. He broke the kiss, licked his dry lips, and tried to say something, but his mouth wouldn't work, and bloody hell, he felt himself go under before he even had time to enjoy having Esmeralda in his arms.

"EARL OF CROWLEY, wake up." Someone was repeatedly shaking his shoulders. Where was he? He vaguely remembered a lady dressed as a courtesan. She had taken him to a private residence. "Esmeralda?"

Several deep chuckles invaded his ears. "If ye want to call me Esmeralda, go right on doing so, but to be honest, my name is Raymond. Esmeralda is my masquerade character."

Nick grabbed the hands as they tried to shake him again and held on tight. His head pounded, and the jarring of his body intensified it. Inhaling several deep breaths, he opened his eyes and took in his surroundings. It was the same room Esmeralda brought him to last night. Several people were asleep on the floor and on the furniture in various stages of undress. All appeared to be men. He looked down at himself and was very glad to see he had his breeches on, even if he was without his shirt. "What the hell is this?" He tried to sound demanding and pompous. He wasn't convinced it worked, as several men nearby laughed.

"Ye are in a den of iniquity for gentlemen and gentlemen only."

He released the man's hands and forced himself to his feet, swaying slightly. He retrieved his shirt from the floor and put it on. "You are mistaken. I was with a woman last night."

The man who said his name was Raymond laughed more, grating on his nerves and exacerbating the ache inside his head and behind his eyes. And lucky him, his stomach joined in the fun.

"Esmeralda is no lady. Now, if ye want to keep this life of yours secret, all I need is five hundred pounds."

Nick considered himself an intelligent person. Yes, he had the reputation of being a rake, which he wouldn't deny, but he had never let his guard down before or been swindled or tricked into something nefarious. Unfortunately, there was a first time for everything. Meeting Esmeralda had been his undoing. No matter what the man—Raymond—said, Esmeralda was a woman. When she'd straddled his lap and he'd pulled her close and kissed her, he had felt the curves of a woman.

It was a trap. These people preyed on rich men who had money to burn and reputations to uphold. Esmeralda must have drugged him. At the masquerade and again here. It left a sour taste in his mouth. Mortification burned his cheeks for falling for her scheme. He had no option but to pay.

But even though he paid, rumors spread rampant in the coming days. The only thing he could do was ignore the whispers and gossip and continue living as he had. Keeping up his reputation would eventually make the rumors disappear.

Except they never really did.

CHAPTER TWO

London 1817

THE FIRST TIME Pricilla heard the rumors about Hollingsworth, she had been eighteen and preparing for her first Season. She'd overheard her mother and Lady Hollingsworth discussing their marriage as usual. Only this time, they questioned their hopes of uniting their two families. That was why she was having a Season instead of marrying Nick. Priscilla didn't completely understand what was happening, and her tender young heart was broken.

She had wanted to marry Nick since she was ten years old. However, he didn't want to marry her. According to him, he regarded her as a sister. It was too bad, because he was the only one with whom she could be her true self. He admired her intelligence and interest in Parliamentary affairs, and she enjoyed their time together. They may not have spent a great deal of time together the past several years, but their friendship had grown even so. It saddened her to think she would marry another man and perhaps never see him again.

As her Season progressed, she noticed that most gentlemen she met cringed when she opened her mouth to discuss a series of subjects. So she had taken to being a giggling fool within the company of the opposite sex. If being intelligent wasn't attractive, perhaps being silly was. So she played at being empty-headed and silly. But it didn't seem to work, because their drawing room had remained empty, to her father, the Duke of Avery's, dismay. But what was she to do to attract a suitor? Her father didn't understand why gentlemen were not barging down their door to court her. She was beautiful, rich, and the daughter of a duke. She was stymied as well as he. The eligible gentlemen of the *ton* disliked intelligent women, and they did not like silly debutantes. What did they want?

She would need to lighten up on the silliness at the next social event and pay attention to other debutants, mimicking how they acted and spoke. Though she disliked pretending to be someone other than her true self to attract a husband. Deception was no way to start a life together. If only Nick would admit they were perfect for each other. His luck in the marriage mart was as grim as hers. Truly, they deserved each other.

For three Seasons, she struggled to make her parents happy by securing a husband. She wasn't all that bad, and her looks were, if not beautiful, at least passable—even pretty. So why did no gentlemen call on her? And it broke her heart when Nick still wouldn't consider her.

It was during this lonely, difficult time of feeling invisible to every person in London that her best friend, Lady Sophia Templeton, who lived in the country with her husband, the Earl of Spencer, introduced her by letter to her cousin, Lieutenant Jasper Montague, a Royal Navy officer and the third son of an earl. They started exchanging letters, and several months later they began meeting secretly when he was in port. She enjoyed being with him. He saw the real person she was and understood her for the most part. When he proposed, she said yes, and they snuck off to Gretna Green, much to her parents' dismay. They never accepted Jasper into the family.

When she returned home after her wedding and Jasper immediately left for his ship, she brought a white kitten, whom she named Snowball, home with her. Snowball was to be her constant companion while waiting for her new husband to return. She was anxious to move out of Avery Manor and start her new life with Jasper. Being his wife didn't seem real with him away.

But three months after their wedding, he died at sea when a French warship attacked his ship. They had had their wedding night together after their nuptials and nothing else. Her mother believed she took to her rooms for so many months because she was heartbroken. Yes, she was heartbroken and devastated, but she hadn't been deeply in love with him. She had liked Jasper very much and was sure she would have come to love him had they had more time together, but she'd never had the chance. That saddened her and caused guilt to eat at her insides. That, more than anything, caused her to withdraw from Society. She had been a failure as a wife. If only she had conceived a child to carry on his name and legacy. He had deserved better.

Though he was not without his own flaws. During their time together, he had admitted to marrying her quickly to get out of an alliance with the daughter of his father's best friend, a young lady he'd abhorred ever since they were children. So his heart was perhaps not engaged as it might have been, either. Still, they got on well together and after his loss, she battled melancholy daily. Jasper should never have died. He was all that was good, brave, and honorable. One such as he should have lived and made his mark on Society.

Time passes, as it always must, and her year of mourning ended, but still she struggled with her marriage and widowhood and, more than anything, Jasper's death. Everything had happened so fast, she felt like an imposter.

"My dear," her mother, the Duchess of Avery, said to her as she entered her chambers one afternoon. "It has been a year since his death. It is high time you reenter Society to find another husband."

Sitting on the chaise longue in her chambers, patting a sleeping Snowball curled up on her lap, Priscilla sighed deeply before replying to her mother's comment. "Why do you never say his name? He had a name, Mother. His name was *Jasper*. Say it!"

Priscilla tried not to feel bad for her mother when she witnessed her eyes close and her face tense.

"Forgive me. It doesn't seem real to me because it happened so quickly, without our approval, and we never had the privilege of meeting him. I sometimes have trouble believing you were married and are now a widow." Her mother sat on the edge of the chaise longue and took one of Priscilla's hands in hers. "I will strive to be more understanding. He died a hero and deserves our respect." She squeezed her hand. "I'm just worried about you. Staying in your room is not healthy. You need fresh air and friends surrounding you. You don't want to hear this, but it is time to enter Society, and I have taken the liberty of arranging it. Tomorrow night, you will attend a ball with your father and me at the Earl and Countess of Langford's. It is the first event they have hosted since their marriage last year. She also belongs to the Ladies' Society of Mayfair, which I have urged you to join. Perhaps you and the countess will become friends since she is close to your age. We will not take no for an answer."

"I have nothing to wear." Several of her favorite dresses and gowns had been dyed black for mourning. And the rest didn't fit her as she'd lost weight since Jasper's death.

"I have taken care of everything. Madam Serena will arrive soon for a fitting with a bevy of dresses and ballgowns she made for you in the current fashion and colors. I gave her carte blanche, for she knows what you like."

"Mother." Bees swarmed her stomach. Priscilla was afraid she wasn't ready to enjoy herself, dance, and converse with gentlemen. Some would be the same men who had disliked her during her first Season, and she didn't relish going through their rejection again.

She understood she was expected to marry and have children, but couldn't she accomplish that without entering London Society? The thought of being held in another man's arms had the bees stinging her. Would Jasper think she was betraying him? How did young widows, such as herself, move on without guilt eating at their insides? Perhaps becoming friends with the Countess of Langford would help her. After all, she had been a widow before she married the current Earl of Langford. "Fine. I will attend. But I should warn you that my days of being silly and giggling like a fool are over. This time I'm being myself, and if I attract no suitors, so be it. I'll not be anything but myself this time around."

Mother rose from the chaise longue, leaned down, and kissed her cheek. "Be yourself, and thank you. I know you won't regret this." As she walked away, her skirts swaying, she said, "Who knows, you might meet your future husband tomorrow night."

Priscilla leaned back on the chaise and sighed. Perhaps, but she somehow doubted that.

NICK WAS THIRTY-SIX. How had he become that age with nothing to show for it except the title of marquess after his father passed several years ago? He had no wife and no prospects in sight. No son to inherit when he died. If God forbid, he died soon, his sniveling cousin would inherit, and Nick knew his father would be waiting in Heaven to kick his arse for not protecting his legacy. And that was the reason he dressed for the Langfords' ball.

When the invitation came a fortnight ago, he hadn't been shocked, but some people would. Before Langford married his countess—nearly two years ago now—Nick had courted her and proposed marriage, even knowing Langford wanted her for himself. Lilly, Lady Langford, refused, and she was smart to do so, as Nick had only used her to irrevocably get out of marrying Lady Priscilla. Which, in hindsight, had been daft on his part. If he had simply married Priscilla then, he would not now be in this predicament of having mothers and daughters avoiding him because of those infernal rumors that wouldn't go away. In fact, they had gotten worse, and he wondered who the culprit was spreading them anew.

The last thing he wanted was to attend the ball and be given the cut direct for something that had never happened. If only he could find the woman who had called herself Esmeralda that fateful night and force her to tell the truth and free him from the noose around his neck. He was tired of the whispers and sly looks. They were worse than when the event happened. There was a real possibility he would never find Esmeralda since he'd been looking for so long already with no luck. Hadn't he paid enough over the years for being stupid? Wasn't it time good things happened to him? He'd learned from his mistake, never taking his status as a marquess for granted. He understood how fortunate he was to have been born into privilege.

Thankfully, he had a handful of friends who either didn't believe the rumors or didn't care. It was a small circle, but they were good friends: the Earl and Countess of Langford, the Duke and Duchess of Blackstone, Mr. James Caldwell and his wife, Lady Beatrice Caldwell. They were new friendships, to be sure, and it was pure luck that they had become so, but one would think that he could find a bride with them vouching for him.

His carriage moved slowly as it approached Langford House. He exited the carriage and joined the receiving line, where Edmund and Lilly greeted their guests. They presented as the perfect, loving couple, and he felt a twinge of jealousy for what they shared. He wanted what they had, even though he doubted it was in his future. At this point, he would settle for any wife if she would have him.

"Lady Langford," he said with a genuine smile as he bowed over her hand. "You look enchanting this evening."

"Hollingsworth," she giggled. "Smooth tongued as always. I'm so glad you could attend."

"As am I." He turned and bowed to Langford. "Langford, you are a lucky man."

He grinned at him, and there was not even a hint of lingering animosity for things that had transpired in their past. They were indeed friends. "Thank you. I know it." He lowered his voice and whispered. "You are the only one left who hasn't found a bride. Perhaps tonight will be your night."

Nick swallowed his laughter. "Perhaps. But don't hold your breath."

The Master of Ceremonies announced his name as he entered the ballroom. Many eyes landed on him, and several ladies whispered behind their fans. He had gotten good at pretending nothing bothered him, and he did so now even though his stomach knotted up tight. Strolling around the outskirts of the ballroom, he made his way toward the Duke and Duchess of Blackstone, as well as James Caldwell and Lady Beatrice, who was the daughter of the Earl and Countess of Hartford. They were all smiles when he approached them.

Once the required formalities were over, they broke out into informal conversation. "I have not seen you in some time, Hollingsworth," said Emmeline, Duchess of Blackstone. "Where have you been hiding and why? Please don't tell me the whispers and rumors are bothering you after all this time?"

"I've not been hiding if that's what you think. I spent some time at my country seat." He nodded his head. "But thank you, Duchess, for your concern."

"I believe I spoke for all of us present."

"Don't feel bad for me. It's my fault I'm unmarried." He could've married Lady Priscilla years ago when she made her come out. Something he'd come to regret. He nodded his head again. "Please excuse me." He sighed as he walked away. He did not like the person he had become of late. He'd never let the gossip bother him before, so why now? And his friends were only trying to help him, and he walked away? He could kick himself for letting his pride get in the way. He deserved to stay at his country estate, wasting away until old age claimed him.

A lady's laughter and voice traveled his way, and he froze in his steps, his ears straining to hear. He hadn't heard that melodious voice in a long time but would never forget the sound of it. He pivoted around, heading toward the voice of the lady he knew as Esmeralda. Her height and overall figure remained the same as he remembered. She stood with Viscount Norton, an elderly man Nick was surprised to find still living. He had to be seventy if a day.

He approached, bowed, and said, "Viscount Norton, I haven't seen you in ages. I'm glad to see you hale and hearty."

Norton chuckled. "Crowley . . . no, you are Hollingsworth now. You always were a rambunctious fellow. Your father could never rein you in. I'm not surprised to hear you are still single."

Nick winced at the look Norton sent him. "Don't believe everything you hear in the gossip rags. I don't believe I've had the pleasure of meeting this lovely lady on your arm."

"Forgive me," he said. "Emma, my dear, may I present the Marquess of Hollingsworth. Hollingsworth, this is my lovely wife, the Viscountess Norton."

Nick's chin almost dropped at Norton's words. How in bloody hell had Esmeralda—no, Emma—managed to go from swindling men for money to marrying a viscount? Perhaps she had tricked him, too, and he had offered to marry her and save her from the streets?

Nick bowed over her hand, never taking his eyes off her deep blue ones, which had haunted his nightmares for years and ones he would never mistake for another. After all these years, he'd finally found her. He tamped down his excitement. He needed to play his cards right. If he didn't, things could go to hell. So, for now, he'd pretend they'd never met. "Viscountess," he drawled. "It is a pleasure to make your acquaintance. If Norton doesn't mind, perhaps you could save a dance for me."

"I don't mind at all," Norton said. "My wife loves to dance, and my rheumatism does not allow my legs to move as they once did."

Nick bowed over the viscountess's hand again, looking for any sign that she recognized him. "Until then." It took all his willpower to walk away nonchalantly and not jump up and down in jubilation. Instead, he meandered to the back of the ballroom, where the wallflowers and their mothers stood or sat. He nodded to them, and they looked away. Even the wallflowers were too good for him. Christ, what had this courting world of the aristocracy become when a marquess got the cut direct from wallflowers?

Stepping out of the double glass doors onto the veranda, where several other people milled around, he put his hands on the railing. He inhaled the scent of the clear night air, trying to slow his heart down. Ever since he heard her voice, it'd been beating triple the regular pace.

"Good evening, Hollingsworth."

Another voice he recognized. He turned around and bowed. "Lady Priscilla." His eyes took her in. It was the first time he'd seen her without mourning clothes in the past year. His pulse jumped at the pretty picture she presented, dressed in a lovely green ballgown accentuating the green in her hazel eyes. She was still tall and willowy as she had been as a child, but her chest had filled out nicely.

"Stop staring at me."

He couldn't help it, he chuckled. "Forgive me. I'm used to seeing you in mourning. Black was fine, but this shade of green has your hazel eyes looking emerald green. It is most becoming, and you look beautiful."

She swatted his shoulder with her closed fan, not caring if anyone saw. He liked that about her. "Stop it. I'm hardly beautiful. And don't pretend you think I am."

Her words brought a frown to his face, and his heart pained. "I'm sorry if I ever made you feel anything less than beautiful, because you are. Beautiful, that is."

"Nonsense, Nick. Stop playing with me." She went to the railing and stood beside him, her gloved hand close to his on the railing, looking out into the lighted gardens beyond.

"You are beautiful, but that's beside the point. What did your parents say to get you out of mourning?"

She exhaled. "That it is time I marry again."

He hmphed. "So we are both still seeking to marry. You for a second time, me for the first." He paused and moved his hand on top of her. "We could marry each other and make my mother and your parents happy."

"I think they gave up on us marrying a long time ago." She tugged her hand from his. "What with the rumors and all."

Was he forever going to have to deal with that one night? "We never discussed it, but you and I know they are untrue. I can't believe the rumors still exist with my roguish ways and numerous mistresses over the years."

It was slight—he would have missed it if he hadn't been studying her overly intently—but her features tightened, and at the same time, her spine stiffened. But why? Was she bothered by the rumors or by his admitted roguish ways? Or perhaps because he'd had mistresses? Although not any longer.

"Someone is purposely spreading them again. I'm sorry for that," she said softly. "If what they say is true, I don't think less of you because of it."

His mouth refused to form words. True? She believed it was true? Inhaling and exhaling several times, he managed to get his mouth to form words. "It is not true. I was drugged by a woman who called herself Esmeralda at a masquerade party and brought to a home I didn't recognize. I was blackmailed, and I paid the sum they asked to keep it quiet. It was a trap. Nothing happened."

A gasp escaped her lips. "Why have you never said anything? Never stood up to the gossipmongers to expunge the rumor? Never proven it a lie? Why have you never done anything?" Her exasperation shocked him.

"I thought it would go away if I ignored it. That another scandal would come along and mine would be forgotten. I didn't think it would still haunt me years later. But I've been searching for Esmeralda for those years, and I finally found her." He didn't bother hiding his excitement. "She is here tonight. I recognized her voice and her eyes. I've never seen eyes like hers. They are a deep blue, so deep they appear nearly black. There is no mistaking I've finally found her."

"Who is she?"

"What I'm telling you is in confidence. Don't repeat it. I don't want her to know I recognized her. Promise me."

"I promise."

"She is the Viscountess Norton."

Priscilla gasped again. "She is married to old man Norton?"

"Yes. I wonder if she schemed him, too."

"If she did, why would he marry her?"

"To save her?" He waved his arms out. "Who knows? All I know is that I will get her to fix this mess. The whispers never bothered me before, but bloody hell, I need a bride, and I can't even get a woman to speak to me. Even the wallflowers snubbed me tonight."

Soft giggles came his way, and he turned to her. "It's not funny. It's humiliating. Marry me, Priscilla, please?"

CHAPTER THREE

PRISCILLA'S HEART STOPPED. Four years ago, when she'd just turned eighteen, she would have given anything to hear Nick say those words. She would have melted into a puddle at his feet. But he had done everything to avoid the betrothal their families wanted. During those years, she'd hidden her hurt and broken heart from him and her parents. She had gotten good at pretending. And she would need to keep on pretending.

"You know you don't mean that. You have made it abundantly clear in the past that you never wanted to marry me. So stand up straight, hold your head high, and find a wife. There must be someone willing to marry you."

His groan hit her ears, and she refused to feel sorry for him. She would admit she'd felt puppy love for him as a child, which had turned into a young lady's blossoming love when she was sixteen. But when she married Jasper at twenty-one, she had buried that love for Nick and threw away the key. She could not revisit that locked-away heart. He would only break it again. Even if he married her, she didn't believe he could be faithful, and that in itself would utterly destroy her. It was better never to have than to have and lose.

"You know many people. Approach someone with a marriage-aged daughter and offer for her. Instead of collecting a dowry, pay the father. I've heard it's done. There must be someone in the *ton* with a daughter desperate for funds. Ask your friends for help. Wouldn't a duke know everything and everyone's personal business?"

His chuckle surprised her. "I highly doubt Blackstone knows all. Perhaps there is a man in his employ who has a daughter who would like to marry me for my title. He does employ past naval officers to captain his ships. Splendid idea. I'll look into it."

"Yes. Splendid idea." She tried to make her voice sound excited but knew she failed. "Please keep me informed."

"I will," he said. "Now." He bowed. "If you'll excuse me, I have a dance to collect from my nemesis."

Priscilla's eyes followed Nick until he was swallowed up by the crush of bodies inside the large ballroom. It took several minutes before her heart returned to normal, but her breathing had yet to. He asked her to marry him just now. Why didn't she say yes?

"Lady Priscilla," said Baron Latham as he approached her and bowed. "What a pleasant surprise to find you in attendance tonight."

She curtsied. "Latham. It is nice to see you." The baron was the older brother to Mr. James Caldwell, who owned Mayfair Imports and Exports with Blackstone and Langford. The baron was known for overindulging in spirits, gambling, and courtesans. However, rumor had it that he had mended his ways. Priscilla wasn't foolish enough to think he sought out her company because he was interested in her. He certainly hadn't been interested in her when she first came out. If he had any interest now, it was in her dowry—intact because her father never paid it to Jasper. Not that Jasper had cared or had time to care. She also received a small pension from the government for Jasper's ultimate sacrifice.

"I was wondering if I could call on you tomorrow?" Latham said, blushing. Priscilla could not believe her eyes. The baron blushed. The poor man had probably never paid homage to a lady of good breeding, and she felt sorry for him. "That would be lovely." She curtsied. "I look forward to your visit on the morrow." It was a lie, but it would appease her mother.

He bowed. "Until tomorrow."

They walked through the double doors into the ballroom together, but Latham then headed to the exit. She inhaled the scent of warm, sweaty bodies, and she covered up a sneeze. Her eyes strayed to the ballroom floor as the first strings of a waltz began to play. It only took her a moment to find Nick escorting a beautiful, dark-haired lady, and Priscilla ignored the tumbling of her heart.

BEFORE SOME OTHER man could claim the next dance from Viscountess Norton, Nick made his way across the room, bowed before her, and held out his hand. "I believe this dance belongs to me." He couldn't help the devious smile that curled his lips as he heard the opening notes of a waltz.

"Why yes," she curtsied. "I believe it does."

Nick led her onto the ballroom floor, placed his hands in the correct positions, and danced her around the room. "I have been looking for you for several years now. Where have you been?" He tightened his grip on her just in case she thought to flee. But he knew she recognized him—her feet paused during the dance briefly before she realized she was giving herself away by her reaction. Her body beneath his hands tensed, and her smile faltered. And still, she was utterly beautiful. No wonder she had been so good at deceiving him into following her that night.

"I don't know what you mean, Hollingsworth. We have never met until this evening."

"Come now, Esmeralda, don't play coy with me. I will never forget your sultry voice or your blue eyes. Please tell me how you came to be married to Norton. Surely you did not drug him also?"

"Please loosen your hold."

It was then that Nick realized he had gripped her waist and hand tightly, and he relaxed his hold. "Don't lie to me. I want the truth, and I want it now."

"There is not enough time. Meet me in the library when the dance is over."

Nick started to laugh, then stopped as he attracted unwanted attention from the other dancers. "I will not fall for one of your nefarious schemes again. Once was more than enough to ruin my chances at marriage."

She huffed. "Fine. It was me. I was desperate after my father died and my protector let me go. I met two men who offered me easy work, and I took it."

He studied her eyes, looking for lies.

"I only did it a few times before I met Norton. And to answer your question, no, I didn't drug him. However, he discovered what I was doing and offered to marry me. What can I say? He was lonely and wanted someone to keep him company in his advanced years, and I needed a husband and money."

"You need to start a new rumor about how you saw someone pour something into my drink at the masquerade ball. Prove that I was drugged."

Her eyes widened in shock. "Why would I do that?"

He leaned close to her ear and whispered. "Because if you do not, I will expose you for who and what you are. Even marrying a viscount will not keep you from being ostracized from Society once they know of your criminal past."

The music ended. Emma curtsied and hurried away from him to her husband. Nick took a deep breath, hoping his future would improve now that he had finally found the woman who called herself Esmeralda.

"HE RECOGNIZED ME," Emma whispered to her husband when she

arrived at his side after waltzing with Hollingsworth.

"There is no need to fret, my dear." Norton patted her hand. "You are my wife now. I will protect you from Hollingsworth. Besides, he is not the sort of gentleman to cause trouble. He is hoping to discredit the rumors, not add to them. Rest assured, all will be well."

THE FOLLOWING MORNING, Nick had a bouquet of hothouse roses delivered to Priscilla. He planned to pay a morning call—he had a favor to ask. An idea had hit him last night as he'd paced around his chambers in the dark, too full of energy to sleep. Since she refused to even consider marrying him, perhaps she would agree to a fake courtship. Between that and the viscountess coming to his rescue about the old rumors, he hoped that his chances of finding a wife would increase. It was all he could hope for at this moment.

PRISCILLA SAT IN the drawing room with her mother, awaiting a visit from Baron Latham. That morning, he'd sent her a lovely bouquet of wildflowers. Nick had also sent her roses, and she couldn't wait to discover why. Was she to expect him to visit? She blew into her steaming cup of tea.

A footman entered the room and announced, "Baron Latham."

Once pleasantries were finished, Priscilla said, "Please have a seat, Latham." She gestured to a chair facing the settee she and her mother occupied.

"Thank you," he said as he gripped his hat in his hands. "Have you ventured outside today? It is quite warm and sunny."

A conversation about the weather. How original. She fought

not to roll her eyes. She had forgotten how she disliked drawing room chatter, the few times she'd had callers to chatter with. "Yes, I rode in the park on my mare, Princess, this morning. It was restorative after the late night at the Langfords' ball."

His fingers tugged on his cravat. Perhaps his valet had tied it too tight. She felt for the man. Priscilla hated anything around her neck, tight or not. Fortunately for her, today's fashion styles favored low necklines, and she could breathe easy most days.

"May I pour you tea, Latham?"

"Yes, please."

The same footman entered. "The Marquess of Hollingsworth."

Once again, the required etiquette was followed. Nick took the seat beside Latham and grinned a questionable grin at her. No doubt he was wondering what the baron was doing here. Did it bother her that the baron was almost certainly after her money? A little. Though she could do much worse as potential suitors or husbands went. Latham had dark-brown hair and eyes, and he was handsome. Instead of him, she could be facing a pockmarked, hunched-over man well past his prime. Thank goodness she wasn't. Since she was a widow, she didn't believe her father could try to force her to marry as he might have done when she'd been a debutante—if she hadn't eloped. All in all, Latham seemed affable enough to warrant considering him as a suitor, provided he had truly mended his ways.

"What a nice surprise to have a visit from you, Nicholas," her mother said with a sly smile aimed at her. "Is your mother well?"

"Mother is well. She sends her best."

"Please give her mine."

"Thank you both for the flowers you sent. My chambers smell divine," Priscilla said as she glanced from one gentleman to the other. Neither appeared happy to be sharing her attention.

After a reasonable amount of time for a call, the baron left, and her mother disappeared, leaving her alone with Nick. "So tell me why you are here."

She was met with laughter but refused to feel anything from it or acknowledge how the sound heated her insides and made her heart sing.

"I have come to beg a favor," he finally said most seriously.

"Go on."

"I was hoping to form a fake courtship with you to spike interest amongst the single ladies seeking husbands this Season. Perhaps if you take an outward interest in me, others will also. That way they won't see me as a pariah or a degenerate."

She had been about to pick up the teapot and pour more tea into her china cup. It was a good thing she'd hesitated, otherwise the teapot would have slipped from her fingers and smashed onto the tray. Never had she expected those words to come from him.

"A fake courtship? I see how it will benefit you. For me, it will turn gentlemen away who may be interested in courting me. They may not want to bother themselves with competition."

"Have you had many gentlemen interested in courting you?" he asked with a knowing but sad look.

"You know I haven't," she huffed.

"Why was Latham here? The man is not worthy of you."

"I heard he has mended his ways and is actively seeking a bride." Not that she was in any way hoping to be his bride.

Nick snorted quite theatrically. "Money. He is seeking a *wealthy* bride. And besides, he has spent his life on the fringes of Society and in bed with lightskirts who have pleasured him. He wouldn't know to satisfy his wife in the bedchamber."

Priscilla felt her entire body burn. Never had Nick ever spoken to her in such a way, crudely and without regard to shocking her. She was no blushing virgin, but still. "Why are you being vulgar? I'm not one of your friends sitting around White's drinking and discussing lightskirts. How dare you?" Her voice trembled, and her entire body shook.

"Forgive me. My behavior was uncalled for. I just wanted you to understand what Baron Latham is like." He waved an arm. "But as you say, perhaps he is a changed man." He rose from his chair and sat beside her, taking her hands.

"I'm sorry." She shook her head. "But I can't agree to a fake courtship. I have agreed to allow Latham to court me, and that wouldn't be proper."

He released her hand and stood. "I understand."

He left without another word—no bow, no goodbye, nothing. She flopped against the back of the settee and berated herself. Latham never asked to court her; she'd lied. Had she really stooped so low as to try and make Nick jealous? When would she learn he was indifferent to her? As far as him asking her to marry him, she knew he truly didn't mean it. And she couldn't marry Nick unless he declared himself properly.

A footman entered the room. "A note for you, my lady."

Priscilla studied the missive and recognized the Blackstone seal. She broke the wax, unfolded the parchment, and read the message.

Dear Lady Priscilla,

The Countess of Langford and I were speaking last night, and we wondered if you would like to join us at the Duchess of Greenville's townhouse tomorrow for a meeting of the Ladies' Society of Mayfair. We are a charitable organization that provides food, clothing, and medicine, and sometimes a place to stay for the needy. We would love to have you join us. The meeting is at ten in the morning. Unless I hear from you, my carriage will arrive a quarter of an hour before ten.

Your friend,
Emmeline Blackstone

She placed the letter on the settee beside her. She recognized the name of the charity as the one her mother had spoken of. Perhaps it was time to give back to the less fortunate. And she looked forward to spending time with the Duchess of Blackstone and the Countess of Langford. They had both been young widows, perhaps they had some words of wisdom to share with her.

Priscilla was so thankful they were staying in that night, especially with her new plans for the next morning, and she retreated to her chambers directly after dinner and went to bed early.

She awoke in the middle of the night and couldn't sleep. Her entire being was unsettled. Her mind kept picturing scenarios involving Latham and Nick. The ones featuring Latham were quite ordinary. Dancing, walking in beautiful gardens, and attending the opera. In every incident, he was a true gentleman. Perhaps Nick was wrong about him. However, she did notice during the two times she'd conversed with him that he didn't appear too intelligent. Could she marry a man who was not her intellectual equal? *Why not? Everyone else did.*

Nick, on the other hand, taunted and shocked her at every turn, even in her imagination. Suddenly, he'd become someone she didn't know at all. Where had the perfect gentleman gone? Every time his face flashed in her head, she saw him stretched out on her bed, on his side, clothed in his breeches and nothing else. He had a sly grin and a naughty twinkle in his molten brown eyes. She kicked off the covers as her entire body became flushed. She also had the urge to touch herself down there. She groaned and rolled onto her stomach. Why, oh, why did Nick still haunt her? She had to get control of herself where he was concerned.

MORNING CAME TOO soon as Priscilla's maid, Eugenia, entered the room with a breakfast tray and flung open the curtains covering the two windows that faced the street. "Good morning, my lady. I've brought you a breakfast tray. If you don't need anything else, I will return shortly to prepare you for your outing."

"Nothing else, Eugenia. Thank you."

She bobbed a curtsy. "Yes, my lady."

Nudging Snowball off her bed before the cat licked her food, Priscilla swiped a triangular piece of toast covered with jam off the tray and stuffed nearly the whole thing into her mouth. She was so starved. Thank goodness no one was there to witness her ill manners. When she had finished her breakfast and drunk the last drop of her hot chocolate, she stood at a window and watched several neighbors come and go. Where did they go at such an early hour?

Eugenia returned and helped her dress in a dark-green linen day dress with matching pelisse, bonnet, and gloves. Then she descended two flights of stairs and greeted her butler in the entry hall. "Good morning, Berkley. I'll wait outside for the Duchess of Blackstone to arrive."

He opened the door and bowed. "Good day, my lady."

Standing on the top step, she tipped her face to the partly cloudy sky and closed her eyes. If her mother saw her, she would admonish her for turning her face into what sunshine there was. But Priscilla was past the time that she worried about freckles. She had yet to see any on her unblemished face, and if she had any, she wouldn't care. The sound of horses' hooves and carriage wheels stopping in front of her made her open her eyes to see a sleek, black carriage with a matching set of four and the Blackstone crest on the door.

One of the footmen standing on the back of the coach climbed down, opened the door, and let down the steps. "My lady," he said, holding his hand to assist her. Inside sat Lady Langford and the Duchess of Blackstone facing front so she sat facing backward.

"Priscilla, may I call you Priscilla?" the duchess asked with a friendly smile. At close to thirty, she still looked youthful. Her dark-as-night hair was striking against her pale-blue eyes.

"Yes, please do."

"Thank you. Please call me Emmeline in private or within our circle of friends."

Priscilla wondered if she would ever find herself within their circle of friends outside of attending Ladies' Society of Mayfair meetings. "Thank you, Emmeline."

"And please call me Lilly," the Countess of Langford said.

"Only if you call me Priscilla, too." She knew Lilly had been widowed at the age of eighteen. She had been married to the previous Earl of Langford, an older gentleman, then after he'd died, she fell in love with his heir, Edmund Weston, the present Earl of Langford. Quite confusing. Except for Lilly, whose title hadn't changed from one husband to the next. As best as Priscilla could tell, she was twenty years of age, two years younger than her. Her blonde hair was thick and wavy, and the green of her eyes resembled emeralds.

"We are so glad you decided to join us," Lilly said as the carriage stopped several streets from Priscilla's home.

When the butler opened the door to the house they'd come to, the Duchess of Greenville greeted Emmeline and Lilly by their first names. When she saw her, she smiled and took her hand. "Welcome, Priscilla. May I call you Priscilla?"

"Yes," she replied as she went to curtsy.

"None of those formalities at these meetings. I only ask that you call me Duchess."

Her body stopped mid-curtsy. "Duchess. I'm honored to be asked to join your charity. My mother speaks so highly about it."

"Yes. Your dear mother is very generous with her monthly donation. I've yet to convince her to attend a meeting, though. Perhaps you will encourage her to accompany you next time."

"I will ask her." Inside the large drawing room were about twenty ladies doing different tasks. Most were familiar to Priscilla. However, there were one or two she didn't recognize. Everyone appeared cheerful and happy to be giving of their time. It wasn't long before Priscilla relaxed and, following the lead of Emmeline and Lilly, began grabbing items and filling bags and baskets with various items. They were to be given to needy families later in the week.

When it was time to leave, her back may have been sore from all the lifting and bending, but her heart was full, knowing what she had done this morning would make a difference in someone's life. Feed a small child, a starving mother, or an infant. Give a husband peace of mind that when he went to work, his family would have food and medicine while he was gone. Or perhaps there was no husband—a mother with children to feed, house, and clothe with no coin to pay for it.

When the carriage pulled up to Avery Manor, Emmeline asked, "What did you think?"

"I think I would like to attend the next meeting. It felt good to do something to help others less fortunate. I believe most members of the *ton* live their daily lives without regard for the suffering of those around them. I was one of them. Not anymore."

"It does feel good to help," Lilly remarked. "Growing up as the vicar's daughter, I helped the villagers in all capacities. And I'm glad to be giving back again. Will we see you tomorrow night at the Trowbridge musicale?"

"Yes."

CHAPTER FOUR

PRISCILLA'S MOTHER ACCOMPANIED her to the Trowbridge musicale, where she knew Nick and Baron Latham would also be attending. Her stomach fluttered at the thought of seeing Nick again, which was foolish.

As for Latham, perhaps she would give him a chance if he did ask to court her, which he still hadn't yet. Ordinarily, potential suitors would request permission from her father, but since she was married before, it was no longer a prerequisite unless they wanted to. But her marriage to Jasper was so short that she had never felt like a wife. Tears threatened to escape her eyes, and she used her gloved fingers to stop them from falling down her cheeks.

"Why are you teary-eyed, my dear?" her mother asked with a worried frown.

"I was thinking about how I'm not your typical widow. Jasper and I never set up a residence or lived together. The only time we shared a bed was on our wedding night. I feel like a fraud. I more closely resemble an unmarried lady than a widow. I have no experience in what married life entails. My heart hurts that Jasper and I were cheated of a life together."

Her mother leaned forward and touched her hands. "I can't begin to understand your loss, but I'm here for you. When you marry again, you don't need to worry about running a household immediately. Whomever you marry will have household servants to handle everything. Your father and I have brought you up as a lady, and I believe a lady can do almost anything. Have faith in yourself. As for Latham, Nicholas, or some other gentleman, choose the one which suits you best. I know I've shown favoritism for Nicholas, but don't let it sway you. After Jasper died and you stayed in your chambers, I worried for you, your health, and your future. All I want is for you to marry well and be happy."

"I know, Mother, and I appreciate your concern for me."

The carriage came to a stop, the door opened, and the stairs were dropped down. The footman helped her mother and then her out of the coach in front of a lovely townhouse in Grosvenor Square. The Earl of Trowbridge had three musically accomplished daughters—or so Priscilla had been told. She would only believe it when she'd heard the girls play.

Her mother saw several of her friends and parted ways with her, leaving Priscilla standing in the aisle between several rows of chairs, wondering where she should sit. Lilly waved at her, which caught her eye, and she waved back. Several unoccupied chairs were near her, Emmeline, Blackstone, and Langford. Making her way toward them, she sat beside Lilly and whispered, "Thank you for noticing me. My mother left me alone, and I didn't know where to sit."

"I'm so glad you joined us." She put her hand on her husband's arm. "Edmund, you remember Lady Priscilla?"

"Yes. It is nice to see you," he said as he dipped his head.

"It's good to see you also, Lord Langford."

Emmeline and her husband had a hushed conversation going on. Priscilla would acknowledge them when the performance ended.

Three young ladies stood in the front of the room, and Priscilla hid her shock when she realized they were triplets. All three girls looked exactly the same, perhaps around sixteen years old. One had a violin, one sat at a pianoforte, and one stood off to the side—the one with the voice.

Nick slid into the vacant seat beside her as they began to play a lively tune. "Fancy meeting you here," he whispered.

Leaning close to him, she whispered back, "You knew I was attending."

"So I did. Quiet now, it is beginning."

Priscilla leaned back into the hard chair and sighed. As far as musicales went, and honestly, she'd only attended a few, this was one of the best. The sisters were good. There were only a few missed notes on the instruments and forgotten words during the singing. Not that Priscilla was judging them. She wasn't all that musical herself. Her pianoforte was passable at best, to her parents' dismay.

"Well, that was fun," Nick said after the music was done, and he stood, his arm out. "May I escort you to the refreshments?"

She placed her hand on his arm and saw Latham sitting with his brother, James Caldwell, and his wife across the aisle and back several rows. The baron watched her intently. Their eyes connected, and he smiled at her, making her think he was very handsome when his features were relaxed. Not as handsome as Nick, but who was? The man was an anomaly.

"Who has caught your attention?" he asked as his eyes followed hers. "Oh. Latham. Do you really believe he would make a decent husband? I'll give him points for being handsome. His clothing is impeccable, although a little dandified for my taste. But to each his own."

"Stop it. You are being rude. I never said anything about marrying him. And how would you like it if people gossiped about you behind your back?" The moment she voiced the words out loud, she wished she could take them back. If anyone knew how it felt to be talked about negatively, it was Nick.

His body tensed. "That is not amusing."

"Apologies, Nick."

"Apology accepted." He hit her with a tight grin. "About those refreshments. Shall we?"

"Yes." And they could not come too soon as her tangled-up

tongue was parched. Making their way through the crowd, they entered what appeared to be a small ballroom, where an orchestra was tuning their instruments. "I didn't know there would be dancing."

"Me either. This is quite a nice change."

Long tables with drinks and platters of foods were set up off to the side of the ballroom. Nick filled a plate with two of everything while Priscilla took two glasses of punch. They returned to the music room, which had already been transformed into a large receiving room full of tables, chairs, and settees.

Nick gestured toward a small table with two chairs. "Over there is perfect."

She knew it was perfect for Nick because no one else could join them, and he would have her all to himself.

"Have you given any more thought to our fake courtship?" he asked while stuffing a small confection into his mouth.

"You are not going to let this go, are you?"

"No. I wouldn't ask again if I weren't desperate. You are my friend and I'm asking a favor from my friend." His eyes widened, pleading with her. "If you do this, I will owe you a favor. Whatever you need, I'll do it."

If she didn't agree to this she was beginning to be afraid he would simply hound her until she gave in. She may as well get it over with. "I will agree if you allow me to court Baron Latham simultaneously. He interests me. This can't be all about you." Nick was good at hiding his emotions, and right now was no exception, except for the little tic in his right eye. When she was a young girl and pouted and yelled about marrying him when she grew up, she'd noticed the tic. She couldn't be the only one who had. She wondered how many card games he lost because of it.

"You know that it is highly unusual for a lady to simultaneously court two gentlemen."

"No, it is not. Debutantes have a slew of gentlemen calling on them on any given day."

"Perhaps, but that is different than taking them for rides in the park and escorting them to the theatre or opera."

"I disagree. Besides, I'm a widow, so I will do as I please. And it pleases me to have you and Latham both courting me. Since your courtship is technically false, what difference does it make? You aren't competing with the baron for my affections, so it shouldn't matter. You would only be courting me so that other eligible ladies will look past the rumors and see the deathly handsome and debonair gentleman you are. In no time, you will be swarmed by ladies, like bees to a hive. Our so-called courtship will end, and you will have your pick of any number of ladies to marry."

"Go on." He grinned and wiggled his brows.

She rolled her eyes. "So many young ladies will be chasing you that you will beg them to leave you alone," she said drily.

He cocked a brow. "I highly doubt it." He leaned forward. "Don't look now, but Latham is coming this way."

"Indeed." Drat, but she felt her cheeks heat. And it didn't go unnoticed by Nick. And drat him as well.

"Good evening, Hollingsworth, Lady Priscilla," Latham said with a perfectly turned-out bow.

Without appearing obvious, Priscilla tilted her head to the side, hoping Nick took the hint and left. After several times, his eyes widened, then narrowed, and he frowned. However, he did stand.

"If you will both excuse me, I feel the need for fresh air." He bowed to Priscilla and winked.

"May I join you?" Latham asked while balancing a plate and cup of punch in one hand.

"Yes, please do."

He sighed once he was settled, with his cloth napkin draped across his lap on his dark-gray breeches. "I never thought Hollingsworth would leave. I've been staring at him for five minutes from across the room."

She almost laughed out loud at his admission. "He finally did. Don't be too hard on him, as he asked me today if he could court me."

The baron's sad, blue eyes met hers. "I'm sorry to hear this. I was hoping to court you myself. I planned on asking you this afternoon, but he arrived before I could do so."

"I can court you both if that is acceptable to you. How am I supposed to know which of you suits me better if I can't spend time with you both?" How her mouth spilled lies so easily these days.

The sadness disappeared from his eyes and was replaced with hope and a little bit of uncertainty. "You have known Hollingsworth your entire life. How are you not certain if you suit one other by now?"

Her stomach dropped. He had her there. "To be honest, until recently, he has never bothered much with me. I may have known him as a child but not enough as a grown woman. Not as a widow." He pulled at his cravat. It was either too tight again or something Latham did when he was nervous. She would bet on nervousness. "Perhaps you can start by telling me why you have set your sights on me?"

His fingers tugged at his cravat again. His eyes darted around the room, and she felt he was seeking a savior. He raised his napkin to his mouth and cleared his throat. "To be honest, I am thirty-one years old, and I have never spent any quality time with a lady. I'm sure you've been told about me by Hollingsworth. I've worked hard recently to redeem myself in the eyes of the *ton*. I no longer gamble or drink hard liquor. I do partake in a glass of wine now and then with dinner. I'm spending time with my property managers. I'm truly trying to be a better man. Thankfully, my brother, James, made me see the error of my ways and how what I was doing was not just affecting me but the people who rely on me." He paused and took a sip of the watered-down punch. "It is no secret that I require funds. And the best way to acquire them is to marry well and come into a dowry." He reached across the table and touched her hand.

"I'm ashamed of my actions before and now. But let me be

honest: I've been smitten ever since I saw you at the Langford ball. And it has nothing to do with you being a duke's daughter. I have this deep desire to get to know you."

Shocked at his long speech, Priscilla sipped her bland punch to give her pause. "I appreciate you telling me all this. And as to your comment, I already knew most of your past. But I think both of us should concentrate on the here and now. Not what was, but what is. Does that make sense?"

He sighed audibly and smiled. "Yes. Thank you for not holding my past against me."

"How can I when I've heard that reformed rakes make the best husbands?" Her hand flew to her mouth, and her cheeks heated. "Did I just say that? Goodness, what's gotten into me?"

He had a nice laugh, and it warmed her skin. "I have heard that as well. But I don't think most people believe it."

He stood and held out his hand. "Perhaps you would like to take a turn around the ballroom, announce to those in attendance that you are accepting of me."

His words rang close to something Nick would say. She took his hand as she stood, then wrapped it around his arm as they strolled out of one room and into the ballroom. There, the guests danced, strolled, and conversed in quiet conversation. Her eyes found Nick immediately standing with Langford, Caldwell, and Blackstone. Their wives were nowhere to be seen.

The bored look Nick sent her didn't bode well to her.

They strolled behind several other couples as they made several passes around the room, attracting the attention of many, including her mother, who nodded her head with a smile. Latham appeared genuinely interested in her for more than just her dowry. She would bet her pin money on it unless he were really that good at hiding his emotions. But if that were the case, wouldn't he have been successful at the gaming tables? And she knew for a fact he hadn't been.

"Lady Priscilla. Did you hear me?"

"Yes. But could you repeat it?"

He chuckled. "I hate to think I'm so boring that you were woolgathering while I was rambling on about taking you for a ride in the park tomorrow. Weather permitting."

"Yes. Forgive me. I was thinking of my mother. I would like that very much. Weather permitting."

He chuckled again. "Thank you. I am honored that you accepted my offer. And I fear I have monopolized your time. I will escort you to your mother."

Having relinquished her to her mother, Priscilla sat in the chair next to her. "Well, you may as well say what's on your mind, Mother."

Her mother hummed. "You know me too well. You and Latham make a lovely couple. There is no doubt about it. But I see more than most. I saw Nicholas following you with sadness and yearning in his eyes. I know he has hurt you, but perhaps he wasn't ready to admit until now that he has feelings for you."

"It isn't true. Let me clue you in on a little secret." She whispered into her mother's ear, "Nick and I have agreed to a false courtship to help other eligible ladies see him in a new light, see him as a gentleman worthy of husband material. To finally bury the rumors."

"Priscilla," her mother admonished. "You can't be serious."

"Don't look at me like that. It was his idea, not mine. I only agreed to go along with it. But I also agreed to a courtship with Latham. So don't be shocked that I am now courting two gentlemen. And I do it proudly."

"I *am* shocked. Are you trying to get me to faint? To take to my bed with a migraine? What will people say?"

"I don't care what people say. For once in my life, I will do what I want."

A gasp escaped her mother's lips. "What you want? Let me remind you that you eloped to Gretna Green with Jasper. Someone we had never met or heard you mention. You have already been gossiped about once before. Do you wish so again?"

"It didn't bother me the first time. And I won't let it bother me this time, either. I'm doing Nick a favor. A favor he asked for. Please, Mother, I'm doing the best I can. I'm helping out Nick and allowing Latham to court me. You and Father should be happy that someone is interested in me. I never confided in you how much Nick's rejection of me hurt when I was eighteen. It took me a long time to get over him. So please don't make this difficult for me."

"I never knew you felt so strongly about Nicholas or that he hurt you terribly." Her mother said in a soothing voice. "I'm sorry. Would you like me to speak to him?"

Priscilla couldn't help the groan that escaped her lips before she covered it up with her gloved hand. "No, Mother. I have Latham interested in me, and perhaps one day he will propose." Her stomach dipped down to her toes. Was she ready to marry someone else?

"YOU LOST PRISCILLA once before," Blackstone said as they watched Latham escort her around the outer perimeter of the ballroom. "By sheer tragedy, her husband perished at sea, and you have another chance to redeem yourself. What are you waiting for? For her to marry Latham and hope something takes his life?"

Caldwell frowned at Blackstone. "I can't believe you just spoke of my brother's death. Besides, if he were going to die, he would've already. He came close several times. Now that he's becoming the man he was meant to be, I like him and would prefer to see him grow old."

"Sorry," Blackstone winced. "I meant your brother no harm or disrespect. I only meant to make a point to Hollingsworth since he seems too daft to see what's right in front of him and what's in here." He tapped his chest.

"You both realize I'm standing right here, and my hearing is perfect." His eyes traveled back to Priscilla and the lovely picture she presented in her stunning blue gown, accentuating her curves on her tall frame. "I wish the baron nothing but the best in pursuing Priscilla while I'm also courting her." He held up his wine glass. "May the best man win."

Blackstone and Langford laughed. "You don't have to court her," Langford said when he stopped laughing. "Just propose and skip all the tedious courting and the rules and marry her with a special license. By this time next week, you can be living in wedded bliss."

Caldwell begged off, leaving Blackstone, Langford, and him standing together, wine glasses in their hands. Nick explained about the fake courtship—more laughter from his so-called friends. "There is nothing amusing about it. Priscilla is helping me, and in return, I'm helping her find a suitor, be that Latham or some other lucky fellow."

"Why on earth are you doing this?" Langford asked, all amusement gone. "Admit you have a tender spot for Lady Priscilla."

"I admit I do," Nick said with a frustrated sigh.

"Have you ever taken her into your arms and kissed her?" Blackstone queried and continued before he could answer. "If you have, you would already know whether you felt something or nothing. And that could answer all your questions regarding Lady Priscilla."

"Well, have you?" Langford asked.

"Lord, give a fellow a break and stop badgering me." He ran a hand through his hair. They brought up a very valid question and point. Why hadn't he ever kissed Priscilla? He'd thought about it a time or two, but then the moment would pass. For the past year, she had been in mourning, and he had hardly ever seen her. Before that . . . he'd been a fool. "No, I haven't kissed her."

"What the bloody hell is wrong with you?" Blackstone said rather loudly.

Several people looked their way. "Be quiet. People are beginning to take notice. There's nothing wrong with me," Nick huffed.

"I suggest," Langford began, "you take Lady Priscilla out onto the veranda, and if any people are around, take her deeper into the gardens and . . . well, I don't think I need to tell you the rest, do I?"

Nick choked on his wine. "I believe I'm well versed in the art of kissing."

"Well then. Kiss her before she runs off to Gretna Green with the baron. After all, she has done it once before."

CHAPTER FIVE

NICK WEAVED HIS way through the crowd to where Priscilla sat with her mother. The closer he got to them, the more the tension inside his body eased. His friends may have recommended this quest, but he was invested completely. Kissing Priscilla was something he dreamed about quite often lately. When he stood before both ladies, he bowed. "Duchess, Lady Priscilla." He paused and inhaled. "Lady Priscilla, may I interest you in a stroll through the gardens?"

She didn't hesitate. She stood and wrapped her arm around his. "That would be lovely," she said, nodding to her mother. "I will return shortly, Mother."

As they made their way out the double doors to the veranda and the well-lit gardens beyond, he noticed how lovely she smelled—making him wonder why he'd never noticed her flowery scent before. Had he truly been such a selfish idiot concerning her? She should hate him. He frowned. Perhaps she did.

"Look at all the stars. I've never seen them so vibrant," Priscilla said, her voice full of excitement.

"The moon is not lighting up the sky making it difficult to see the stars. They are also not covered up with the usual clouds."

They stopped along the stone path and smelled the night jasmine. "It is strange some jasmine plants only bloom at night."

Priscilla leaned forward and breathed in the white flower's scent. "Heavenly. It's one of my favorite scents. I'm wearing it tonight."

Before thinking about what he intended to do, he buried his nose against her neck and inhaled. "You smell divine."

Her body shuddered, and he prayed it was a good shudder and not one of repulsion from him sniffing her.

"I have something to ask you, and I'd like an honest answer," he said.

She picked a jasmine bloom and tucked it around her ear. "I'll be honest if I can."

Here goes nothing. He hoped like bloody hell she didn't laugh in his face. "Have you ever thought about kissing me?" Her face went from shocked to blushing in a matter of moments. He had his answer before she spoke. The tightness in his chest eased.

"Truthfully, yes, I have."

"When?"

A gasp escaped her. "That is none of your business."

"Fair enough. Since we entered the gardens, it's all I can think about." Her eyes widened, then her lashes lowered to fan against her delicate skin.

"I see."

"May I?"

"Yes."

Nick took her hand and pulled her into a little alcove of shrubs and trees away from the path and potentially prying eyes. His insides vibrated, and he was shocked to find his hands shaking as he cupped her cheeks, stroking his thumbs across her jaw. She trembled, closed her eyes, and leaned forward, giving him the necessary courage. He bent, touched her slightly parted lips with his, and became lost.

The kiss started gently and sweetly until she curled her arms around his neck. He moved his hands to the small of her back and pulled her tight against his body. They touched everywhere, and he knew she would feel his desire for her evident in his trousers. She gasped, and he took advantage by sweeping his tongue inside her mouth and tasting the sweet punch she had drunk, fueling the fire burning through his body. He deepened the kiss. He devoured her mouth with his. Nothing mattered but tasting all of her. He nibbled her bottom lip with his teeth, and she moaned, gripping his shoulders tight.

"Nick," she sighed.

His lips skimmed down her neck and throat to the other side. Her nails dug into his skin, feeding his desire for her exponentially. He licked across the swells of her breasts, peeking over the top of her low-cut gown, and her head rolled back, forcing her chest forward.

"Priscilla," he breathed as he cupped one breast, tugged the fabric away from the twin, and snuck his tongue inside to lave her taut nipple. "You taste so good."

"Oh my God, Nick," she purred as she tugged on his hair, pulling him up and kissing him. She devoured him this time, and it was all he could do not to strip them out of their clothing and take her right there beneath the bright stars.

Instead, he let her lead the kiss. He slid his leg between her thighs, and she instantly rubbed her womanhood against it.

His control was breaking, and he slid his leg back and forth between her thighs; the more she moaned into his mouth, the more he did it. His hands needed to be busy. He cupped her cheeks, tilted her head, and took the kiss beyond anything he had ever experienced. Breathy sounds kept escaping her lips, and her entire body trembled. Afraid she may collapse, he moved his arms around her waist, holding her up while she rode his thigh. He kissed her to smother up her cries of pleasure, as there was no doubt she'd just orgasmed.

She buried her face in his neck, panting as her body's trembling peaked and eased.

Suddenly, he didn't know what to do. They'd just experienced an intimate moment so profound he never wanted to let her go. If only he had known . . .

"Well, that was unexpected." He didn't know what else to say.

"Hmmm," she murmured into his neck. "I would say so. Who knew a leg could do that?"

He expelled a nervous chuckle as he kissed the top of her head, wondering if his heart would ever be the same. "Yes. Who knew?"

"Nick?"

"Yes?"

"Why did you take me into the gardens and kiss me?"

"HONESTLY?" HE SAID in a voice still seductively deep in tone.

"Yes. I expect no less from you."

"I wanted to know if there was a spark between us. If we would be a good fit in the bedchamber."

Nervous giggles escaped her lips, and she tried to swallow them down because as far as she was concerned, they would fit well together. If his thigh and kisses could arouse her, she could only imagine what being unclothed in a bed with him would be like. Still, she hesitated before asking, "Do you have your answer?" Her breath whooshed from her lungs as she waited for him to respond.

He chuckled into the top of her head, then kissed her. "I believe I do. I truly believe we would have a very interesting, active, and satisfying married life."

The air escaped her lungs, and she inhaled and exhaled several times. "I believe that to be true, also." She desperately wanted to ask where they went from there but didn't want to spoil the intimate mood.

"Too bad I never kissed you before, when our mothers expected us to wed."

She stepped away from him and cupped his cheek, looking into his eyes. "We were not the same people as we are now. Life experiences have played a part in who we have become. Frankly,

I wasn't ready for you and your sexual prowess then. And you weren't ready to settle down."

"Still. We could consider it now. Properly, not just a fake courtship."

As much as she wanted to believe Nick wanted a real court-ship, some part of her didn't believe him. She had hidden much pain and disappointment regarding him and she didn't want to go through it again. She closed her eyes, regretting what she needed to say. And it was hurting her more than she thought it would. She wasn't the starry-eyed eighteen-year-old girl she used to be. Nor did she want to be. She'd been vulnerable then, she wanted to think she was strong now. "I promised Latham he could court me. I can't go back on my word now."

His head fell forward and he inhaled and exhaled making her know he wasn't happy with her. "I don't like it. But I understand. You committed and must honor it. As you must honor to continue our fake courtship."

"I will honor our arrangement." With those words, she left him standing in the gardens as she entered the house and hurried to the ladies' retiring room. Standing in front of the large mirror, Priscilla tried to smooth out the wrinkles in her gown, as tears started flowing at remembering how those wrinkles came to be. Drat, she'd never been a watering pot and refused to turn into one. Damn Nick for kissing her and making her want him.

She pulled several pins out of her hair and replaced them, making her look presentable again and not like she'd had a tryst in the gardens. Her hand flew to her heart.

Ducking out of the ladies' parlor, she ran into Baron Latham. She actually bumped into him. His arms came out, gripping her to steady her. "Forgive me, Lady Priscilla, you came out of nowhere. Are you hurt?"

Was she? Besides her heart, she was right as rain. "Forgive me, as I'm the one who bumped into you. And no, I'm not hurt. Are you injured in any way?"

He dropped his hands to his sides. "No harm done. But while

I have run into you, I wonder if you would like a bit of fresh air. I hear it is lovely outside. Clear skies and hardly a breeze in the air."

Could she survive another gentleman's attentions tonight? If she were to give the baron a chance with her and get to know him better, she needed to do this. In all fairness, she needed to give him the same privileges she gave Nick while courting. "Why yes. That would be lovely."

Placing her hand on his arm, they walked back into the ballroom while the guests danced a lively minuet.

"If you'd rather dance, we could do that instead?" he asked.

"I would prefer the fresh air."

"As would I," he said with a smile. His blue eyes sparkled, making him look younger. He was extraordinarily handsome and debonair.

The veranda was quite crowded, more so than when she'd recently been there. So they walked into the gardens and down the same stone pathway she had earlier with Nick. She breathed evenly, trying to keep her body from tensing and her mind from comparing the two—not very successfully.

She knew both men could be gallant and friendly—Nick openly and Latham hesitantly. But both of them also had a dark side. She had recognized Nick's at a young age. From her vantage point, he didn't let many people close to him. After the incident that was gossiped about, he became worse. It was as though he couldn't open up to anyone or let anyone in. He guarded his emotions, and his smiles rarely reached his eyes.

She didn't know Latham all that well, but she knew he had nearly ruined his life and bankrupted the barony, which was why he needed to marry and marry well. She didn't know the extent of the depravity he had fallen into. Could there be more than the drinking, gambling, and his propensity for lightskirts? How badly had he slipped into the darkness? She was most curious to find out and perhaps she would ask him soon.

Either way she looked, her suitors were enigmas, and she

would need to puzzle them out. Dig into them until they released their secrets, their darkness, and joined the sunshine.

"What a beautiful night," Priscilla remarked as they approached a bench. She sat down, adjusting her skirts.

"It is," Latham joined her on the bench, his hands resting on his thighs. Thighs that filled out his breeches nicely, if she were being honest. "If I'm not being too forward, I was wondering if I could call you Priscilla when we are in private?"

Her hands tightened around her fan as she realized she didn't even know his name. "Yes. May I call you by your given name as well?"

"Yes. It's David."

"David."

"I'm named after my grandfather on my mother's side. He was a great man. Loved his family and the Crown." He paused, leaned back against the bench, and sighed. "I worry that he is watching from Heaven and shaking his head at how I've messed up everything. He was the Marquess of Gloucester."

Her heart pained at the sadness and self-hatred she heard in his voice. She placed her hand on one of his and gently squeezed. "If he is watching, I'm quite convinced he is proud of you for overcoming your vices and working hard to make everything right again." She squeezed his hand again. "I can't imagine how hard that must have been. You should be proud of yourself for turning your life around."

He snorted. "Yes, well, if it weren't for James, I would probably be dead. Either by a duel of honor, because I had none, or by drinking myself to death. Or by hundreds of other ways."

"Caldwell is a good brother to have. Thankfully, he came back to London when he did."

"Yes. That is my only saving grace."

She turned toward him, their knees bumping, and she cupped his cheeks. Suddenly, she had the urge to kiss him. To kiss all his pain away. Did that make her a bad person for kissing Nick one moment and then kissing the baron next?

They both leaned toward each other at the same time until their lips met. The kiss was gentle. His lips were soft and firm, which was a contradiction she knew. His arms cupped her cheeks and tilted her head to deepen the kiss. She exhaled into his mouth as his tongue swept inside, tasting her. With her eyes closed, his large, warm hands resting on her cheeks, his tongue twirling around the inside of her mouth, her body relaxed, and her insides tingled. He pulled back.

"Forgive me."

"There is nothing to forgive. I initiated the kiss. I wanted you to kiss me."

He kissed her again, not as deeply, but it was no less enjoyable.

"We should go back before your mother starts to wonder where you have gone," he said, standing with his hand out.

Taking his hand, she let him assist her in rising from the bench. "Thank you."

"Are you still willing to go for a ride in the park tomorrow?" he asked, uncertainty vibrating in his voice.

"Yes. I'm looking forward to it."

He bowed once they went through the doors into the ballroom, the musicians playing a waltz. "Until tomorrow." He brought her hand to his mouth and brushed his lips across her fingers, causing her to sigh.

Her eyes followed him as he walked around the room, exiting toward the staircase, which she knew brought him down to the entry hall and outside. Feeling exhausted all of a sudden, she shuffled her feet to her mother and said, "May we go?"

"Indeed, we may," her mother replied.

The ride home in the carriage was silent. Her mother nodded off and Priscilla was glad, because she knew her mother, and if she were awake, she would inquire about what transpired in the gardens with Nick and Latham. And Priscilla wasn't in any mood to discuss it.

When they arrived home, she bid her mother goodnight and

made her way to her chambers where her maid waited for her to help her prepare for bed.

Lying beneath the pretty blue floral coverlet with Snowball purring loudly beside her, she touched her lips as she remembered kissing two men that night. Nick's kisses made her lose all reason. The world had disappeared, and nothing had existed but the two of them. It was dizzying, and she'd almost panicked at the feelings bombarding her from all angles. It was amazing and terrifying at the same time. Handing over control to another person didn't come easily to her. However, she had given over control to Nick. When his thigh gave her unimaginable pleasure, that was the only thing she had thought about. Nothing else mattered but using his thigh to her advantage. Was that selfish? Perhaps. It also frightened her to be so lost to her surroundings that only her needs prevailed.

As for kissing David, at first, it was sweet and gentle, a light caress. When it deepened, her body had tingled in all the right places, but the sensations didn't take over her every thought or desire. He didn't try to touch her or arouse her in any way, but she did learn one valuable lesson: She would welcome David's advances. If she married him, the marriage bed would not be a chore. She believed she would enjoy his touch. And she wouldn't lose her mind over his caresses, which would be good. Being with Nick—her inner being taking over, pushing all reason aside—frightened her. He could wield such power over her, and that was worrisome.

During her wedding night with Jasper, she did not lose control the two times they made love. The first time was uncomfortable, and the second time she was so worried about it hurting, she couldn't relax. So she didn't have much to go on, but she believed she would enjoy the marriage act with whomever she married, be it Nick, David, or some other as-yet-unnamed gentleman.

Not long later she had trouble keeping her eyes open and succumbed to the pull of sleep tugging her under.

HIS CHEST PUFFED out with pride, Latham left the dreadful musicale and made his way to his mistress's home. He'd accomplished what he set out to do. Get Lady Priscilla to agree to a courtship. And with any luck, she would agree to a marriage proposal. Yes, he needed funds, which was why he was considering marriage. However, marrying Lady Priscilla wouldn't be a hardship.

He was attracted to her, and the kiss they'd shared affected him more than he thought possible. His blood ran hot when he was close to her. Her tall, lithe body had curves he wanted to explore. He could envision her long legs wrapped around his waist as he sank into her warm heat.

He exited his coach and hurried up the stairs as the butler opened the door with a sour look. "Good evening, Baron. My mistress awaits you in her boudoir."

Thinking about Lady Priscilla had his body ready, and he ran up the stairs to the welcome arms of his mistress.

CHAPTER SIX

AFTER LEAVING THE Trowbridge musicale, Nick stopped by Brooks's for a nightcap. He was stalling returning home because there was nothing for him there. He sat in a quiet corner by the fireplace, sitting in a comfortable, overstuffed chair and nursing a glass of brandy. His eyes stared into the amber liquid, hoping to find answers for his life.

For many years, he'd felt damaged. His heart was unable to feel anything, which was why he never married Priscilla. He felt she deserved someone who could love her, and for most of his life, he was incapable of loving anyone. He always wondered what was wrong with him, why his heart didn't work correctly, and why it was damaged.

After tonight, he wished it didn't work. During his time with Priscilla tonight, his heartbeat had changed course. It had veered from the damaged path it had been on and turned in another direction. His heartbeat had reset. He could feel the rhythm change during their kiss. His feelings had overloaded him, and he'd had to fight the need to make her his in every way possible. The intense need was difficult to ignore in those gardens.

He now thought back to the blackguard he had been to her since she turned ten. That was the first time she'd announced to him that she would marry him. What a defiant child she had been.

Tonight, once his heart reset, he couldn't get enough of her. It wasn't just his heart. Everything changed. The gardens came alive with sounds and scents. His eyes saw things differently. Not just Priscilla but everything around him.

When she left him in the gardens, a painful crack split his heart in two. Who knew one could actually experience pain from inside one's heart? How had he lived in the dull gray of life up until now? And would he want to go back? Part of him did because it was easier to live in the darkness where your feelings could not be hurt than to live in the light and be vulnerable. He had protected himself so well since his Eton days, and then from the gossip that started seven years ago, that he hadn't realized what the darkness had done to him until it was lifted.

He brought the cut crystal brandy snifter to his lips and downed the drink in one gulp. The burn going down his throat and spreading into his belly was comforting. It didn't solve his problems, but he felt better for it. He left Brooks's, collecting his hat, gloves, and coat from the doorman, and went to his carriage. "Home, Fitzroy."

THE FOLLOWING DAY turned out to be a miserable, rainy, and windy day—the kind where the rain pelts sideways. Nick called upon the Viscount and Viscountess Norton. After relinquishing his rain-soaked coat, gloves, and hat to the butler, he was led up the stairs and into a burgundy drawing room, where he found the married couple sitting together on a settee enjoying a light repast.

"To what do we owe the pleasure of your company, Hollingsworth?" Norton said as he sipped what smelled like strong coffee. Nick would kill for a cup.

"I have something to discuss with the viscountess."

"Please sit," Viscountess Norton said with a flourish. "Would you like tea or coffee?"

"Coffee, if it's not too much trouble." He could almost taste it already.

"Nonsense. I have a pot right here. How do you take it?"

"Cream and sugar," Nick replied.

She handed over the cup and saucer. He took a sip and sighed. "This is delicious."

Norton agreed, and the viscountess laughed. "If you say so. I find the taste of coffee too similar to dirt. Not that I've eaten dirt, mind you."

Nick found himself chuckling and relaxed as he sipped the hot coffee. "May I speak privately with the viscountess?" he asked, watching Norton closely.

"My wife and I have no secrets. In fact, she told me about your night with her previous cohorts. And I must apologize for what you went through. My dear wife had no choice but to take to extortion to make a living. She refused to sell her body, which I highly commend her for. But still, I realize what she did was wrong, and it did irreparable damage to your reputation. Seven years is a long time for the *ton* to remember such things."

"What I ask of her is to spread gossip about her attending the masquerade ball and recall witnessing a lady drug me and help me leave." He paused and exhaled. "That is it. The gossipmongers will fill in the rest. It will make people doubt what they thought happened, and perhaps I can finally find a wife to give me sons to carry on my title."

"Do you think it will work?" Viscountess Norton asked, her deep blue eyes wide with curiosity.

"I do. Members of the aristocracy are fickle creatures. If it doesn't work, no harm is done. What else can they say about me to make matters worse?"

"I understand you were to marry Lady Priscilla Amesbury when she came of age. If you don't mind me asking, why didn't you?" Norton queried over the rim of his cup.

"Because I was foolish."

"I understand she is widowed. Why not make her your marchioness now?"

"It's complicated." He rose and bowed. "Do we have an agreement?"

Viscount and Viscountess Norton both said yes simultaneously.

"Thank you, and I bid you good day."

Nick made his way to Avery Manor to pay a call on Priscilla. Thank goodness the rain had let up, and he didn't arrive resembling a wet dog. To his dismay, he arrived to find Latham sitting beside Priscilla on the settee while the Duchess of Avery sat in a chair across from them embroidering.

"Good day," Nick bowed and glared daggers at Latham, who grinned and shrugged his shoulders.

"Good day to you, Nicholas," the duchess replied. "Please take a seat. Can I offer you refreshments? The cook just prepared a fresh tray with tea and cakes."

He was liable to float away on the Thames if he drank anything else. And then he really would resemble a wet dog. "No, thank you," he said as he took the chair beside the duchess. His eyes took in Priscilla and how beautiful she looked in her pink-and-white day dress. How he wished he sat beside her instead of Latham. Even though his heart had transformed last night, he could still be a blackguard and selfish.

He didn't trust Latham. He appeared to have mended his ways, but he'd spent years living in hell and lying. Could someone truly change? He couldn't have cared less if only his intentions were on anyone other than Priscilla. Nick felt a certain responsibility for her. A specific need to ensure she married well and was not used only for her money, even if she didn't choose him. Latham needed her dowry, but did he have feelings for her? It wasn't easy to tell. The man was nearly as good as he was at hiding his emotions. If Nick were assured that Latham's attentions were honorable and in Priscilla's best interest, could he walk away? That was a bloody fine question. He could walk away if that were truly what she wanted. If she loved Latham, he would give her up to make her happy.

Until he knew what was in Pricilla's heart, he would continue with their fake courtship. And if his plan with Viscountess Norton worked, he could continue seeking a bride. Perhaps tonight, at the soiree given by the Duke and Duchess of Blackstone. Damn, if the idea of marrying someone other than Priscilla didn't cause his heart burn.

"HOLLINGSWORTH MUST BE desperate to show up here and propose his plan," Norton said once their uninvited guest took his leave.

"Do you think he suspects anything?" Emma asked as she held her husband's bony hand. She'd met Edward at her lowest point in London, and he'd taken her in and saved her. Several years later, she'd wept with relief when he'd married her, securing her future. They were true partners.

"If he did, he wouldn't have come here today."

"But?"

"But nothing, my dear. I married you to keep you safe. The likelihood of us being tried for our crimes, if they ever become known, is remarkably slim. There are advantages to being members of the aristocracy."

"I understand, but sometimes I fear for the future," Emma said as a chill invaded her body. "I didn't expect Hollingsworth to come back into my life all these years later. We should never have attended the Langfords' ball."

Edward turned his hand over and intertwined their fingers. "Nonsense. You were bound to run into him. If not that night, some other night. We decided not to keep you hidden any longer, and I stick by that decision."

Emma understood Edward's desire to enjoy what time he had left since he had recently turned seventy. He enjoyed showing off his young and beautiful wife. Yet, she worried. Although she may have retired from the business, Edward was still involved. It was where he received the funds to live. He was the mastermind behind it all, even if he sought his replacement.

⊱⊰

SITTING BESIDE DAVID, fidgeting with her hands on her lap, Priscilla tried not to stare at Nick. More precisely, she tried not to stare at his lips. The lips that kissed her senseless last evening. Looking at him now, all she could think about was grabbing him by the hand and dragging him up to her bedchamber. She could only imagine the extent of their shared pleasure if they were naked and in her bed.

Oh, dear. She twisted her hands to keep herself from fanning her heated cheeks. She must think of a cold, snowy day to cool off. She took her eyes off Nick. He had stared at her the entire time she'd stared at him, making her wonder if he was thinking about their time alone in the gardens as well.

"Are you both attending the Blackstone soiree this evening?" she asked, hoping to distract herself.

"I am," Nick replied. "Would you save me a waltz?"

Oh, to be in his arms again. Drat, her cheeks melted again. "Yes."

"Will you save me one as well?" David said. "Assuming they play two. If not, another dance, perhaps?"

"Yes, of course."

She needed to concentrate on David, but how could she when Nick looked like he wanted to devour her? What a pickle she was in. She had never experienced two suitors at the same time. Come to think of it, she had never had a suitor ever. You couldn't count Jasper. Their courting was done through letters and quick secret meetings. No wonder some of the young debutantes strung along several suitors during the Season. The attention was exciting. It made Priscilla's heart warm to know someone cared for her.

"I believe I will take my leave," Latham said as he bowed. "Until this evening. Perhaps we could take that ride in the park tomorrow, weather permitting?"

"I would like that," she replied.

After Latham exited the drawing room, Nick muttered as he stood, "I thought he would never leave." He picked up her newly arrived cat and plopped him on her lap. Then he sat beside her on the settee.

"Why do you dislike him?" she asked, patting Snowball as she watched her mother pack up her embroidery.

"I'll give the two of you some privacy," her mother said as she left the room.

Priscilla had mixed feelings about being alone with Nick. Would Snowball save her from making a fool of herself?

"It is not a matter of liking or disliking him. I know he has redeemed himself in the eyes of the *ton*, but what if he slides back to his previous vices once again, pulling you down with him? What if you marry him, and he ruins you and everything he had the privilege of being born with? What would happen to you then?"

"I understand your worry," she said with a frown. She truly did. But as far as she was concerned, Nick was getting ahead of things. Latham was courting her, not marrying her. At least he hadn't proposed yet. "You are looking too far forward. We have hardly started courting and getting to know one another. If and when our relationship becomes serious enough for his proposal, I will not answer immediately until discussing things with my father, who you know is a very pragmatic man and will not allow me to enter into a marriage if he believes it will be detrimental to me."

"But?"

"I am quite capable of taking care of myself and making good decisions. Even though I eloped once, it wasn't a rash decision. I knew deep inside my heart that if Jasper had lived, we would have had a happy and loving marriage." She rubbed her chest at the sudden pain plaguing her at the memory of him. "The only time I ever let my emotions get the better of me is when it comes to you." Oh dear, she wished she could retract that last comment. It wasn't something she'd meant to share.

"I'm sorry things didn't turn out as our mothers planned. I wasn't ready for a serious courtship, never mind the wedding they planned. I never meant to hurt you, and I'm sorry if I ruined the life you thought you were to have."

She snorted in a most unladylike way, and at the same time she blinked back tears. "Don't flatter yourself. I always knew you only placated our mothers and me regarding our supposed wedding." What had come over her? Why was she taunting him with words meant to wound him? She knew why. She was retreating inside herself to protect her heart.

His hand shot out, and he grabbed hers. "Don't. Don't turn away from me. I thought we shared something special last evening."

"Once again, don't flatter yourself. I am hardly a virgin, and I took what I wanted."

She refused to look at him and see the hurt in his eyes. Knowing his body stiffened up as he tore his hand from hers was enough to know she insulted him and, worse, hurt him. She, of all people, knew what being hurt by someone you cared for or even loved felt like. He had done it to her. She hadn't intended to say those things to him. And she wasn't retaliating for the hurt he caused her. It just happened. The words flowed out of her mouth before she could stop them.

Just when she thought they had made progress in their relationship, her words had him retreating inside himself again, and she had only herself to blame. He hadn't deserved her cruel words, truth or not.

Standing, he nodded his head, his features and eyes guarded. Once again, his emotions were bottled up from the world and her. "I will see you this evening. If you want to renege on that waltz, feel free."

He pivoted around and exited the room before she could respond. *Renege?* No. She wanted that waltz. They had never waltzed before, and as far as she was concerned, it was high time they did. Giving up on holding back her tears, she let them flow. She had no one to blame but herself for how things turned out with Nick just now. Perhaps she would apologize tonight if he came to collect on his dance.

CHAPTER SEVEN

EUGENIA SEEMED TO take forever to do her hair and help her dress for the soirée, while Snowball sat curled up, purring on her lap, and she rubbed his ears.

"Snowball is going to wrinkle your gown, my lady."

Priscilla continued to swirl her fingers around Snowball's ears. "No, he won't." Priscilla had decided to wear a cream and gold ballgown with gold ribbon woven throughout her braids, which brought out the gold in her auburn hair. She was dressed to impress, but which gentleman did she want to impress the most? Why did the answer always have to be Nick, no matter how he put a sour taste in her mouth when he put her off or angered her? He used to say she was more like a sister to him than a potential bride. This afternoon proved it with him sharing his concerns regarding Latham as a potential husband. He was looking out for her best interests as a brother would. When it came from Nick, it turned her stomach and made her lash out. Brother to her he was not and never would be.

On the other hand, hadn't he been the one to say they'd shared something special last night? And she was the one who'd made light of it. Would the two of them forever be in turmoil?

Finally, Eugenia finished and left her alone to her jumbled-up thoughts. Men? They were so infuriating, and they said women were. Quite the opposite. She picked up Snowball, placed him on the bed, and grabbed her gold reticle, fan, and shawl off the foot of her bed. She petted Snowball one last time and went downstairs to meet her parents. Her stomach buzzed with bees as she hoped the night would go well. Out of respect from one duke to another, even her father would attend the soirée tonight, even though she knew he would rather stay home.

They arrived at the Duke and Duchess of Blackstone's elegant and enormous London home with many other carriages dropping off their occupants. Anyone who received the lucky invitation to the soirée would never dare to refuse the Duke of Blackstone, who seldom entertained. And this was the first time since his marriage to his duchess.

Getting through the receiving line outside the ballroom was surprisingly quicker than she anticipated. Priscilla was very thankful to have the duchess as one of her friends since joining the Ladies' Society of Mayfair. They stood outside the ballroom, waiting for the Master of Ceremonies to announce them. As usual, the man had a loud, booming voice that resonated throughout the room, making no mistake about who he announced.

Priscilla's eyes darted around the room and landed on Nick standing with Lord and Lady Langford, Mr. James Caldwell, and Lady Beatrice. David stood on the other side of the room with several gentlemen she recognized but could not name. Before she had taken ten steps into the room, Nick locked eyes on her and smoothly walked her way, looking dashing in his black evening wear.

"Goodness," her father said. "Hollingsworth is wasting no time in seeking you out. Perhaps your mother frets for nothing, and a marriage between you two will happen."

"Father, I refuse to fall into Mother's delusions of me marrying Nick. The time passed many years ago. We are merely friends now."

"Pish-posh," her mother remarked. "I see the predatory way he looks at you. Trust me, your father will announce your betrothal before the month is out."

"Mother," she moaned. "I disagree."

"Duke, Duchess, Lady Priscilla," Nick said as he reached them and bowed.

"Hollingsworth." Her father nodded his head. Her mother curtsied, and so did she. "Your mother and I are going to take a turn around the room."

They were gone before Priscilla could say anything, leaving her alone with Nick. She felt slightly uncomfortable after their quarrel that afternoon.

"Shall we take a turn as well?" His eyes beseeched her to say yes.

"If you wish." She placed her hand on his arm and joined the promenade of others doing the same.

"I must apologize for upsetting you this afternoon, regarding my opinions on Latham," he said in a low voice. "I don't know what got into me. Forgive me."

"I will forgive you if you forgive me." She looked around the room and noticed David watching them intently. "You visited me, and I was rude. There is no excuse."

"I asked you to speak your mind, and when you did, I became upset. That is what I'm apologizing for. I had no right to be cross when I pressed you to share your thoughts and feelings with me. I understand you are interested in Latham, and I must accept it."

"Yes. Just as I will have to accept it when you become interested in another lady." Her eyes had not missed the looks he'd received from several beautiful young ladies while they walked. "Do you see what I see?"

"Yes. I never had the chance to tell you about Viscountess Norton." He relayed their conversation from earlier that day. "She certainly didn't waste any time spreading her story. And it must be working."

"It appears so. How freeing for you to be rid of that stigma that has followed you for so long." She hoped he was correct in his assumptions regarding Viscountess Norton.

"Yes. Between our so-called fake courtship and the viscountess, perhaps my life is changing for the better."

Her heart sped up at the thought of seeing Nick courting someone who wasn't her. The only time she'd experienced it was when he'd pursued Lady Langford, and that had only lasted a short time. Her stomach hurt with guilt. Why, oh why, did she and Nick have such a problematic relationship that was impossible to define? And the night in the garden—a night she was not likely to forget anytime soon—had only made it worse.

Lost in her thoughts, she hadn't realized Nick had led them to their friends. Once greetings were over, Lady Langford said, "It is nice to see you again, Lady Priscilla."

"You as well, Countess."

Lilly wrapped her arm through hers and lowered her voice. "Please call me Lilly. And how are you? Rumor has it you are courting both Latham and Hollingsworth."

Hearing it said out loud had her wincing. "Yes, well, can I be honest with you, Lilly?"

"Yes, of course."

"I don't know if Nick mentioned it, but our courting is fake. We hope to make him more attractive to other young ladies. He is not getting any younger and needs to marry and produce heirs."

Lilly said softly, "Yes, I suppose he does. However, something Viscountess Norton said has been going through the gossip chain, which will greatly improve his chances. I see several unmarried ladies looking at him with interest. He will undoubtedly be besieged by many ladies hoping to become his marchioness now that the truth has been revealed."

"Oh, look," Priscilla said. "Here comes Lady Wilmington with her eldest daughter, Grace, who has yet to make a match. Not that I can understand why. She is positively lovely."

"Grace is lovely," Lilly agreed. "Although not as graceful as her name implies. But her mother is a terrible gossip and thinks she is above everyone else. I met her for the first time when I'd just come out of mourning for my first husband, and all she wanted was to get information about me. She was not very pleasant. Emmeline warned me about her, and I have stayed far away. If Lady Wilmington has set her sights on Hollingsworth for Lady Grace, he should run for the country. Not from Grace, but from her shrew of a mother."

Priscilla watched the exchange between Nick, Lady Wilmington, and Lady Grace with interest. The longer the three conversed, the harder it became to breathe. Truly, she was happy for Nick to be free of his burden, but it still hurt to see him openly flirt with another woman. The opening strains of a waltz began, and she knew she owed the dance to Nick. To her dismay, he offered his arm to Lady Grace and escorted her to the dance floor. To his credit, he looked over his shoulder at her and shrugged as if to say he didn't have a choice.

"Lady Priscilla," David said, as he approached her side. She'd been so engrossed in watching Nick she hadn't seen or heard him walk over. He turned toward her and bowed, a tentative look was in his eyes. "May I have this dance?"

She buried her disappointment at not dancing the waltz with Nick and smiled at David, placing her hand on his arm. "Yes. I believe I owe you a dance."

David knew the steps but was stiff and slightly awkward. She didn't take notice of it, but tried to pay attention in case he stepped on her toes. She also tried to ignore Nick dancing across the room with Lady Grace, who turned out to be as ungraceful as Lilly said—the poor thing. Fortunately, Nick was patient and would never chastise her for missed steps.

"I apologize if I misstep or step on your foot," David said as he winced. "I don't normally partake in dancing. I'm more of a watcher."

"You are doing fine. Just try to relax and feel the music."

His features softened. "Thank you. I needed to be reminded of that. I have trouble relaxing. Sometimes, I can't believe what a mess I made of my life and what I missed out on. I truly hope you know how much I have come to care for you, and that I will never return to the wastrel I was before. That man doesn't exist anymore." His eyes bore into hers, begging her to believe him. She did. Even if Nick's words from that afternoon penetrated her mind, trying to make her disbelieve.

"I believe you. I never knew you then and find it difficult even to comprehend the man you have described as the same man in front of me now." It was true. She couldn't. Nick entered her peripheral vision, and she fought with all her willpower not to turn her head and look. She barely succeeded.

"I'm forever grateful you never met me then. Out of many of the people I know and knew then, only a few have good things to say about me. I will take my embarrassment and regret to my grave."

As they talked, his steps became less forceful and his body less stiff. She believed he only needed to practice dancing to become comfortable at it. He had the steps and the rhythm she noticed. Not that she was an expert. Quite the contrary.

"Do you still want to ride in the park tomorrow if it's not raining?"

"Yes. Did I not make that clear this afternoon?"

He snorted. "Yes. But I didn't know if you said it to annoy Hollingsworth or if you meant it."

She smiled. "Of course I meant it. I rarely say things I don't mean. I have been accused many times of being outspoken and blunt." Again, she was tempted to look at Nick as they came close on the dance floor again. Her eyes stayed on David.

He looked taken aback. "Who would say such a thing?"

She giggled. "My parents, my husband, Jasper, God rest his soul, and who else but Hollingsworth." She paused. "Oh, and perhaps Lady Langford and the Duchess of Blackstone. That may be it."

"At least they are people you know and care about. It is different when it comes from a stranger or someone who is barely an acquaintance. They only say those things to be mean and hurtful."

"Indeed."

The music ended, and David escorted her to an adjacent room where refreshments were being served. Supper wouldn't take place until midnight, and she suddenly felt parched.

"Which would you prefer, wine or punch?" he said inquisitively as he stared at the choices.

"I think punch would quench my thirst better than wine," she replied.

He picked up two glasses of punch and led her outside onto the veranda. The torrential rains of earlier had dissipated, along with the clouds, leaving a bright sky full of stars and a tiny piece of the moon. He handed her the glass of punch as she stood at the railing looking out into the pretty gardens beyond. "Thank you."

"My pleasure," he said, downing half his glass in one sip. "Finally, someone who knows how to make punch. It has a nice fruity flavor."

"I suspect the duchess would serve nothing less than a flavorful punch," she said as she sipped. "Hmmm. It is good."

He finished his glass and gave it to a servant circling with a tray on the terrace.

"Tell me about yourself," he said as he stared into the gardens, his body close to hers. Her eyes fluttered to him, and she admitted to herself how handsome he looked in his evening attire. If nothing else, David had a good eye for fashion. *If nothing else. Not very nice, Priscilla.*

"There isn't much to tell. I spent much of my childhood in London. My mother preferred it to the countryside. Probably because her closest friend, the Marchioness of Hollingsworth, did as well. I was introduced to the theater and opera at a young age. Other than that, I was bored. I had one close friend, Lady Sophia Spencer, to play with, but my mother disapproved of her mother, so we didn't see each other often until we both came out at the same time. She is married and living in the country, so I still don't see her, but we write to each other frequently. She is the one who instigated my relationship with my husband by suggesting we begin corresponding by letter."

"Tell me about your husband. Is it true you eloped to Gretna Green?"

"Yes." She explained how the marriage came to be. "It was Jasper's idea to elope. It sounded exciting and romantic. I also didn't want to allow my parents to deny his proposal. So off to Gretna Green we went. They thought I was spending several days visiting my friend, Lady Sophia, who was in London at the time. Needless to say, when I returned married, they were unhappy with me. But they said they would welcome him into the family. After all, they knew his family. His father is the Earl of Barnstable." She paused, ready to steer the conversation into more cheerful waters. "There is one more thing I should mention. Before I married Jasper, I was quite the spoiled, demanding brat, according to some."

He chuckled. "I find that hard to believe. You are nothing at all like that now."

She giggled, and she meant to giggle. It wasn't false. "Yes, well. Perhaps I still have a little bit of the spoiled, demanding girl in me. And I left the most shocking detail for last: I insisted Father hire a tutor for me. So I have learned most things young men have. For years, I have begged my father to let me take over his accounts, but he refuses. Not because he doesn't think I'm incapable, quite the contrary. He knows I'm better at figures than he is, but he refuses to admit it."

"I would turn my books over to you immediately. I don't have a head for figures, nor am I organized. I will hire a secretary to take care of those duties as soon as I can. Or, if I have a wife who . . ."

His words had her insides jumbled up with contradictory emotions. She was flattered and excited at the slip of his words regarding a wife, because she knew he had to mean her. And at the same time, part of her hungered for Nick. Caring for two men was very confusing. Could her feelings for David overtake the ones she had for Nick? That was the biggest obstacle she had to overcome.

"Now it is your turn to tell me about your life growing up with your brother, Caldwell."

He turned his head and smiled at her with soft blue eyes. "James and I were inseparable. I'm only fifteen months older than him, so we were each other's best friends and playmates when we were young." He chuckled. "We were holy terrors, according to our mother and our governess—not in a mean way, but in a mischievous way. We liked to put things in our governess's bed. Of course, she anticipated it and never climbed into bed until she'd stripped the bedding. She loved us, and we loved her. She stayed with us until we no longer needed her." Sighing, he continued. "I remember the day she left like it was yesterday. It was right before I left for Eton, and I was embarrassed that I hugged her and cried real tears."

"Real tears. As opposed to fake tears?" Priscilla teased.

"You know what I mean."

"Do continue."

"James was unhappy that he had to wait another year before going to Eton. It was the first time we came to blows. He was so hurt and angry it came to fisticuffs, and we both sported black and swollen eyes. Mother and Father weren't happy sending me off to school looking like I was beaten."

"My days away at Eton were fine. There's not much to say about my time there. When James did join me the following year, he made friends with Blackstone, Langford, and Mr. Aiden Fitzpatrick, the Duchess of Blackstone's first husband. I had my friends by then. Sadly, we were no longer as close as we once were."

"That is sad," she said wistfully. "I'm an only child and would've given anything to have a sister or brother."

"Even though I'm the eldest, James has come to my rescue too many times to count. It is something I am truly ashamed of. I'm also very proud of James for his accomplishments with Blackstone and Langford. He knew what he had to do to secure his future, and he did it."

"He has accomplished much. He seems happy being married to Lady Beatrice."

"He does."

"We should go back inside. I did promise Hollingsworth a dance."

"Go on in. I'm going to enjoy the peace outside a little longer."

Entering the ballroom from the veranda, Priscilla looked around the crush of bodies for Nick, and her stomach dropped when she couldn't find him. Her feet moved forward, having spotted Emmeline and Lilly together.

"Priscilla," they both said together when she stood beside them.

"Emmeline, Lilly, have your husbands deserted you?"

"Caldwell wanted to speak to them, so they went to my husband's study. I thought it was business talk, but Hollingsworth accompanied them, so perhaps not," Emmeline replied.

"Oh." This time, her heart fell alongside her stomach. Soon, she would be hollow inside. It didn't appear that she would waltz with Nick tonight.

Before the gentlemen returned to the ballroom, her mother and father approached to inform her that it was time to leave.

While sitting in the carriage, Priscilla realized again how disappointed she was that she didn't get to dance with Nick, although she did enjoy her time with David. The more she got to know him, the more she enjoyed his company. And the more difficult it became to visualize him as the wastrel and debauched gambler he once was.

"WHAT IS ON your mind, Caldwell?" Blackstone asked as he poured and handed out four glasses of brandy once everyone was settled inside his study.

"I'm worried about my brother," he said as he downed his glass and refused another.

"Is he . . .?"

"No," Caldwell interjected before Langford could say more. "Not that I believe. I haven't seen him drunk, nor any proof that he is gambling. However, I believe he's taken a mistress."

Every nerve and muscle in Nick's body tensed up. How dare Latham keep a mistress while courting Priscilla? And how the bloody hell could he afford a mistress? "I'm not sure I want to hear this. Not since he's courting Priscilla, and she likes him."

"Perhaps you should leave," Caldwell said. "I wasn't thinking."

"Bloody hell if I'll leave now!" Nick bellowed louder than he intended. "Sorry, I didn't mean to yell."

"It's all right," Blackstone said. "I understand. You feel responsible for Lady Priscilla."

"I'm wondering where his influx of coin is coming from to afford a mistress," Caldwell asked no one in particular. "I'm paying for his household and Latham House's expenses until his estates start thriving again. I can't imagine any profits coming in yet."

Langford took a sip of his drink. "You know it's not from gambling since you pay spies at all the gambling hells to report to you if they see him."

"Right," Caldwell agreed. "So where is the coin coming from?"

"How convinced are you that he took a mistress?" Nick asked.

"Not completely. It's just a feeling," Caldwell began. "Since Beatrice and I moved into Latham house, I've become accustomed to his routine. There are nights he doesn't come home. The only reason I can come up with is a mistress. That and he sometimes reeks strongly of lady's perfume at breakfast."

"He could be visiting a brothel. He used to frequent them

often enough," Blackstone said.

Caldwell frowned and looked thoughtful. "That is true."

"Well," Langford began. "How can we help you?"

"You can't. I just needed to vent my worries." Caldwell stood. "Sorry to take you away from the soirée."

"Think nothing of it," Blackstone said as all four men exited his study.

"YOU WANTED TO see me?"

"Yes. Please sit," Viscount Norton said to his late-night guest.

"I understand you require funds and have many connections with . . ." Norton paused, ". . . how can I put this delicately—the seedier side of the *ton*."

"I do. Or I did until recently. I'm trying to prove to my brother that I'm a worthy gentleman and have left my vices behind."

"And have you?"

"For the time being, I have. I'm courting the daughter of a duke in the hope of marrying her."

"Will that give you the funds you desire? Enough to live the life you want?" Norton asked.

"Truthfully, no. But it's a start."

"What if I said I've run a lucrative business for nearly fifteen years, giving me the life you see before you?"

"I would wonder if this business is legal."

The old man laughed, then coughed. "Far from legal. Does that bother you?"

David took time to answer. What if Lady Priscilla found out he was doing business illegally? If he joined Norton in business, could he marry Lilly and still keep his mistress? It would be ideal. "Illegal dealings don't bother me."

"How do I know I can trust you?" Norton asked with beady eyes that saw all.

David didn't think the man missed anything. "You wouldn't have invited me here if you didn't already trust me. Nor would you have sent me money to keep, regardless of whether I took the job or not."

"Correct. Let us have a whisky, and I'll tell you a story."

CHAPTER EIGHT

FOR THE FIRST time since his days at Eton and his one night of blackmail, Nick felt his life was out of control. He had always prided himself on being in control—except for those times.

And now.

He sat behind his desk, looking into the eyes of his ex-mistress, Anne Brooks. He experienced the world around him fade to black and sway from side to side until he grabbed a small trash receptacle and relieved his stomach of his breakfast.

"I'm sorry I had to come to you and share the news. I know you last visited me six months ago, and you promised to care for me until I found a new protector, and I meant to find one." She wiped her eyes with her handkerchief. "I truly did, but as you can see by my burgeoning belly, no one wants a castoff with a bastard in her belly."

If he hadn't already emptied his stomach, he would now. Anne, his mistress of three years, with whom he'd broken off relations six months ago, was carrying his child. He swore to himself when he first took a woman to bed that he would do everything in his means not to sire a child outside of wedlock. It wasn't fair to the child—being a by-blow wasn't an easy life. He would take care of them both for life, of course, but as much as he didn't want to subject the child to being a bastard, he couldn't marry Anne. Being a selfish blackguard turned his stomach, but that's what he was.

"I will buy the house I rent for you and put the title in your name, pay the taxes and upkeep, and continue paying for the household servants. On top of that, I will settle five hundred pounds yearly to be paid in quarterly installments. I will pay for the child's nurse, governess, and education. If it is a boy, I will set up a trust for his future. If it's a girl, I will set aside a dowry to ensure she marries well." He paused and continued. "There is one thing, though. If you become another man's mistress, which is your right to do, your yearly allowance and all the household expenses will stop."

"Nicholas," Anne said with a relieved sigh. "Thank you. You are being most generous."

He leaned forward, put his elbows on the desk, steepled his fingers, and studied her. He met Anne when she was eighteen years old. She was the daughter of a talented and well-known tailor. She welcomed customers into her father's shop. A shop she could never take over because she was a woman.

The first time he saw her, he knew he wanted her. Her hair was black as night, and her eyes were just as dark, with the tiniest slant on the side giving her a unique look. She had the palest skin and a round figure. Nick visited the shop more than necessary to see her. A flirtation started, and before he knew it, she begged him to take her away and make her his mistress.

"Why are you staring at me?"

He shook the musings out of his head. "Sorry. I remember the first time we met. I should never have gone back to the shop."

"I would still be greeting my father's customers and living with him on top of the shop if you hadn't. Cleaning, cooking, and being his slave. I don't think he would ever have let me go." She rested her hands on her round belly. "No. It is better this way. Although I never wanted to bear a child out of wedlock. I am truly ruined now. Not that I wasn't the day I walked out of my father's shop with my hand in yours."

His insides tightened. "I'm sorry. I always used a French

letter. It must have failed on our last night together." Anne had come to him chaste; as far as he knew, she had never been with another man.

"I understand you are looking for a bride." Her face fell, and he'd never heard her sound so sad.

"I am. And I'm sorry. It can't be you. I'm obligated to marry someone within my social standing. As a marquess, I have responsibilities to uphold."

"I know. But a girl can dream, can't she?"

Rising from the chair, she headed toward the exit.

"You will send word when the baby is born?" he queried, his heart hurting for Anne and her situation. However, she would be set for life and need not be mistress to another.

"Of course, Lord Hollingsworth."

The hour was early, but he grabbed a bottle of brandy, poured half a glass, and downed it. He poured more and stared into the amber liquid, pondering his future. A future that was rapidly spiraling out of control.

⟫⟪

"You seem out of sorts today," Emmeline said to Priscilla, sitting next to Lilly as they rode in Blackstone's well-designed carriage toward Bond Street.

"I am. My mind is preoccupied with two gentlemen." Fidgeting in her seat and adjusting her skirts for the third time, Priscilla exhaled. "How does one choose between two?"

Lilly and Emmeline exchanged a knowing look.

"It should be easy. But alas, it is not," replied Emmeline.

"Not easy at all," added Lilly.

"Have either of you encountered such a dilemma?"

Both ladies laughed. "Have you never heard the story about how I met my first husband?" Emmeline asked.

"I don't believe I have. Only that he died several years later in a riding accident."

"Indeed. But there is so much more to the story than our marriage and his death. On the first night of my first Season, I met Blackstone and Mr. Fitzpatrick, Andrew and Aiden. I was smitten with both of them." She sighed wistfully. "More than smitten in the months that followed. I fell in love with both of them as they did with me. I received two marriage proposals. What you may not know is that Andrew and Aiden were the best of friends. I never wanted to cause friction in their friendship, and what I say next needs to stay between us. I was prepared to accept Andrew's proposal, except he rescinded it." She wiped a tear from her cheek with her gloved hand. "I was heartbroken, yet I still had Aiden's proposal, which I gladly accepted, as I also loved him.

"I tried to be the best wife. Regardless, Aiden grew uncomfortable with Andrew and distanced us from him. But not only from Andrew but also from Caldwell and Langford. I felt guilty for this. Then, not long before the house party we attended where he died, I miscarried."

Gasping, Priscilla reached out and touched her hand briefly. "I'm so sorry."

"Thank you. Anyway," she took a moment to glance out the window before turning back to her. "He took it hard, as did I. But he dealt with it differently. He got angry, drank, and we quarreled, which we seldom did. But I was glad at least that all four friends were finally together again at the house party. They went hunting—or at least planned on it. They got drunk instead. Andrew and Aiden raced, and Aiden fell from his mount and broke his neck."

"How horrific for you."

"Yes. My heart broke in half that day."

"How did you come to be married to Blackstone?" Priscilla asked. A pain settled heavily in her chest at the sad story of Emmeline's first marriage.

"Six long years passed, and I waited for him to come to me. He did once before leaving for the West Indies for nearly three years. Andrew battled his own demons, which nearly destroyed him. His father almost disowned him. Thankfully, he turned his life around and came back to me. I love him now more than I ever thought possible."

Priscilla sighed at the second-chance love story. "I see that every time you are together. Or even now, when you speak of him. Your eyes and face glow with love."

She blushed. "How embarrassing."

"Nonsense," Lilly chimed in. "It is lovely."

"You do the same when you are with Langford," Emmeline said.

"I know. I can't help it."

"How do I choose between David and Nick? David is very nice and acts gentlemanly when in my presence. I enjoy his company. There is an easy companionship that is forming between us." She sighed and closed her eyes to picture his face, but the only one that came to her mind was Nick. "Though I know he is only courting me in hopes of obtaining my hand in marriage for my dowry."

"That may be true, but it's not the only reason," Emmeline said. "I have seen the way he looks at you. He is smitten."

"That is kind of you to say. But as for Nick? I care for him deeply." She exhaled. "I've been half in love with him for half of my life it seems. He does not need my dowry. He does, however, need someone to marry and bear his heirs. Either way, I am being used for something when I only want to be loved."

"What about your first husband?" Lilly asked with sadness in her eyes. "All three of us have been widowed."

"I cared deeply for Jasper, but the chance to fall completely in love with him was stolen from me. Although I know, given time, it would have happened. He was that type of man. Honorable, kind, and considerate. He put others before himself. He died a hero trying to save another man from drowning. Their ship was under attack by the French. A sailor had fallen overboard, and Jasper jumped in to save him. Sadly, they both perished."

"How tragic. I'm sorry his time on this earth was cut short," Emmeline said. "Too young to be taken from you, as Aiden was from me. Yet, when I see my future, I can't visualize it with Aiden, only Andrew."

"When I see the man of my future, it is blurry. I want to believe it is Nick. It would be easier to see Latham." She paused. "I don't think Nick sees himself with me." Regardless of what he said to her about wanting to court her for real, it would be for all the wrong reasons. They were comfortable together, and what she attributed to possible love, he saw as friendship.

"You never know," Lilly replied. "I hated Langford when we first met. Look at us now."

"You hated him?" Priscilla couldn't believe that.

"Yes. He accused me of stealing from his uncle, the previous Earl of Langford, who married me as a favor to a dying man—my father."

"How had I never heard all of this?"

"Oh, look," Lilly leaned forward, looking out the window just as the carriage stopped. "We have arrived."

Priscilla realized Lilly didn't want to talk about what led to her marriage to Langford. Perhaps it was too painful for her. They exited the carriage and made their way to the milliner's shop. The weather was in their favor for shopping, which made Bond Street crowded, and the milliner's shop was even more of a crush.

"Look at these white lace gloves," Lilly said as she tried on several pairs. "They are nice and thin and soft. And a perfect fit. I must have these. My hands sweat in my cotton gloves during the heat of summer."

Emmeline giggled at Lilly's comment. "I know what you mean. I could use a pair of lace gloves as well." She tried on several pairs and chose a pretty pale-blue pair and a white pair.

"You have both convinced me I need them, too. I'll take this cream pair," Priscilla said as she tried them on. "Perfect fit. I need a cream bonnet and perhaps some ribbon to go with them. Do you mind stopping at Madam Serena's? I have a final fitting for a gown for the Greenville Ball."

"Not at all," both Lilly and Emmeline replied. "We do as well."

"Will it bother you to return to where Viscount Redford attacked you?" Emmeline asked Lilly.

"Perhaps."

"Attacked?" Priscilla gasped.

"Yes, well, I courted Viscount Redford briefly. He was after my money and would not take no for an answer to his marriage proposal. So he accosted me at the Greenville Ball at the Vauxhall Pleasure Gardens two years ago and then tried to kidnap me to Gretna Green and force me to wed him. Fortunately, my dear husband, Edmund—though he wasn't my husband then, of course—fouled up Redford's plans and rescued me with Cald-well's help."

"How dreadful. Thank goodness you were saved," Priscilla said as chills crept up her arms at the tale.

"Yes, indeed," Lilly said.

When they arrived at Madam Serena's, she called for Priscilla to have her fitting first, and she went through the curtain into the fitting room. Madam Serena and an associate pinned the beautiful blue-and-silver ball gown, ensuring it would fit her perfectly once the stitching was done.

When Priscilla was finished, Emmeline went in and she joined Lilly in the front of the shop. "Why are people looking at us and whispering?"

Lilly glanced around and nodded her head at several ladies. "They whisper about Emmeline and me because we were widowed at such young ages and are happily married to a duke and an earl. As for you, I imagine it is because you ran off to Gretna Green to marry a naval officer who died in battle. I believe they find our tragic lives intriguing. And as for Emmeline and me, our love matches are also fascinating compared to many of their loveless marriages."

"Truly, do they not have something else to gossip about?"

"Sadly, no. Lady Wilmington loves to gossip and make one feel uncomfortable. She is staring at you because she knows you and Hollingsworth are good friends and courting, and she wants him for her daughter, Lady Grace, who looks as though she wants to be anywhere but here. Be careful; Lady Wilmington is quick and cunning and not beyond resorting to inventing rumors to suit her plans."

"I've never talked to Lady Grace, as she is shy, but she appears nothing like her mother," Priscilla said as she smiled at Lady Grace to let her know they weren't adversaries. Except they were where Nick was concerned. Oh, dear. She didn't want to be rivals with her. She wanted to be friends with Lady Grace because she appeared genuinely lovely and would probably make a good friend. That was if she was ever without the company of her mother.

"I don't know her well either," Lilly added. "But when I first met her, I planned on joining her as a wallflower."

"What happened?"

"Langford swept me off my feet. I never had time to stand on the outskirts with Lady Grace. Too bad, really. We could have become friends."

Emmeline swept through the curtain separating the front of the store from the fitting room. She looked striking with her black hair, blue eyes, dark-blue walking dress, pelisse, and matching bonnet. Priscilla was jealous of her looks and lush figure. Priscilla was tall for a woman and always felt she stood out for that reason alone.

"Your turn, Lilly," she said with a wide smile.

As Lilly left to take her turn, Emmeline approached Priscilla and grimaced. "Lady Wilmington is making eyes at you. I believe you have gained an enemy."

Priscilla found all this quite shocking. Did everyone have ulterior motives? Did most people hide behind a façade? "If Nick wants or doesn't want Lady Grace, that is his business. I've no say in it either way."

Emmeline looked at her with narrow eyes. "Don't you? You are in his favor and courting him. That makes you Lady Grace's rival. Lady Grace may not see you that way because she is too kind, but her mother is something else entirely. She might even stoop so low as invent things to keep you and Nick apart. Even so much as start false rumors."

"Lilly said the same thing. Surely, she cannot be all that bad?"

Emmeline wrapped her arm through Priscilla's. "She can. A determined Marriage Mart Mama can and will be ruthless."

Her insides trembled at the thought of Lady Wilmington setting her sights on her, ruining her chances with Nick, David, or anyone else for that matter, inventing rumors meant to crush her socially. How could someone be so cruel? Looking at the lady in question now, Priscilla shuddered at the hatred spurring from her eyes. Oh, yes. She had an enemy.

Emmeline's driver met them outside with the carriage and took them to Berkeley Square, where Gunter's was.

"Thank you, Thompson. We shall be back in an hour," Emmeline said to the driver.

"Would you like to order and take our ices back to the park? We can return the cups and spoons when we finish. It's such a lovely day," Emmeline asked as they crossed the street.

"That would be lovely. I do so admire all the trees," Lilly said.

"Trees?" Priscilla queried.

"I grew up in the country and miss all the trees and woods."

"I see," she said. Since Priscilla spent most of her life in London, the woods and forests appeared scary to her. When she needed to feel nature, taking to a park was perfect for her. Not to mention, most of the streets of Mayfair were lined with trees.

All three ordered lemon ices and sat on a bench in the park to enjoy the frozen treat.

"Tomorrow morning, I'm delivering baskets to the rookeries," Emmeline said as she finished her ice. "Would you care to join me, Priscilla? I believe the duchess would appreciate me having another person to help me."

Her father always warned her about the seedier parts of London and how she was never to travel into them. But he need never know. "I would like to do my part for the cause. I will devise an excuse for my parents if they ask where I'm going."

"Wonderful. I'll pick you up at half past eight."

"That early?" Since the Season began, Priscilla had been staying in bed late. It was a good thing there was no social event on her calendar for that night which would keep her out until the wee hours of the morning.

"Are you attending anything tonight?" Emmeline asked.

"No. Half-past eight will be fine."

"Good."

CHAPTER NINE

P RISCILLA ARRIVED BACK home after Gunter's just in time to prepare for afternoon visitors. David and Nick would arrive soon if today were like any other in the past two weeks. Eugenia helped her change into a medium-pink day dress with matching slippers. She combed out her hair, teasing it to fluff out the flatness on top from wearing a hat most of the day. Leaving it loose, she went down the stairs to the drawing room, where she found her mother chatting with Lady Hollingsworth.

Priscilla curtsied. "Lady Hollingsworth. It is a pleasure to see you."

Lady Hollingsworth laughed. "Sit down, Priscilla, no need to be so formal with me. After all, you are like a daughter to me."

"Thank you." She sat in a relatively comfortable chair facing the settee where her mother and Lady Hollingsworth ate small sandwiches and grapes. Priscilla studied Lady Hollingsworth and, for the first time, saw a resemblance to Nick.

Priscilla picked up a clean plate and placed two sandwiches and several grapes on it. All she had had since breakfast was the ice at Gunter's. She nibbled on a sandwich, sans the crust, while listening to the ladies gossip about one thing and another.

"Did you hear that Viscount Norton passed in his sleep last night?" Mother said. "I think his viscountess poisoned him. She has a rather mysterious past."

Priscilla nearly choked on her food. "Mother. Be kind. Perhaps she loved the man and is devastated by his death."

"Oh, pish-posh," her mother said as she waved her arm out. "He was ancient, and she is rather young. Perhaps only in her twenties. They wed some years ago. Perhaps she was tired of waiting for him to keel over, so she helped him a bit."

"Once again, Mother, don't be spreading rumors."

"I didn't start them; they are already spreading throughout the drawing rooms of London."

"Still. You don't need to repeat it."

"She has ties to my son," Lady Hollingsworth said. "And I would love to know how. She states she saw him drugged and dragged from that awful masquerade party that ruined his reputation. Why did she only speak about it and come to my son's aid now? What does she want from him? Most likely, she wishes to be the next Marchioness of Hollingsworth. Over my dead body will she marry my son."

"Be careful," her mother said. "If she poisoned her husband, no telling what she will do if you get in her way."

"Oh, dear," Lady Hollingsworth clutched her chest.

Priscilla's heart seized up. What if she managed to marry Nick and she poisoned him? She disliked this conversation and her wayward thoughts. As she forced the image of Nick with Viscountess Norton out of her mind, he was announced. It was laughable because when he saw his mother, his eyes widened, and for a second, she thought he would turn around and exit the room. If he'd been smart, he would have done that. Both their mothers in the same drawing room should frighten anyone.

"Mother," he bent and kissed her cheek. "What a pleasant surprise to find you here."

"And why should it be a surprise?" his mother huffed. "The duchess and I are very good friends going back to our childhood."

He bristled. "I didn't mean it that way. It was just something to say when I saw you here, that is all."

"Please have a seat," Priscilla's mother said, freeing everyone from the uncomfortable moment.

"Thank you, Your Grace," he said as he sat in the chair beside Priscilla. "Hello, Priscilla."

"Hello, Nicholas."

"I'm rather shocked Baron Latham is not already present," he said. "Do you suppose he is skipping a day to seek out other . . . avenues . . . of entertainment?"

She glared daggers at him and lowered her voice. "You are a vile man."

"Thank you." He grinned. "I try hard."

"Did you hear that Viscount Norton died?" Oh dear, she sounded like her mother.

He turned somber. "Yes. Unfortunately for him. He was rather old, though. And keeping up with a young wife couldn't have been easy."

"It would appear so since he is dead."

"Are you mentioning this because you want to recruit her into the Ladies' Society of Mayfair?"

"Hardly. And not all the members are widows. I also don't believe she's up to the Duchess of Greenville's standard."

"Careful," he said as he toyed with his hat. "Your horns are showing."

"My what?"

"Never mind me." He frowned. "I'm in a dreadful mood today. Forgive me for taking it out on you." He turned, looked at her, and hit her with his beautiful smile and mischievous eyes. "How would you like to take a walk in the park? The weather is quite nice."

"Yes, I know. I went shopping with Emmeline and Lilly this morning and only just arrived home before you showed up."

"Well, would you?"

"Mother, could you please make my excuses to Baron Latham if he calls? Nicholas and I are going for a stroll in the park."

Priscilla should have known the look their mothers would share at this announcement. They were forever hoping for the fairytale ending, the one where Nick rode off into the sunset with her sitting on his horse before him, his arms wrapped around her. They would travel through magical forests with animals that could speak until they arrived at their castle in the clouds. If only fairytales came true.

She excused herself to hurry up the stairs to retrieve the pelisse and hat that matched her dress and change into half boots. If she kept her slippers on, she would feel every pebble she stepped on through the thin soles.

Once they were out the door, she wrapped her arm around his elbow, and they began to walk toward Hyde Park. "I would imagine the park is a crush with this weather." Her insides flinched at her silly words about the weather. For some reason, Nick was making her nervous today. She'd never truly had competition for his affections before. Even if she'd never truly had his affections, at least no one else had, either, except for his longtime mistress.

Priscilla used to be envious of his mistress. She had Nick all to herself. But when Priscilla considered their relationship, she felt sad for the woman who would never be more than his mistress. He would never marry her. Did she love him? "Can I ask you a very intimate question?"

His entire body tensed, she felt it. And his breath hitched inside his chest. "You may ask. It doesn't mean I'll answer it."

"Do you still have your mistress?" There, she said it. She hadn't thought about his mistress in forever; however, the conversation about the viscount had her wondering.

He coughed. "Christ, what the hell made you ask such a thing And how did you even know about her?"

"I don't know why I asked." She sighed. "I overheard our mothers speaking about her once. And you didn't answer me."

"It's none of your business, but the answer is no. I called it off months ago. Six months to be exact."

She couldn't think of a thing to say in response.

"No comment on my answer?" Nick continued when she

didn't. "You know I wouldn't waste my breath by answering anyone else who dared ask such a personal question. But I thought being honest was wise because you mean something to me."

The low timbre of Nick's voice during that last—and what he said—sent pleasant chills throughout her entire body. It reminded her of the way he sounded when he kissed her in the gardens at the Trowbridge musicale.

"Forgive me. It was rude of me for wanting to know." She pulled her arm from his, then wrapped it back through and sighed once again. When or if they ever kissed again, she had wanted to know if his lips had recently been on another's. Not that she had the right to think that way. They did not belong to each other. And hadn't she kissed David? What right did she have to want Nick all to herself?

He turned his head, his features softened as he gave her a crooked grin. "There is nothing to forgive, and I could tell something was bothering you so I'm glad you were brave enough to ask."

"How did you know something was bothering me? I hardly knew it myself."

Why did he have to be so handsome, charming, annoying, and so many other things? If only she could lock up her heart again against him. But their private time in the Trowbridge gardens had shattered the locks encasing her heart, and she was so very susceptible to having it broken into smithereens, never to be whole or beat correctly again. She needed to keep reminding herself her courtship with Nick was fake and the courtship with David real.

"You forget I've known you since you were a wee babe. I notice all your tells," he said with that silly half grin still on his face.

"My tells? Please enlighten me!"

"When annoyed with someone or something, you narrow your eyes and wrinkle your nose. Quite cutely, I might add."

Well, she'd asked for it. "I do not wrinkle my nose."

"You do. And when you are happy, you smile, and your eyes sparkle. The hazel color turns more green."

"I'll agree with that. What else?" Oh, lord, did she ask for more tells?

"When you are truly exasperated, your body trembles and you look down your nose at whoever is the cause."

"I tremble—I hope you are the only one who notices that. Looking down my nose at people is easy since I'm taller than most ladies and even some gentlemen. Seriously, though, I don't think others notice any of these tells."

"There are other tells. Intimate tells I noticed for the first time the other night in the garden when you . . ."

She smacked his shoulder with her free arm. "Don't you dare say it!"

"I won't. But when you . . . you know, your face became flushed, your eyelids closed, and your lips pursed as you moaned."

"Enough of my tells or bringing up the other night," she warned as she hit him again. "Are you trying to make me die of embarrassment? Because that is what will happen if you continue."

He patted her hand, the one entwined through his arm. "Not at all. I like getting you riled up. However, since the entrance to the park is up ahead, we must cease this talk and speak of nothing but the boring weather and who danced with whom at the latest society function. Otherwise, people will notice something stirring inside my breeches."

Do not look at his breeches. Do not! Her eyes lowered, then widened at the noticeable bulge. She chose not to comment on his predicament. "What a silly, unaccomplished life most of the *ton* live if all they talk about is the weather and such stuff."

"Not you, my dear. You have your charity now. And I admire you for it. Thinking of those less fortunate is one thing, but to actively help is another. I hope you take all precautions when traveling into the slums."

Was he worried for her safety? Her heart tingled at the thought. "I've hardly done anything besides attend one meeting. We'll see how tomorrow goes."

His brows pinched as he turned his head down and looked at her. "What happens tomorrow?"

"Tomorrow will be my first time venturing into St. Giles. Please don't let it slip around Mother or Father. If they knew, they would forbid me from going."

"Your secret is safe with me."

"Emmeline is picking me up in the morning. I'm excited and terrified."

"As you should be."

"Nick, don't frighten me."

"Sorry. Just please be cautious."

"I will."

"You were correct when you said the park would be crowded," he remarked as they entered the gates. His body tensed, and he groaned. "Perhaps we should head back. I hate crowds."

"Nick, what's wrong?" Then she saw what caused his hackles to rise. A lovely pregnant woman walked toward them with an older gentleman.

"I fear it's too late to turn around," he said, his voice vibrating in panic, which puzzled her. Nick panicked?

The couple was upon them. The woman had a beautiful smile for Nick, which changed to a frown and a glare at her. Priscilla had no idea who the woman was, but the stranger spewed venom at her. When the gentleman noticed Nick, he looked ready to pounce like a lion on his prey. Chills climbed up Priscilla's spine. Nothing good could come from the expressions on these strangers' faces or by Nick's behavior.

"Well, if it isn't the supposed gentleman who stole my daughter," the man snarled, "set her up in a fine home and used her for nigh on three years, then left her with a baby in her belly. A bastard for a blackguard."

"Sir—"

"Don't *sir* me. You don't get to address me after what you did to my Anne. You ruined her. You saw an opportunity and took it without regard for my daughter and her reputation. Not that you have a good reputation, either. Although I heard it has been restored. She could have married a fine, upstanding shop owner, but no, you had to have her for your plaything."

Priscilla stood there, her body tense, her heart pounding. As much as her jaw wanted to drop open, she kept her mouth shut as she listened and realized what this conversation was about. This young lady was Nick's previous mistress. And the man with her was her father, whom Priscilla now recognized as her father's tailor, Mr. Brooks. What she couldn't come to terms with was that she carried Nick's child. She'd always known they'd shared a bed. Wasn't that what a mistress was for? But seeing the proof of it had the sandwiches she'd eaten threatening to reappear.

"Come, dear," Mr. Brooks said as he started walking, practically dragging Anne, who looked wide-eyed and apologetic to Nick as she mouthed, "Sorry."

"I need to go," Nick said in a weary voice she'd never heard from him. "I'll escort you home."

"Was that your ex-mistress?" For some reason, she needed verification; she needed to hear it from his lips. And how coincidental they had been just discussing her.

"Yes. She was my mistress. She showed up at my house the other day. I hadn't seen her in six months."

"She came to see you?"

"Yes. Obviously, she had news to share."

"Nick. What will you do?" She squeezed his arm. "Will you marry her and keep your child from being born a bastard?" Oh dear God, her knees almost buckled at the thought.

"I would be doing her an even more disservice if I married her. She would never be accepted into our world. One doesn't marry one's mistress, child or no child."

Her insides fell. Not that she wanted Nick to marry his mistress, but for some reason, she expected him to be more emotional . . . more sensitive . . . more caring. "I see."

He tugged her over to stand beneath a tree away from prying ears and eyes. "I don't think you do. Anne is a lovely woman. And regardless of what her father said, I didn't steal her away. She begged me to become my mistress. She hated her father's shop and all it entailed. She didn't want to marry a shop owner and work night and day. She dreamed of a pampered life, and I agreed to give it to her. She entered our relationship knowing what would happen then and in the future." He paused, took off his hat, and combed a hand through his hair. "What I did do was promise her I would support her and the child."

"Nick." She touched his shoulder.

"Let me finish." He exhaled. "I'm not a bloody blackguard. I'm doing everything I can to help her and the child. I'm not the monster her father made me out to be."

She wanted so badly to hug him as he wiped away tears that escaped his eyes. She'd been wrong. He was emotional.

"I used a French letter every time we were together. I know they do not always protect against conception, but at least I tried to keep her safe."

"Did you love her?" Oh dear, how hard it was to speak those words out loud. And it would devastate her to hear him say yes.

"No. I cared for her. But I never loved her, and she knew it."

"Does she love you?"

His fingers combed through his hair again, and he groaned. "She told me she does. I told her not to fall in love with me, but she did anyway. And for that, my insides are in upheaval. The guilt eating at my stomach is excruciatingly painful. Nothing more than I deserve for not protecting her better. When I made her my mistress, I swore to her and myself I would never get her with child."

He placed his hat back on his head, wrapped her arm through his, and began walking briskly. "I must apologize for what you found yourself in the middle of. Mr. Brooks should have spoken with me privately. But I also understand that she is his only child, and he raised her alone after her mother died of a fever when Anne was young. Still, I'm sorry you had to hear what you did."

"It wasn't your fault."

"Isn't it, though?"

"Fine. It is your fault, but you are not to blame for Mr. Brook's outburst. Thank goodness no one else was around to hear him. Otherwise, you would find yourself entangled in yet another scandal. Although I don't understand why. Gentlemen of the *ton* have bastards with their mistresses quite often, and it is widely accepted. Gossiped about but not scandalous."

"Which is sad. I hope her father will convince her to marry one of his assistants. My settlement on her will not change, and she can continue to live the life she wants while giving our child a name. When I return home, I will send a message to him immediately stating just that. Perhaps he will hate me a little less."

"You are a good man, Nicholas Pierce, Marquess of Hollingsworth."

He groaned, "You can think I am, but I'm not. You may want to remember that when you think otherwise. I'm less likely to hurt you that way."

AFTER RETURNING HOME from the walk in the park that never happened, Nick sat in his library with a full bottle of whisky and thought about his troubles. When he first recognized Anne and her father approaching him and Priscilla, he almost turned and ran. However, he was no coward. He did have to fight not to cast up his accounts, though, because he had known what was coming.

Mr. Brooks was a good man, but Nick had done the worst thing imaginable to a parent: He had taken his daughter as his mistress. Nick had already sent a footman to him with a message and hoped to hear back soon. He would do all he could to make things right. Anne deserved a husband, even if only to give the child a name and Anne respectability.

When Nick had asked Priscilla to walk in the park with him, he had hoped to pry her feelings for Latham out of her. He needed to know how serious she was about him. Because of running into Anne, he didn't know any more about her feelings for Latham than he had before. It added another thing to worry about.

He poured a generous amount of whisky into a glass and was so thankful he had no plans for the evening. If he had, he would have had to cancel because he planned to get drunk.

CHAPTER TEN

"A RE YOU FEELING all right?" Emmeline inquired the following morning when Priscilla took the seat opposite her in a nondescript, black carriage she'd never seen before. Her head spun after she met the driver and guard, both in disguise. They were brothers, apparently, and Emmeline did not know their real identities.

"I had trouble sleeping last night. But I'm fine. I'll nap before the Greenville Ball tonight. I can't wait for my gown to be delivered today."

"Nor I," Emmeline replied. "Was your troubled sleep because you were anxious for today?"

"No. It had something to do with Hollingsworth, but I can't share."

"You are too good to him, and he doesn't deserve it."

She started to do what Nick said she did when annoyed and relaxed her face and body. "I probably know him better than anyone, and he is a good man. Misunderstood at times, I think. He internalizes his emotions and appears cold or cynical, but truthfully, he is not. I realize when he briefly courted Lilly, he spoke unkindly of me and not wanting to be stuck in a marriage with me, but I don't think he meant it."

"You are right. I see the way he looks and smiles at you. He doesn't do that with anyone else. Now let me tell you about today. When we arrive, Flynn will open the door, and we will get out to a crowd lined up on the side of the street. He will hand us the donations, and we will give them out. It's as simple as that. The hard part is when we run out, and people are still lined up waiting and we send them away empty-handed. I tell them to come back earlier next time. We deliver on Mondays and Thursdays. On another note, has the duchess told you about Amelia House? It's a home that she runs in her sister's name for mothers and children with nowhere to live or who were abused. Those who live there are trained in a profession so they can eventually support themselves and have a better life."

"I have heard about Amelia House but not about the training. The duchess is the most kind and generous person."

"She is. It all came about because her sister became with child, and the man refused to marry her. She ran away, and both she and the baby died from disease in a rickety tenement in St. Giles."

"That is so sad." Priscilla refused to compare the duchess's sister with Nick's mistress. Nick would take care of her and the child. Unfortunately, not all men did.

"We are here," Emmeline said as the coach stopped. "Do not wander off under any circumstances. I did that once and was almost run down by a coach. If it weren't for Blackstone, I would be dead. As it was, both of us nearly died." She shivered. "I still have nightmares about that day."

"I do remember hearing something about that. How dreadful. And thankfully, Blackstone was there to save you. He is truly your hero."

"Some days, yes, he is."

When Flynn handed Priscilla the fourth basket to disperse, she was positive she knew him from somewhere but couldn't pinpoint it. "Have we met before?" she finally asked him.

He smiled, his teeth slightly crooked, and said, "Not that I know of."

Emmeline chimed in with a smile at Flynn. "Even if you have

met, he will never admit it. He and Mitchel are mysterious to the core."

"I see," Priscilla said, eyeing the two brothers. She was confident she would figure it out eventually. She never forgot a face or name. It was a talent if you wanted to remember and a curse if you didn't.

It didn't take long to finish distributing the baskets, and Mitchel helped them back into the coach. As they began to move Emmeline said, "Thank you for accompanying me today. Will you consider going again?"

Not that it took up much of her time or was as frightening as she thought it might be, but she needed to think on it. She disliked keeping things from her parents, and she knew they'd be worried for her safety if they discovered it. Emmeline's tale of nearly being hit by a carriage flashed in her mind. She wanted to help, but perhaps donating more funds and packing the baskets with goods and clothing would be a better route for her. "Perhaps. Would you be disappointed if I preferred not to?"

Emmeline reached forward and patted her hands, which were entwined and resting on her lap. "Not at all. The Ladies' Society of Mayfair is appreciative of any help you can give."

Priscilla relaxed against the squabs, feeling relieved. She hadn't wanted to disappoint her friend and was glad to know she wasn't. "Thank you for understanding."

The carriage stopped in front of Avery Manor, and Mitchel helped her down. She gave him a second look and shook her head. She still couldn't place him.

Before she made it to the top of the granite stairs, the butler opened the door. "Thank you, Berkley."

She hurried upstairs to her bedchamber and, with Eugenia's help, washed up quickly and changed into a pink day dress. Once presentable, she made her way to the family parlor, where she knew her mother would be embroidering or needlepointing something or other. She also expected lunch to be served at any moment, and Priscilla was ready for it. Her stomach had growled for most of the morning.

"Mother," she said as she swept into the room.

"Where were you off to so early this morning?"

"The Duchess of Blackstone picked me up, and we rode through the park. Then we visited Lady Langford." Snowball snuck into the room, climbed onto her lap, curled up into a ball, and purred contentedly.

"I'm glad you have new friends, especially as they're widows who went on to make advantageous second matches. If dear Nicholas would come up to snuff, you could join them."

"Mother. I can't make Nick do something he doesn't want to do, nor can you or Lady Hollingsworth. You have tried for years, and it has caused nothing but friction between us."

"But you love him—do not deny it. I see it in your eyes every time you are together."

"You could be witnessing feelings left over from my girlhood infatuation." She would not admit that which she did not know herself completely. "I know Nick cares for me, but Baron Latham does, too. And there would be nothing wrong if I married him."

Her mother frowned. "By the way, I forgot to tell you that he came by yesterday and was disappointed that he'd missed you. He said he would see you tonight at the Greenville Ball."

"Good. I thought perhaps he was giving up on courting me."

"You know how your father and I feel. A joining of our family with Hollingsworth's would please us. That being said, if you choose Latham, we will welcome him into the family graciously."

"Thank you. It's good to know—if it comes to that. Then again, perhaps I will meet someone new tonight and be swept off my feet, and I will forget all about Latham and Nick."

"I highly doubt it. Your heart is invested in Nicholas."

She could tell her mother all about girlhood infatuations and lie to herself about not knowing whether she loved or didn't love Nick, when the truth was she did love him. Always had. But time and circumstances had changed the way she perceived things. Whether she loved Nick or not, marriage was not a forgone conclusion. It if were, she would have married him at eighteen. Her feelings for him didn't sway his feelings, and she would not marry him without his love. But she would marry someone else without theirs.

After luncheon, Priscilla went to her chambers and, with Eugenia's help again, undressed down to her chemise and crawled beneath the counterpane to rest. It took some time for her mind to settle down. Too many faces flashed in her mind. Finally, she had had enough and forced them away as she drifted into a much-needed nap to the sound of her cat purring.

DAVID ARRIVED VIA his carriage at Norton Hall half an hour after receiving the message from the viscountess informing him about her husband's death. She received him in the library.

"Please have a seat, Latham."

He sat in a wingback chair—one of two in the room. The new widow occupied the other. "Thank you for coming."

He hadn't believed he'd had a choice. "Please accept my condolences on the passing of your husband."

She dabbed at a tear with her lace handkerchief. "Thank you. It was quite shocking when he didn't awake this morning."

"I imagine."

"I understand you met with my husband recently. He left me with the details. Have you made a decision?"

"I have."

"And?"

"I'll do it."

The viscountess broke out into a smile. "Wonderful." She handed over a thick packet of papers. "This is a copy of everything you need to know. Study it, memorize it. We never swindle the same person twice. Come back in two days."

Knowing he was dismissed, he exited her townhouse, climbed

in his carriage, and signaled the driver to take him home.

Once back home, David locked himself inside his study and shuffled through the numerous pages, picking the ones he wanted to read carefully first. Two men would report to him directly. Gieves and Fergus. Presumably not their real names. According to Norton's notes, they were men who had been working for Norton from the outset and were reliable and trustworthy. Norton, under many false names, rented properties throughout London. For the swindles to work, they needed to move constantly, and they needed the swindles to change in nature.

David worried that Gieves and Fergus would want to strike out on their own now that Norton was dead. Except it seemed they hadn't the connections to do so. That was the one thing Norton expressed during their initial meeting, which had David considering taking over for the viscount. His death only accelerated the timeline.

His mind worked fast as he read over the papers. He understood all the logistics regarding the players, the scams, and the blackmail. David laughed when he saw the date and the amount swindled from Hollingsworth. So he wasn't as bright as he thought he was. And now David understood the rumors surrounding Hollingsworth. The list of gentlemen who had fallen prey was staggering. Not just members of the aristocracy. Members of the gentry as well as members of the clergy. David had fallen into a windfall of knowledge and the potential to make thousands of pounds monthly. Old man Norton had been brilliant in creating such a lucrative business. David would gladly take it over and reap the financial rewards.

THE GLIMMERING BLUE-AND-SILVER ballgown Priscilla wore shimmered when she walked as the lights reflected off the silver sparkles adorning the tulle overlay on the skirt and in the thin pieces of silver tulle woven throughout her hair, which she wore half up with the rest of her auburn curls cascading down her back and across her shoulders. A matching shawl, gloves, heeled shoes, fan, and reticle finished her elegant ensemble. One last glance in the looking glass had her heart soaring with confidence. If Nick and David didn't lose the capacity to speak when she arrived in this gown, nothing could accomplish it. It was the most daring ballgown she'd ever worn, and she was afraid if she took a deep breath, she might pop out the top. Madam Serena assured her it would never happen, but still. She felt indecent.

Her mother looked her up and down with a frown but refrained from giving her opinion, which shocked Priscilla. Perhaps her mother hoped if she bared most of her breasts to Nick, he would go crazy with lust, lose himself, and take her in the Pleasure Gardens, sealing their future together.

Even if they did succumb to their lustful urges, she would never force Nick to marry her. She was a widow, not an innocent debutante.

"The carriage is here," her mother said as Berkley opened the door to the cool evening air.

Priscilla pulled her wrap across her chest as the cool night air caressed her bare skin. Indeed, if she glanced down, she would see her nipples pebbled. Oh dear, that would be something she would have to keep in mind tonight. She did not want some lecherous older gentleman leering at her breasts.

The ride to Vauxhall Gardens on the south side of the River Thames took longer than usual because of traffic. Anyone who had received an invitation from the duke and duchess would not dare decline—the Greenvilles were valuable acquaintances. The duke was twenty years the duchess's senior, but even at fifty-five and thirty-five, they made a strikingly handsome couple. One would have to be blind not to see how the duke doted on his duchess, and with good reason. Since joining the Ladies' Society of Mayfair, Priscilla had a great respect and affection for her.

"Look at the queue of carriages," her mother said, leaning

forward, holding the curtain open on the window.

"Emmeline and Lilly said this would be the largest event of the Season."

"Well, it is certainly the place to hold such an event. I imagine if the weather were foul, it would have been rescheduled. You can hardly have a ball outdoors in inclement weather."

"No. I don't suppose you can." She exhaled as butterflies flew inside her stomach as their carriage pulled up in front of Vauxhall Pleasure Gardens. The name in itself provoked naughty thoughts. They disembarked the carriage with a footman's help and followed the bevy of people lining the Grand Walk, waiting to greet their hosts. Priscilla gasped when her eyes traveled down the line of trees glowing from hundreds of glass lanterns hanging from the branches. They finally reached the front of the colonnade where the duke and duchess were greeting their guests. The colonnade was a three-terraced building, the top of which resembled a crown. On the first-floor terrace was the large orchestra. Her insides hummed with the desire to dance the whole night away.

Priscilla approached their hosts and curtsied deeply. "Your Graces. It's an honor to be here this evening."

"Lady Priscilla, please rise," the Duchess of Greenville said with a kind smile and touched her hands. "We are so glad you could come. Please enjoy yourself and partake in the entertainment."

"Duke, Duchess." Her mother curtsied.

"Duchess." The Duke of Greenville took her mother's hand and bowed over it. "We are pleased you could come and that you brought your lovely daughter with you."

The Duchess of Greenville curtsied. "You honor us with your presence, Your Grace."

"Thank you both for your kind words," her mother said with a smile.

It wasn't long before the Master of Ceremonies announced their names, and Priscilla sighed with relief. She had been so frightened the Duchess of Greenville would say something about the Ladies' Society of Mayfair. Not that her parents didn't know she belonged, but she feared the duchess would comment on her traveling into St. Giles that morning. Her mother would have needed her smelling salts.

Now that they were through the receiving line, Priscilla took in more of their surroundings, and she smiled wistfully at the magical appearance everywhere she looked. A large wooden dance floor had been constructed in front of the colonnade. Numerous tables and chairs were clustered around the dance floor. The tables were decorated with beautiful hot-house flower arrangements. Also, tables and chairs were tucked here and there into the gardens, lit up with more glass lanterns. Flowers and shrubs of every conceivable color were blooming and disbursing their flowery scent into the air. The grandeur and vision took her breath away.

"The duke and duchess outdid themselves this year," her mother said. "The white-and-gold tablecloths and accents complement the colorful gardens instead of trying to outshine the vibrant blooms. The choice of flowers on the tables works perfectly as well. They must have bought out every hot house in London. I've never seen such beauty." She paused and scanned the crowd. "I see Lady Hollingsworth seated with several other ladies. That is where I'll be if you need me."

Before she could acknowledge her mother's words, she vanished. Her mother made the worst chaperone ever. Good thing she didn't need one. She looked around at all the tables and groups of people until she found her friends gathered around a table on the perimeter of the gardens. Her insides relaxed a bit. Standing tall to give herself an air of confidence when she felt nothing remotely resembling confidence, she glided toward them. Well, it was not precisely gliding, but it sounded better than walking. She'd seen ladies glide across a crowded room, drawing all eyes toward them. She pretended to be that person.

Just as she approached, Emmeline and Lilly stepped forward,

each taking one of her hands and leading her toward their table. "Isn't this place magical?" Emmeline said with a smile and a twinkle in her blue eyes. Her deep sapphire-blue gown played off her eyes, making them seem ethereal in the twinkling lights. "Your gown is stunning. Nick had to wipe the drool off his chin as you floated across to us."

She fought not to giggle like a love-sick fool. "I highly doubt it. Both you and Lilly look beyond beautiful." Lilly wore a deep ruby-red gown accentuated with transparent tulle and gold sparkles. Madam Serena had outdone herself with their three gowns.

That wasn't to say the gentlemen didn't look handsome in their evening attire. All wore black cutaway coats with tails, black breeches with hose, and black shoes with either silver or gold buckles. The three waistcoats varied, as did their shirts and cravats. Nick wore a gray-and-white striped waistcoat and a white linen shirt and cravat. She'd never seen him so handsome and formal.

"Lady Priscilla," he said in a smooth, smoky voice that did indecent things to her woman parts as he bowed over her hand. His deep brown eyes seared into her soul. "You look enchanting. You are a princess in a garden full of fairies; their sole purpose is to grant your every wish and desire."

He still held her hand when she curtsied. "Lord Hollingsworth. Are you spouting poetry these days?"

His deep, throaty chuckle warmed her heart. After their encounter in Hyde Park, she had been afraid he would treat her differently now that she knew about his personal affairs.

"Perhaps I should. It would give me something else to do with my time. Will you save me a waltz this evening? I don't see a dance card attached to your wrist."

She knew she didn't have one, yet she looked at her wrist out of habit. "They did not supply them. Perhaps tonight one may dance with whom they wish as many times as they want."

He chuckled again and winked at her. "Wouldn't that be a

pleasant change from Society's strict rules?"

It was then that Priscilla noticed Baron Latham, Mr. Caldwell, and Lady Beatrice joining their little party. Her eyes locked with David's, and her cheeks flushed at the thought that he might have heard her and Nick flirting. She smiled at him. He smiled back with one brow cocked. Drat. He must have heard.

He walked toward her and bowed, his blue eyes taking her in from head to toe. "Lady Priscilla. You look stunning."

"Thank you," she said, curtsying, as Nick took his leave. Her cheeks burned from David's intense stare, but even so, she perused him as he had done her. He looked handsome in his evening wear. He had added several fripperies to his ensemble. A gold handled walking stick, a gold pocket watch, bows on his shoes, and several rings on his fingers that only he could make look fashionable. He cut a dashing enough figure to give even Beau Brummell competition. She could not fathom how he managed to pay his tailor since he'd admitted to needing her dowry.

"I can see the gears working inside your curious mind," he said softly. "You wonder about my extravagant tailoring bill."

"I . . ."

"You were," he said with a chuckle. "Fear not; I haven't purchased anything new for my wardrobe in over a year. Gentlemen are fortunate in that respect. Switching waistcoats and cravats makes an outfit look fresh and new. Also, my valet is a miracle worker regarding men's attire."

"Forgive me," she murmured, feeling awful about her assumptions. But how could she not, given the way he dressed? Though he spoke truthfully about men's wardrobes. They had it easy when it came to wearing things more than once.

"Of course. On another note, will you save a dance for me? Preferably a waltz?"

"Yes. I promised Hollingsworth a waltz. After I dance with him, you will be next."

He didn't do a good job of hiding his disappointment in coming in second to Nick.

The sound of footsteps approaching and a clearing of a throat got their attention. "Forgive my intrusion," Nick held out his hand, his head tipped down, his amused eyes on her. "Lady Priscilla, I believe this dance belongs to me."

The opening cords of a waltz tickled her ears. "So it does," she said as she took his hand, and he led her to the already crowded dance floor where graceful couples floated as though their feet hardly touched the ground.

Soon, she and Nick joined them. "I hope you will wear this lovely gown again. It is most becoming," he said, his eyes falling on her low-cut neckline, which exposed her breasts nearly to the tops of her areolas.

Her nerves had her giggling. "Pardon. I hadn't noticed how daring the neckline was until my final fitting, and Madam Serena forbade me from adding lace. She said it would spoil the gown's effect." The heat of her blushing encompassed her entire body.

His hungry eyes met hers, and the heat increased dramatically. "Perhaps we can sneak away to a private part of the pleasure gardens, and I can find out if you taste as good as you look."

Her steps faltered. Nick tightened his grip on her to keep her from falling flat on her face. A face that must be red as a berry. "Don't say things like that to me. Are you trying to shock me?"

His chuckle was deep and rumbly. "Guilty. You are easy to rile."

"If we weren't on a dance floor in sight of half the *ton*, I would slap you across the face. Please remind me to slap you later when we are in private."

"Promise," his eyebrows rose, and he grinned, looking devastatingly handsome.

"Have you never grown up?"

"Most definitely, but sometimes it's fun to let my guard down and enjoy life's little pleasures." He winked at her. "Such as a dance with a beautiful, desirable lady like yourself."

"Are we ever going to talk about us?"

His muscles tightened up beneath her hand. "If you recall, I mentioned something about us sharing something special in the Trowbridge gardens, and you didn't want to discuss it then. You reminded me our courtship was fake. But fake or not, I enjoy my time with you. It's nice to be myself around you."

Her insides tingled. It wasn't that she didn't want to talk about their special moment when he mentioned it. It was just that her feelings were too raw from their intimate tryst. In her own way she was protecting herself from the feelings she had for him. It would be too easy to let herself fall, but she couldn't let that happen unless he declared his love for her. Not the love of friends, but the *I love you with all my heart, soul, and everything I have* sort of love. Sadly he didn't love her that way, which was why she was courting David. David was kind and considerate to her and she enjoyed his company. It wasn't a hardship to spend time with him.

Since it seemed clear they weren't going to talk about the sort of love she longed for, she would ask several other questions she wanted answers to. "Perhaps we should speak of something else," she said, a little breathless from dancing. "How are you handling the issue with your ex-mistress?" Issue didn't seem like the right word, but it was all she could come up with.

Now it was his turn for his steps to falter, but he recovered quickly. "As well as can be expected. I dread the day my mother finds out. Ever since I was sent down from Eton, I've tried not to disappoint her." He shrugged one shoulder. "At least not too much."

"You were sent down from Eton? How did I not know about that?"

His eyes turned troubled. "I was expelled for fighting. End of story."

There was definitely more to the story, but she would drop it for now. However, her interest was piqued and she would look for a moment to bring it up again. "Have you made any decision about whether you wish to court Lady Grace?"

"She is a sweet, kind person—nothing like her mother. I haven't made up my mind about her though. The only thing I do know is she deserves an equally kind and caring gentleman. And I'm nothing resembling that."

Priscilla frowned at his last comment. When had he begun to think so little of himself? Indeed, he had his moments of being selfish, arrogant, and unkind, but she had also caught glimpses of his caring and kind soul.

Because of her woolgathering, she didn't realize when the orchestra stopped playing.

Nick stepped back and held out his arm, which she took immediately. "Instead of returning you to your friends, would you care to visit the gardens? I feel as though I owe you a stroll through them to lighten the mood and beg your forgiveness for making you uncomfortable while we danced."

Now that he mentioned it, she had felt uncomfortable, but she was to blame as well for her personal and intrusive questions. "Yes. I would like that." Her heart beat so fast it ricocheted inside her chest at the possibility that he might kiss her while they were alone again in a garden. They meandered down a stone path flanked by beautiful plants and flowers. Glass lanterns were glowing every five feet, illuminating the stone pathway. They arrived at a copse of shrubs and trees, entirely private from onlooking eyes.

"Let us stop for a moment." Nick looked around and laughed. "Do you think the gardeners planned this little section for private rendezvous? It is the perfect place for a man to ravish a lady." His hands circled her waist, and he tugged her close to his hard body so their hips pressed together tight, and she gasped. Her body had tensed up when they first made contact. Now, her body liquified, and she wrapped her arms around his neck. All she could think about was kissing him. Her eyes flittered from his eyes to his mouth and back to his eyes.

"Perhaps a lady can have her way with a gentleman of her choosing in this very spot as well," she teased, completely shocked she'd said such a thing.

"Do you think so?" he breathed as he lowered his head and took her mouth in a kiss that left nothing to the imagination. His teeth nipped her bottom lip. His tongue tasted every secret hideaway in her mouth, his lips punishing her with their assault. A moan escaped her as she curled her hands into his hair, holding him tight. Everything around her vanished as she leaned as close to his body as she could. If she could crawl inside him and never leave, she would. Everything about this kiss resonated more. Feelings of more. Wanting more. Needing more. She broke the kiss just long enough to whisper, "Touch me."

His answer was a deep, primitive growl. His mouth retook hers, only this time he made passionate love to her with his kiss. Slow, languid strokes of his tongue had her body trembling. Large hands traveled up and down her sides, pausing briefly to rub his thumbs across her breasts. He broke the kiss as they both gasped for air. Her chest rose and fell with her inhale and exhale. He stepped back, his eyes dropping to her exposed neckline. "I could devour you. The taste of your mouth is intoxicating. I want to taste you everywhere. Especially down here." He cupped her through her dress. "I imagine it is sweeter than honey and as addicting as the nectar of the goddesses during ancient times."

Wetness pooled between her thighs, right where his hand touched her. Before she could beg him to touch her again, he reached for the hem of her gown and ran his hand up the inside of her thigh, causing her knees to nearly give way. He took his time, staring into her eyes as his fingers danced up the inside of her thighs. He had that crooked grin that always turned her insides to mush. Her breath suspended inside her lungs as she waited and waited until finally, he found the opening in her pantaloons and inserted a finger inside her womanhood. She exhaled. "Ohhhh."

Their eyes were still mesmerized by each other. She whined when he removed his finger. He brought it to his mouth and sucked on it. "Just as I thought. Sweeter than honey."

When he pulled the skirt of her dress up again, he didn't take his time. He parted her folds until he found the heart of her womanhood. He swirled his fingers around and around.

"You're so wet," he moaned. "What I wouldn't give to have you in my bed right now. I would make love to you all night until neither of us could move."

"Nick," she murmured, "I love you." The second the words escaped her mouth without her permission, she knew she was doomed.

She had promised herself when she was sixteen that she would never admit to Nick that she loved him without him saying the words first. Though at the tender and impressionable age of sixteen, it really was more of an infatuation than love, and since she had always been led to believe they would wed, she assumed she loved him. But recently, since they had been spending time in each other's company, her girlhood infatuation had come back. She knew she falling for him, but the last thing she wanted to do was give him any sort of control over her. Not when he didn't feel the same.

She also had David to consider. While she didn't have strong feelings for him—nothing close to love—she still liked him.

Nick withdrew his hand and smoothed down her skirts. At least he didn't step away completely. He held her close and kissed the top of her head.

CHAPTER ELEVEN

"Forgive me, my wayward hands. I lost myself. You make me forget," Nick said, as though she hadn't just professed her love for him. The idiot!

She wanted to cry so badly. She battled back the tears, refusing to cry in front of him. She didn't want him to accuse her of manipulating him with her tears. She also wanted to hit him in the chest repeatedly to work out her frustrations. Why had he touched her so intimately, making her entire being come alive, only to then retreat, leaving her hurt and chilled down to the bone? But if he wasn't going to acknowledge her declaration, she wouldn't either.

No, it was a lie. She had to.

Swallowing down her disappointment, in both herself and him, she stepped back and out of his arms. "Perhaps we should return." He would not meet her eyes. She cupped his face, forcing him to look at her. She struggled to speak and then the words flowed. "Don't look away from me, Nick. It makes me feel less than who I am. I'm sorry I said those words, though it's not as if you couldn't have deduced the truth of it. I had suspected it, but didn't admit it to myself or you till now. I will not regret, when we kissed the first time, that I refused to admit the intense connection we shared, but I now understand how disappointed you were that I wouldn't discuss it. And now I believe our fake courtship has run its course. Because, as you said once, we both have trouble remembering it's not real. I'm not upset. So don't concern yourself with me."

Her lips brushed across his, then she pivoted and walked back the way they came. Her feet shuffled, heavy and awkward. She could barely lift them off the ground. Her heart, which beat steadily inside her chest, wanted to cease to exist. Her mind called her a love-sick fool. But alas, she smiled as she joined the guests enjoying this wonderful ball. If only she could enjoy it. She had become good at masking her emotions and would tonight. She refused to give Nick any satisfaction in seeing her hurt by his rejection. He may not have spoken his rejection aloud, but his silence said it all. Tonight, they had turned a pivotal corner in their relationship. There was no doubt he wanted her physically, and God help her, she wanted him so desperately her entire body ached for his touch. Yet, he was unwilling to profess his love or offer for her hand. They could have an affair, except that she knew she would never recover if she gave her body fully to him. With him, she was afraid it would be all or nothing. Unfortunately, it looked as though nothing had won.

Finally understanding this, she would look to the future, though she felt nearly paralyzed from a broken heart. It was time to seriously consider David as a potential future husband and father to her children. There was no time like the present as another waltz began to play, and she looked around for him. He was at her side in seconds, bowing and offering his arm. "My dance, I believe."

Her hand rested on his forearm as he led her onto the wooden dance floor. He held her gently as they danced around gracefully. His dancing had improved since their last waltz. "I've been looking for you. You disappeared on me," he said without condemnation. "Hollingsworth took you into the gardens, I presume."

How refreshing to be with a man who spoke his mind. He didn't accuse her of anything either, only stated facts. She hoped his lack of jealousy wasn't because he hadn't true feelings for her. "Yes. We strolled through them."

"Would you do me the honor of showing them to me when the dance ends?"

"I would like that very much. And just so you know, Hollingsworth and I are no longer courting."

One brow rose. "Is that so?"

"Yes." That was all she would say about the matter.

"Then I look forward to spending more time with you. You do realize we have yet to take that ride in the park. Perhaps you would allow me to escort you tomorrow."

"Oh dear, I forgot about the park. It seems as if the weather or some other interference is always against us. I will sleep tonight praying for a warm, sunny day."

"Thank you. For giving me a chance. For not just seeing the man with the damaged reputation. For seeing me for who I am now and not holding my past against me."

"I didn't know you then. All I see is the man before me." And it was the truth. She had trouble equating the man before her with the man she had heard unpleasant things about. She didn't always believe gossip, but by David's own admission, the gossip was true.

"Once again, thank you."

"The music ended. We'd best leave the dance floor. People are beginning to stare."

"Let them," he said with a laugh. He offered his arm, and she wrapped hers around it.

Priscilla didn't want to go down the same path she went with Nick, so she maneuvered David into the gardens toward the back of the dance floor. "This is a different path. That way, we can explore together."

DAVID, AGAINST HIS nature, let Priscilla choose the garden path. He must not show his domineering personality until they were married. He had taken a hiatus from gambling and visiting dens of iniquity for the time being. He had to prove to everyone that he had changed, mostly his brother. But James was tough, and David was still trying to convince him that he'd changed. If he managed to fool his younger brother, he could fool anyone. Especially Priscilla, who tended to believe everything he said. And now that Hollingsworth was out of the way, he could step up their courtship, seduce her, and wed her. Once he bedded her, she would be his.

The dowry she came with was generous, but it wouldn't last long with his lavish lifestyle. Taking over Norton's lucrative crime business had come at the perfect time. Realizing he'd been musing longer than he should have, he said, "You were correct when you said the gardens are beautiful."

"Indeed. It must have taken dozens of workers to plant wagonloads of flowers and plants to make such a vibrant display of color and blooms."

"Yes." How droll to be talking about flowers. Such insignificant things.

She tugged her arm from his and stuffed her face into some white flower he recalled seeing in many gardens around London. "Jasmine is one of my favorites. The scent is potent for such a delicate flower."

Ever the gallant gentleman, he plucked a flower from the plant and handed it to her. "It is as delicate and beautiful as you are, my dear."

Her eyes lowered, and her cheeks turned red. "Thank you. You are too kind."

"Not at all. What I say is true. Shall we continue? I see a small alcove made by some tall shrubs. Ever since the other night, I've been dying to kiss you again."

Her face turned even redder. Whoever thought blushing was becoming was an idiot. She resembled a lobster cooking in a pot of boiling water to him. Not attractive at all.

When she hesitated a moment, he forced himself to relax and smile that smile he had that no lady seemed to refuse. He'd practiced it in the mirror and perfected it years ago, and it never failed to get him what he wanted. In this case, *whom* he wanted. And he wanted Pricilla. Not because he cared for her but because one female was as good as the next, and he needed to solidify his claim for her hand in marriage, and he needed a son to inherit the title. Eventually he would send her to his country estate to raise his heir and any other children, and he'd be free of her.

He reached for her hand and led her into the opening created by a wall of trees or shrubs. He didn't care what she called them. "Ahhh, we are finally alone," he whispered into her ear. And he grinned when he saw her relax. She was not very good at hiding her feelings and emotions. "May I kiss you?"

"Yes," she said as she leaned into him.

He enveloped her within his arms, pulling her tight to his hard body, and kissed her. He tried to take it slow and use finesse, but her scent suddenly had his senses scrambling. He fought to control himself and eventually won. "Forgive me. I lose my mind when I kiss you." It was the first time in his life that a woman had made him forget himself. It was unsettling, to say the least. He would have to be careful around her in the future.

"There is nothing to forgive," she said softly. "I enjoyed the kiss."

His lips caressed the soft skin of her neck. His hands made a path up and down her back and eventually to her side. He eased his hands between their bodies and cupped both breasts with his large, warm hands. One moment, a sigh escaped her lips, and the next, she stepped out of his reach.

"I shouldn't have come here with you. Because if you are only looking for a tryst, you may as well bow out of this courtship."

What the bloody hell? He ran his hands—which he was shocked to see were shaking—through his hair. Where the devil had his hat gone? He looked behind him, picked it up, and stuffed it on his head. He took Priscilla's hands in his. "Look at me." Her eyes fluttered up to his, and she looked wary. "Forgive me." He turned on the charm. "I care deeply for you. I would never take advantage of you."

"But . . ."

"I know. Saying is all well and good, but doing is another matter. It won't happen again. If our kisses lead us down this path again, you have my permission to slap my cheek." He said it with a smile and teasing nature, and she smiled shyly back at him. She was making it too easy.

"It's good to know I have your permission." She glanced down at her feet and back up to him. "Perhaps we should return."

When the gardens were behind them, and they joined their group of friends. Priscilla's friends really, although his brother and sister-in-law were part of that gathering. He forced himself to bow. "Lady Priscilla, I enjoyed our time together immensely. But I must leave. Goodnight."

She curtsied, giving him a peek at the breasts he had recently fondled ever so briefly. "Goodnight."

David left the gardens and made haste to his lover. If he were capable of caring for anyone, it would be her. According to her, she loved him, and she didn't need his money. She had a provider who no longer shared her bed but continued to pay her living expenses and a quarterly stipend. The man was a fool to think the child she carried was his.

CHAPTER TWELVE

"WHAT WERE YOU doing in the gardens with Latham?" Nick demanded between clenched teeth as he curled his hand around her wrist.

She pulled out of his grasp. "Are you trying to attract unwanted attention?" What had gotten into him? He looked ready to come to fisticuffs with someone. "You need to calm yourself."

"Forgive me." He scrubbed his hands down his face. "I don't trust him."

"That is your prerogative. But I can think and make decisions for myself," she said while her heart still pounded. It hadn't stopped since David had taken her into his arms. She refused to be swayed by Nick's dislike of the man, but in truth she had witnessed something in David's eyes tonight that contradicted his words of caring for her. He'd looked bored when he declared them, which concerned her.

But Priscilla wanted to believe what he said and give him a chance . . . a real chance to court her properly. So, she had decided she would allow the courtship with him to continue. However, she would pay close attention for any tells or signs of dishonesty from here on out. She refused to let another gentleman make a fool out of her.

"I'm going to find Mother." She curtsied. "Goodnight, Hollingsworth." As she walked away, it felt like a tether was pulling her back to him. Could he feel it, too?

Mother sat at a table with Lady Hollingsworth and several other ladies. She greeted everyone, then said, "Mother, may I speak with you?"

Duchess Avery rose. "If you will excuse me, ladies."

When they were standing off to the side, Priscilla said, "I would like to go."

Her mother gripped her hand. "Is all well?"

"Yes. I have a slight headache and don't wish it to turn into a migraine. If you prefer to stay, I will send the carriage back."

"I will stay, but there's no need to return the carriage. Lady Hollingsworth will bring me home."

Once Priscilla found privacy inside her family's coach, she leaned against the soft squabs and closed her eyes. She concentrated on her breathing. In and out. In and out. She ignored her chest rattling with unshed tears. When the conveyance stopped, she heaved a big sigh of relief. She'd never been so thankful for a night to end. When Berkley opened the front door she asked him to send Eugenia up. Before Eugenia arrived, Priscilla removed the pins from her hair and the blue sapphire jewelry that matched her gown and placed them on the dressing table. She then plopped down on her bed, pulling Snowball close and snuggling him. He responded with loud purrs.

"My lady, you are earlier than I thought," Eugenia said when she came into the room. "Do you mind standing so I can remove your gown?" While Eugenia undid the buttons, she asked. "Are you unwell?"

"Just a little headache. When we are done here, could you bring a tray of tea, fruit, and biscuits? I find I'm famished. I left before supper was served."

"Yes, my lady."

Priscilla was very thankful when her corset was removed and she could actually breathe freely. Next went her chemise and pantaloons and on went her night rail and robe.

Eugenia left to get her a tray, and Priscilla sat on the chaise longue facing the cold fireplace and shivered. It was full of kindling and logs, all set up to be lit. So she rose and did just that. As a child, she learned how to build and light a fire in the hearth. Her mother was aghast when she found out, and Priscilla had stated, "What if I'm lost in the woods someday and need to build a fire to stay alive?" She would admit it wasn't the same as lighting the fireplace, but it was close. She refused to always rely on servants when she could do things herself.

The tea tray came not fifteen minutes later. Cook always had hot water simmering.

"Thank you, Eugenia, that will be all for tonight. You may collect the tray in the morning."

"Goodnight, my lady."

She hadn't lied when she told her mother that she had a headache. Or at least, if she didn't have one then, she did now. She relaxed on the chaise longue, sipped her tea, and nibbled on raspberries and a delicious butter biscuit. Just as she placed her teacup and saucer on the table beside her, she heard her door creak. Before looking, she said, "Eugenia, please go to bed. I promise I don't need you anymore tonight."

A chuckle she recognized had her sitting up and her heart thumping wildly. "Nick, what are you doing here?"

"I hate the way we left things tonight. I couldn't go home without fixing it."

"Are you foxed?" It was most certainly not a question.

"I may have drunk a little too much." He hiccupped loudly.

"Come sit down before you fall."

"Your bed looks comfortable. I'll just lay down for five minutes, then I'll leave," he said in garbled words. She was surprised she understood them.

Before she could protest him lying in her bed, he fell back, his booted feet dangling off the side. Strangely, he had worn shoes at the ball. He must keep a pair of boots in his carriage. His loud snores reverberated throughout the room. And her traitorous cat curled up against his side. Oh dear, what if her mother checked on her? How would she explain Nick's unconscious body draped across her bed? Not that her mother would mind. Priscilla was surprised that, since she was a widow, her mother hadn't pressured her to seduce Nick and force his hand into marriage. Laughter bubbled up at remembering Emmeline telling her that her mother kept pushing her to seduce Blackstone. What a conversation for mothers and daughters to have. Emmeline's mother, Viscountess Connolly, was a forward-thinking woman.

She smiled down at Nick's relaxed and sleeping face. She could undress him and tell him they'd made love. She didn't believe he would remember it at this point, even if they did. However, she couldn't deceive him. If they ever made love, she would want him sober and present in the moment. She would like him to remember that when they were joined, they fit perfectly, and they belonged together for all eternity. But that was a big *if.* As it stood after that evening, he was done with her. At least, she believed so until he showed up in her chambers inebriated.

She entered her dressing room, found an extra blanket, and made herself comfortable on the chaise longue, which was toasty warm from the blazing hearth. Snuggling beneath the soft blanket, she closed her eyes and pretended Nick's snoring was thunder and Snowball's purring the rain. She always loved a good nighttime thunderstorm and fell asleep to the rhythmic sounds coming from her bed.

Coughing noises in the middle of the night startled her awake, and when she realized the sound had come from Nick, she jumped up and ran into the dressing room, came out with a chamber pot, and shoved it at him. Snowball jumped off the bed, frightened. "Don't you dare cast up your accounts on my bed! If you do, I'll never speak to you again." She hurried around the room, lighting candles.

Nick rolled onto his side and sat up, his hands gripping his head. "Where the hell am I?"

"Really, Nick. What a terrible thing to say. You visit a lady in her chambers in the middle of the night, and you don't remember?"

"Priscilla? What am I doing here?"

"That is a fine question. And I'll tell you. You showed up around midnight quite drunk and immediately proceeded to fall asleep on my bed, forcing *me* to sleep on my chaise longue." She paused. "You, sir, are no gallant knight in shining armor."

"Please, Priscilla, stop badgering me. My head hurts something fierce. And what is the reference to knights? I'm in too much pain to make sense of your words."

"I'm sorry to disturb you, but you were coughing, and I thought you meant to be sick. I did you a favor by bringing you a clean chamber pot. And if this is the thanks I get, I'm returning to my chaise longue and going back to sleep. Please refrain from disturbing me. Goodnight."

She never realized how much fun it was to tease Nick. She thoroughly enjoyed herself, even if she was exhausted and it was the middle of the night.

"I can't stay." He moved to stand, swayed on his feet, and collapsed back down on the bed with a groan. One hand went to his stomach and one to his forehead. "I'll just rest a little longer if you don't mind."

Before she could even reply or give a snide remark, he began snoring. She placed the chamber pot next to him on the bed. Her eyes fell on his boots, and feeling guilty, she tugged them off, brought out another spare blanket from her dressing room, and covered him. It was the best she could do. He would have a dreadful headache in the morning. She would ask Mrs. Cummings to make him the miracle drink she gave Father when he overindulged. If she did that, though, how would she explain his presence? Which made her wonder how Nick got into the house in the first place. Had Berkley let him in? Did the whole household already know Nick was with her? She would worry about it in the morning.

She returned to the chaise longue, slipped beneath her blanket, closed her eyes, and hoped to sleep. If she didn't, she would be exhausted tomorrow. Not that she had plans, except for the ride in the park with David. After several moments of staring at the ceiling, Snowball climbed onto her stomach, kneaded the blanket with his front claws, and rudely fell asleep.

At the soothing sound of his purring, her breathing slowed and her eyelids, once wide open, now were too heavy. They drooped little by little until she was shrouded in darkness and dreams.

When Priscilla saw the sun's rays the next morning, poking into the room where the curtains gapped in the middle, she was shocked. She had believed she would never fall asleep the night before. Priscilla arched her back, her arms over her head as she stretched the kinks out of her body from being curled up into a ball on the chaise. She popped up as she remembered . . . *Nick.* She glanced at her bed, and her stomach fell. The only signs that he had been there were an empty chamber pot, a discarded blanket, and the impression of his body on the counterpane. When had he snuck out? The last she'd spoken to him, he'd been in no condition to leave and find his way home.

An hour later, Priscilla broke her fast with both her parents, and Nick was not mentioned, nor did any household servants glance at her slyly. Nick must have magically entered their townhome last night and exited in the early morning the same way he'd come.

THAT AFTERNOON, PRISCILLA entered the drawing room dressed for a carriage ride with David to find her mother entertaining him while they waited for her arrival. She had put off coming downstairs for as long as she could, unable to entirely shake the unease with him she'd felt the night before. The moment David saw her, he stood and bowed, looking dashing in buckskin breeches, brown clawhammer coat, cream shirt, cravat, and riding boots. Too bad clothes had no sway over a gentleman's personality or honesty. "Lady Priscilla, are you ready for our outing in the park?"

She curtsied. "Yes."

He indicated the doorway. "Shall we?"

"Yes. We shall not be long, Mother."

"Take your time and enjoy this rare sunny day," her mother replied.

It *was* sunny, and David drove them in an open-air phaeton. He appeared quite adept at driving, and she tried to relax, but all the while, she kept thinking that he was parading her around in the park, showing her off as his. She politely nodded her head in acknowledgment to anyone who did the same. Some other riders blatantly stared and whispered. Was it because she was not in Nick's company or because of David and his prior reputation as a ne'er-do-well? All she knew was that it wasn't an easy, comfortable ride with David, as it was when she rode with Nick. Halfway through the park, he pulled the carriage over and turned to her, taking her gloved hands into his.

"Priscilla," he said in all seriousness, "I've been waiting for the right time for this. I spoke to your father and received his permission." He paused and cleared his throat. "Priscilla, my dear, will you marry me?"

She did not gasp out loud in shock, even though she wanted to, because truthfully, she was not shocked. Her intuition warned her this was coming today, which perhaps was why she had procrastinated in leaving her chambers. She could not believe her father had not warned her about something so monumental as a marriage proposal. No doubt he was disappointed that it wasn't Nick asking permission but probably also glad to have someone, anyone, ask for her hand.

"Is it too much to ask if I may have some time?" He had been nothing but a gentleman, yet she still had doubts about him. She was not in a hurry to get married, not until the person and time were right. Or her doubts about David were solved. She also wanted a few answers regarding Nick. After his visit last night, clearly the two of them had things to discuss.

David squeezed her hands, and she realized she'd been woolgathering in the middle of a proposal, which did not bode well for the man.

"If you said yes, I would be the happiest man alive." He gently squeezed her hands. "But I understand you need time. After all, this is your second marriage and should not be taken lightly. I've come to care for you deeply and would be honored if you chose me. I promise to spend my life proving I am worthy of being your husband."

"Thank you," she whispered as her stomach knotted up tightly. For some reason his words didn't ring true. He released her hand, took up the reins again, and flicked them. The carriage entered the traffic flow meandering along Rotten Row. Thank goodness they were on their way. It had turned into one of the most difficult rides ever. Neither one spoke for the entire ride back to her family's townhouse. David had said he was fine with her needing time, but the tension radiating from him told her otherwise. Did she blame him? No. It could not be easy for someone to propose. Thankfully, women need not do so.

When the carriage stopped, David climbed down and helped her exit the phaeton. He bowed. "Please send word to me when you have an answer, as I am most anxious."

"Forgive me." She curtsied. "I don't mean to cause you distress. Good day."

As she ascended the stairs, the door opened, and she was glad when it closed behind her. It felt as though David's eyes bore needles into her spine.

"Priscilla," Mother's voice called out from the top of the staircase. "A word."

Her hand moved up the banister, pulling her body up one stair at a time. Mental exhaustion weighed her body down, and she wished she could crawl into bed and stay there for days . . . weeks . . . months.

She followed her mother into the family parlor, where a fresh tray was on a low table. They both sat on the settee. Priscilla waited silently as her mother poured tea, put several biscuits on a plate, and handed the plate to her. "You look pale. A little sugar should help. Now, tell me what happened."

Laughter bubbled out of Priscilla's mouth, and she smothered it up with her hand as it quickly turned into sobs. "I do not want to marry Latham." Drat, but she was crying again. However, if there were ever a time to cry, it was now when her future was in the balance. "Why didn't you warn me he would propose today?"

"My darling daughter," her mother said as she patted her hand. Her hand was overly warm from the teapot. "A marriage proposal is meant to be a surprise."

"Yes, but it is not my first marriage proposal or marriage."

"You knew the baron planned to propose."

"Yes. But not so soon." Deep inside, where she kept her secrets and wishes even from herself, she had hoped David would lose interest in her and find another lady to marry—one with a more considerable dowry. Why had she encouraged him? She had misled him and now she had to make it right.

"I married once, knowing the future was uncertain. Jasper was a wonderful man. I was young, and the thought of eloping was exciting. Deep down, I know part of me married Jasper because I wanted to hurt Nick, and a small part of me hates Nick because it did nothing to him. And when Jasper died, I realized I cared for Jasper deeply and that we were both robbed of a future together that would have turned to love.

"But now—I don't want to settle and marry Latham when I know I will never love him, and I do know it. I like him and enjoy his company, but I can't foresee it moving beyond that. I almost had love once, and I want the chance again. There must be someone else out there besides Nick for me to love. I need to pay attention to other eligible bachelors and find someone new. I hope you and Father won't be disappointed when I refuse Latham."

"Drink your tea. It will help calm you down," her mother said. "And no, we will not be disappointed with you. You are still young and have time to marry and have babies. We will respect your decision. And I promise I will stop pushing you and Nicholas together. He is certainly old enough to know what he wants. He has had years to marry you and chose not to. I will get over my hopes of merging our families. Starting today, I will not mention him unless you do first."

At hearing her mother's words, her heart constricted in pain. But what she said was true. Nick had had years to make up his mind about her. "Thank you. Excuse me, I'd like to rest before dinner." Her hand went to her stomach as she stood. "What day is it?"

"Yes, I realize what tonight is."

"Please make my excuses." Tonight was the monthly dinner when they hosted Lady Hollingsworth and Nick. But she couldn't face them, not tonight.

"Will you not feel uncomfortable hiding in your chambers?"

"Perhaps, but I'm going to."

"Very well. I'll come up with something to explain your absence."

When she entered her chambers, she didn't bother ringing for Eugenia. She removed her hat, gloves, boots, and spencer and climbed into her bed, dress and all. She wanted nothing more than to be alone and fall into a dreamless sleep where David and Nick didn't exist.

CHAPTER THIRTEEN

NICK HAD WOKEN in Priscilla's bed with something tickling his face. He'd swung his arm out, and the thing screeched and landed on the ground with a thud. He'd rolled onto his back and moaned at the pounding in his skull, the dryness of his mouth, and the knot in his stomach. Then large white beast had come back and plopped heavily on his chest and proceeded to knead its claws into his chest and purr. Nick winced at the sharp pain the claws caused. He was going to have marks on his chest from the beast. He'd nudged the cat off, rolled over, rose from the bed, and caught himself before he tripped over his own boots. The last thing he wanted to do was wake up Priscilla and have to explain why he'd shown up drunk in her room in the middle of the night.

He'd tugged on his boots and left as quietly as he could. Exiting the house, he could make out orange on the horizon. Dawn was upon them, so he'd hurried home and climbed into bed.

Ignoring the blacksmith pounding inside his head that afternoon, he visited Viscountess Norton. He hadn't seen her since her husband's death, and he felt he owed her his condolences on the loss of her husband. And a thank you for what she had done for him. He tried like hell not to remember that she was the cause of his fall from Society in the first place.

He placed his calling card on the silver tray the butler held in his hands and was shown to the drawing room on the second level. Standing with his arms behind his back, he stared out the window which faced St. James Park.

"Lord Hollingsworth," Viscountess Norton's voice reached his ears. He turned to find the lady dressed in mourning, her face lit up with a smile. "To what do I owe the pleasure of your company, Lord Hollingsworth?"

He bowed. "I thought it was time I paid my respects for the loss of your husband."

"Please have a seat," she said, indicating a chair facing the settee.

"Thank you. I will." He sat down and placed his hat on the empty chair beside him while she sat on the settee.

"I have not had afternoon tea. Will you join me?"

"Yes, thank you," he replied.

"A tray will be delivered soon. And please do not be so formal on my account. After all, we have seen each other at our worst."

Her words caused him to frown. "Indeed. Has the new viscount taken over yet?"

"Reaching my husband's nephew in America will take some time. Once he gets word, no doubt he will board the first available ship."

"Do you plan to retire to the dower house?"

She burst out laughing. "Goodness no. I'm too young to live in the country. My husband was most generous with his private funds, and I have purchased a townhouse several doors down from this one. I should be settled in soon. I should be set for life with the funds he left in trust for me and my allowance from his nephew."

"That is good news. I would hate for you to return to your prior employment." His comment was ignored as a footman arrived with the tray.

"How do you like your tea?"

"Black."

He picked up the cup and saucer and studied her over its rim. He'd never really taken a good look at her before and wondered how she had ever gotten into the predicament she had. He surmised her age to be close to twenty-five. She was petite with a full figure. While she wasn't as beautiful as Priscilla, she was pretty and held herself elegantly, making him wonder about her background. "If I might ask, where did you grow up?"

The whole time he'd studied her, her eyes had been on him.

"I can't imagine why it would interest you where I grew up. My upbringing was rather boring." She held up her hand and twisted her wrist. "But since you asked, I'll tell you. I grew up just outside of Kent. My father was a tenant farmer. Wealthier than most. My mother was a midwife. I was their only surviving child." She paused and nibbled on a biscuit.

He leaned forward in his seat. "Go on."

"Mine is a story you have heard before, I'm sure. I fell in love with a lord's eldest son. He seduced me, and when I became with child, he tossed me aside." She frowned. "A story told many times since the dark ages."

"What did you do?"

"My parents sent me away to a convent. After I delivered a stillborn child, I left and never returned to my parents. Somehow, by the grace and goodness of strangers, I made my way to London. Penniless and with only the clothes on my back, I didn't know what to do. I was frightened and didn't want to become a prostitute on the streets of St. Giles."

"That is not a life, but a death sentence."

"I have nightmares sometimes when I remember what those women and girls live through. One day, I witnessed an older woman being pelted by pebbles by some street urchins, and I came to her aid. She and her husband ran a tavern. She rewarded me with a pallet to sleep on in their storage room and food to eat, and I become a barmaid."

"How did you meet the criminals you worked with?"

"They were regular patrons at the tavern. They said I would wear beautiful clothes and attend upper-class balls. I might have to expose myself occasionally, but I would not have to bed anyone, and the money would be good. They convinced me to work with them, and I didn't look back."

"How long did this go on?"

"Four long years. Although I can't complain. Everything they said was true. Except after the night with you, my conscience got the better of me. I met Viscount Norton shortly after; he took pity on me and married me. Unlike you, he preferred men, so the marriage benefited both of us."

Nick choked on his tea. "I had no idea."

"He kept his secret safe by having a longtime lover in his employ."

"What happened to him?"

"He died this past year. Broke Norton's heart. He never got over it."

Nick picked up his hat and stood. "I should go. Thank you for seeing me."

She stood as well and walked with him to the door. Just as he was about to exit, she touched his forearm and faced him. "Hollingsworth." She leaned into him and kissed him. "You need a wife." She kissed him deeper. "I can make you happy." She trailed her fingers down his chest to his stomach and . . .

He grabbed her hand to stop her from going farther. "Viscountess Norton," he said with an exhale. "While I appreciate your offer, I must decline."

"Why?"

He did not want to make an enemy of her, because he remembered what she was capable of. "I'm already considering two ladies for my marchioness. I don't need a third. I will choose from one of them." He stepped back and bowed. "Thank you for seeing me."

His feet ate up the distance between the upstairs drawing room and the door. When he was outside, he paused, inhaling and exhaling several times to get himself under control. Her unwanted kisses and her hands had done nothing but chill his insides. They would make a terrible couple. Not that he had even considered it when she mentioned it. It was the farthest thing from his mind.

When Nick entered his house a short time later, the butler, Robbins, said, "Lady Hollingsworth wanted me to remind you about your monthly dinner engagement with the Duke and Duchess of Avery. She will be ready promptly at seven."

Tension coiled throughout his body. How could he have forgotten? More importantly, what would he say to Priscilla about last night? Shaking his head, he ascended the stairs two at a time and requested his valet, Hughes, to ready a bath. The vileness clinging to his body from Viscountess Norton needed to be washed off before he faced Priscilla.

Nick went to his mother's chambers at half past seven to collect her. "You are late," she said with a scolding look. "You know how I hate to be late."

"Mother," he said as he wrapped her arm through his and led her out into the hall and down two flights of stairs. He paused to collect his hat and gloves from Robbins. Mother already had her hat, gloves, and cloak on. After assisting her inside their carriage, he took the seat opposite hers. "I'm thinking of proposing."

Mother gasped, started coughing, and covered her heart with her hand. "Are you trying to put me in my grave?"

"I thought you would be pleased."

"Pleased? Yes, I am very pleased. Yet, with you, I know there is much more to a proposal than simply asking a question. You do nothing easily."

"Yes, well, I pride myself in taking my time and mulling over my decisions."

"For years. Yes, how well I know," she said with exasperation.

"I need to be certain I am choosing the lady for all the correct reasons."

"And who, pray tell, is the lady?"

If only he weren't stuck inside a carriage. He wanted to jump up and pace around. Instead, he mumbled to himself like a deranged person. Lately, that was how he felt when it came to Priscilla. His emotions were jumbled up inside, making him do and say the wrong thing around her. He felt too much. She was too much, and he didn't know how to deal with it. Sometimes it seemed he had spent his entire life numb inside.

That is why marrying Lady Grace was the perfect solution. He could return to being numb. He liked numb. Didn't he?

"I'm thinking of Lady Grace." His mother sat silently, not saying a word, which told him she was stunned. "Say something."

"I'm thinking," she said. "While I admit that Lady Grace is a lovely young lady, her mother is another thing entirely. I had hoped . . ."

"I know what you hoped," he interjected, "but I don't know if I can survive being married to Priscilla. Lady Grace is easy and would not demand things of me. Priscilla would force things on me and not take no for an answer. She is a force of nature."

"My dear boy. You are not making sense. Tell me the real issue."

He dug his hands into his hair. "I do not forget myself with Grace. She doesn't make me lose my mind," he huffed. "Priscilla . . . she makes me forget everything. She is demanding and annoying. She speaks her mind and refuses to let me hide within myself. She sees things in me I don't want anyone to see. She thinks she knows me, but she doesn't. No one knows me. I keep my true self hidden deep inside. Not even I know how to find the real me."

"Nicholas," his mother whispered. He leaned back against the squabs and forced himself to look her in the eyes.

"What?"

"Are you truly in that much pain that you hide yourself from everyone, including yourself?" Nick was shocked to see tears streaming down his mother's cheeks.

"I didn't mean to make you cry. Forgive me."

"Forgive you? I should be asking for your forgiveness. How could I not see the pain you struggle with? You are my son; I should've noticed. You have always kept your mind and feelings to yourself. But to feel cut off from emotions completely, that must be lonely for you."

"In a way, it is. I never had real friends until I tried to court Lady Langford. Blackstone, Langford, and Caldwell are the only friends I have now, and yet, I am still on the outside looking in most of the time. Those three grew up together since their first days at Eton."

"Did you know them then?"

"I'm four years older than them and only attended one year. So the answer is no." And normally Nick did everything in his power never to think of Eton and what had become of him there. What someone had tried to do to him.

"Well, I'm glad you tried to court Lady Langford. At the very least, you now have friends," his mother said. "And from what I can tell, Lord and Lady Langford don't hold anything against you."

"Of course not, because I never had any chance of marrying Lady Langford."

"Let's discuss Lady Grace and Priscilla. Why do you fight your feelings concerning Priscilla?"

Perhaps he didn't hide his feelings as well as he thought. "I believe I just explained it. Weren't you listening?"

"Yes, I was. But there must be more to it."

"Do you know I sometimes have nightmares from when she was ten and announced proudly that she was going to marry me and the fit she threw when I told her I didn't think so?" He laughed aloud even though it wasn't a laughing matter.

His mother laughed as well. "I remember that day. She did throw such a fit. Stomping and screaming. She knew her mind even at the young age of ten."

He paused, then said quietly, "If I marry Lady Grace, will I feel guilty for the rest of my life."

"Guilty why?" his mother asked. "Guilty because you married her, or guilty because you love another? If you choose to marry

Grace, I'm quite convinced your marriage will be whatever you put into it, Lady Grace would never complain because that isn't who she is. However, will you be happy letting the great love of your life get away because she makes you feel too much? Can you stand by and let another man, Baron Latham perhaps, call her his? Can you watch him marry her and get her with heirs that are not yours?"

He groaned, "Thanks for putting those visions in my head."

"If those visions bother you so much, perhaps you should revisit your proposal to Lady Grace. The carriage stopped several minutes ago—we should get out," his mother said, wiping away the remnants of her tears.

"I suppose, although I would give anything to be anywhere other than Avery Manor." Nick exited the coach and prepared himself for a difficult night ahead.

"I do so wonder if you will ever grow up, my dear boy," his mother said as she took his offered hand and alighted from the coach.

"Not if I can help it."

Berkley opened the door as they approached and relieved them of their outer garments. "Please make your way to the green parlor. The duke and duchess await your presence there."

It was not lost on Nick that Lady Priscilla's name was left out. Was she not attending this evening? Was she out with Latham? He refused to acknowledge the jealousy coiling up inside him at the thought of her with Latham. Perhaps if she courted anyone but Latham, he could live with it, but he had never cared for the man and never would. Something was not right with him. He was hiding something. Nick was convinced of it.

"Nicholas, Rose," Duchess Avery said. "Let us go into the dining room. Dinner is ready."

"Thank you," Nick said. His heart sank as he entered, scanned the table, and saw four place settings. So she really wasn't attending.

Before he could inquire over her whereabouts, the duchess

said, "Lady Priscilla is not joining us. She is under the weather."

"I hope it's nothing serious?" his mother asked with a glance in his direction.

"No. Not at all." She motioned to the chairs. "Please sit."

Course after course came and went, and Nick wished he could go up and see Priscilla. He needed to know if she was ill. The usual conversation went around the table, and he blocked it out as his thoughts intruded. Was she faking illness to avoid him? Was she at another engagement, and they'd used sickness as an excuse? Then he scolded himself. Why should he care if he was proposing to Lady Grace? Poor Lady Grace. He had been neglectful of her lately. She would be most flabbergasted at his proposal. He must visit her tomorrow.

It was challenging to keep up with his emotional ups and downs. Even though he was so very thankful the gossip from seven years ago had gone away, sometimes he wished for the peace and solitude he'd had due to those whispers.

If he had been asked immediately after dinner what he'd eaten, he could not have answered. He picked up his utensils and ate without tasting or really seeing the food. Before he knew it, they were retiring to the parlor, and he wondered how he would survive the rest of the evening. Hopefully, his mother would request that they leave soon. And per usual, the duke excused himself and left. No doubt to hide in his study, drinking his port or brandy in silence. How Nick envied him.

Nick stood at a window, looking out into the darkness, and sipped his port while the ladies talked. They talked constantly while in each other's company, and Nick could not fathom how they never ran out of things to say.

"Would it be an imposition if I visited the library?" he asked the duchess.

"Not at all, Nicholas. You know where it is."

He bowed. "Thank you." He went down the hall to the library and, to his surprise, found a fire glowing in the hearth. He sat in a chair close to the fireplace and took a sip of his port, nearly spitting it out when he noticed Priscilla looking at him from across the room.

"What are you doing here?" he asked. "I thought you were sick."

She blushed and crossed the room. Her hair was loose and she was dressed in a simple cream dress. She sat in the chair beside his. "I was feeling ill, but I am better now and didn't want to stay in my chambers anymore." She paused and looked at him. "I thought you and your mother had left." She shrugged her shoulders. "Obviously, I was mistaken."

He raised his brows. "Obviously."

"Are you leaving soon?"

"Do you wish to be rid of me?"

"You left before we could talk this morning." She sounded hurt, and he hated that.

"I'm sorry. I should never have come in the first place, and I figured if I left before you awoke, it would spare both of us from an awkward conversation."

"Why would it be awkward? Nothing happened between us."

Oh, how he wished something had. Not that he could have done much in the state he was in. He hadn't been that drunk in forever. "I don't know. I just thought it would be. Unless you often find men in your chambers in the middle of the night."

She giggled. "Hardly. You would be the first."

"Well, that's a relief." And by the way his body reacted, it was indeed a relief to know Latham had never snuck into her rooms at night.

"I have something to share," she said, her cheeks again infused by the color pink. "Latham proposed today."

He downed his glass of port, wishing it were something more potent, and breathed through the pain piercing his chest. "Are congratulations in order?"

She clasped and unclasped her hands several times. "Not exactly."

"And what does that mean?"

"Just what I said. I haven't decided what my answer will be."

"Oh." The pain eased up a tad. "If you truly want to marry him, wouldn't you know already?"

More hand clasping. She stood and went to the sideboard across the room. He couldn't see what she was doing until she turned around, holding two glasses of amber liquid. She strolled his way, and he noticed her feet were bare and peeking out beneath her skirts. She handed him a glass. "I'm sure you wouldn't mind having a brandy with me."

"Not at all." They have known each other a long time, but he never knew she indulged in brandy.

"Don't look at me like that. Women enjoy brandy now and then."

"Forgive me."

THEY SAT SILENTLY while they sipped their brandy, and Priscilla wondered what Nick was thinking. He had seemed surprised to see her up and about. Had he really fallen for Mother's excuse and believed she'd taken ill? Did he not realize that women could manipulate things and men as they pleased? He should—Lady Hollingsworth and her mother were masters at it. Perhaps one day, she would join their ranks.

"Tell me more about Latham's proposal."

"If you must know, I requested time to think on it."

"I'm planning on proposing to Lady Grace."

A buzzing sound in her ears deafened her. Had she heard him correctly? She swallowed the tears clogging her throat, stiffened her spine, and downed the glass of brandy vibrating in her hands. "Congratulations. She is lovely." What else could she say without yelling and screaming at the top of her lungs? Could he not hear her heart cracking in two? Because it was the loudest sound she'd ever heard.

"Don't congratulate me. I haven't asked yet, and she hasn't accepted. I've barely spent any time with her. I think she'll be so shocked she'll faint dead away. I'm truly terrible at courting."

"She will accept. She would be a fool not to." And she had first-hand knowledge of what being a fool entailed. She was at the top of the list. "Would you care for more?"

He held out his glass. "Please."

She took her time at the sideboard, hoping to mask her feelings when she rejoined him. It wasn't easy. Ever since the night in the Trowbridge gardens, her heart was near to bursting with feelings for him. She could hardly contain them. And her tells, as he called them, would give her feelings away to him. All he had to do was look into her eyes, and he would see bright red hearts. She was sure of it. Never mind that she told him she loved him last night at the Vauxhall Pleasure Gardens.

Closing her eyes, she inhaled and schooled her features. She needed to project boredom and indifference. It was more difficult than she thought because she was dying inside. After handing over Nick's glass, she sat again and sipped her brandy, enjoying the slow burn. Perhaps it would burn her love for him right out of her.

"When is this proposal taking place?"

"Soon." He paused and stared into his glass. "Have you done any more volunteer work with the Ladies' Society of Mayfair?"

She doubted he was interested in her charity work. More likely he just preferred a change in topic. Well, so did she. "I helped Emmeline hand out donations recently. The recipients were very appreciative. I didn't know what to expect. They are people, such as us, but born and living in deplorable conditions with no hope of improving their lot in life. It's sad. It made me appreciate my life as the daughter of a duke."

"Yes. You are fortunate to have been born an aristocrat, and so am I," he said.

She finished the rest of her drink and stood. "I should return to my chambers before Mother or Father find me here after begging off dinner."

Nick also stood, took the glass from her hand, walked to the sideboard, and placed both on a tray. "One moment, please."

Her eyes were riveted to his intense brown ones as he walked toward her. Swaggered really. The man could certainly swagger. He stood close enough that she could see the rise and fall of his chest as he breathed. His hand reached out, cupping her cheek gently. The light touch made her melt inside. She wanted to tilt her head into his hand and get as close as possible.

"I want to say a proper goodnight. It may be the last time."

As she opened her mouth to speak, his mouth fused with hers. All she could think was that he devoured her every breath. Her hands wrapped around his neck, and she curled into his body. His hands, now around her waist, pulled her tight against him even more, melding them together until they became one.

This. This was what she wanted, what she craved. She could not imagine living without this. She broke the kiss, turned and hurried from the room, ignoring Nick calling out her name. She needed the privacy of her chambers because her chest heaved, trying to release great sobs of despair. Tears were already rolling down her cheeks. She would not give him the satisfaction of seeing her shatter. He knew he was breaking her heart. He didn't need to witness it.

Once in her room, she flopped onto her bed, face down, hugged her pillow, and sobbed into it, hoping no one could hear her. She did not want to explain to her mother why she was in such a state.

CHAPTER FOURTEEN

NICK STARED WITH his mouth open as Priscilla ran from the room. No, not from the room. From him. From his embrace and kiss. He didn't blame her. He was such a contradiction. Hurrying from the library, he made his way to the parlor. Finding his mother saying her goodbyes to the duchess, he sighed with relief.

When the carriage stopped outside Hollingsworth House, he said, "I will see you in the house before I leave for White's for a nightcap."

After arriving home and escorting his mother inside, he reentered the carriage and signaled his driver with a tap on the roof. His driver knew White's was his destination.

He walked into White's and made for the back of the room where he would find Blackstone, Langford, and Caldwell if they were present. His face fell when the chairs they usually occupied were empty. So instead of sitting in that grouping of chairs, he sat off to the side in a large fabric chair that blocked him from view and afforded him a little privacy. An attendant came by and poured him a brandy. Per his request, he left the bottle.

Lost in his scrambled thoughts and staring into his drink, he couldn't seem to bring the glass to his lips when he heard two gentlemen approach behind him and sit not far from him. When they spoke he recognized one of the voices—it belonged to Baron

Latham. The other voice he didn't believe he had ever heard before. By the loudness of their voices, it was clear they believed they were alone in this section.

"I asked Lady Priscilla to marry me today," said Latham in a bored voice. The type one used when discussing the weather. Unless, of course, you were a weather enthusiast.

"What did she say?"

"That she needed time. What the bloody hell does she need time for? She had better not be stringing me along. I put everything I had into courting her. I've been attentive and nice, and I've kept my hands to myself for the most part. And how does she thank me? She says she needs time."

"Ladies can be fickle. You need to have patience."

"I lack patience. I've kissed her several times, and she seems to enjoy my kisses. I even touched her breasts, and she moaned, which I took as a positive sign. Having children with her won't be a burden. She is beautiful and responsive. Not that I'll spend much time with her since I plan to send her to the country and focus my attentions on my mistress and a new business venture I have underway with the Viscountess Norton."

Nick's blood boiled at hearing the conniving scoundrel whine on and on about Priscilla. It was too much to sit back and listen to him speak about Priscilla like that. How dare he openly discuss kissing and fondling her where anyone could overhear? He slammed his glass loudly on the table beside his chair, stood up, and turned to glare daggers at Latham.

"I say, I didn't know you were there, Hollingsworth," Latham drawled out with a tight-lipped grin. "I hope you didn't take offense to anything I said about Lady Priscilla."

"I didn't take offense, but the lady in question might." By now, he stood directly in front of Latham's chair. Latham looked up with a smug expression. The man had no conscience or scruples. Nick reached down, grabbed his cravat, yanked him to his feet, and punched him right in the nose.

"You cad!" Latham cupped his nose with his hands, which

bled nicely. "You broke my nose!"

Once again, Nick's hand curled around his cravat, and he tugged him close to his face and sneered. "If you ever speak disrespectfully about Lady Priscilla again, I will break much more than just your nose. Actually—" He seized Latham's wrist, twisting it behind his back, giving him no mercy. Just before it snapped, he released it. Too many men had gathered around, placing bets on who would win—pity to anyone who bet against him.

Nick stepped back and bowed graciously. "Good evening, gentlemen." His gaze remained fixed on Latham's, which burned with animosity. What was one more person who didn't like him? As he exited White's, he nearly collided with James Caldwell, Langford, and Blackstone. *Now they show up.* "If I were you, Caldwell, I'd head inside quickly. Someone just broke your brother's nose." He waved to his driver and departed without saying another word to the three men he considered friends. After tonight, his circle of three friends might shrink to two or even zero.

When he returned home—in the foulest of moods—he sat in his study and penned a missive to Priscilla. Whether he sent it or not remained to be seen. But he needed to write down what had happened and get it off his conscience.

My Dearest Priscilla,

After I left your house this evening, I went to White's for a nightcap. As I sat alone, minding my own business, your baron and his friend sat nearby, not having seen me. Latham began discussing very personal matters that have transpired between you two in private. I could not listen to him shame your reputation or disrespect you. And all of this coming from a man who proposed to you today. After all, if I could hear what he said, perhaps other members of White's could hear as well. I will spare you by not repeating anything he said.

As you might expect, I approached him with great control, my temper entirely in check, and proceeded to break his nose. If it weren't for the attention we drew from other patrons at White's, I would have broken his arm. Fortunately for him, he was spared further pain and embarrassment.

I hope you are not upset with me or think unkindly of me for my actions against the man you might marry. My actions were not rash but necessary. I was protecting your honor, and I will always do so.

What I ask of you now is something I have no right to ask, but I will anyway. I ask you not to marry Latham. He is not worthy of you. He will make a terrible husband and father. You deserve someone who will put you first and always be there for you. I hope you find that man someday.

Your humble servant,
Nick

He folded the paper, poured hot wax on the edge and pressed it with the Hollingsworth emblem. He scribbled her name on the front. She would never know what the man said about her if she refused Latham. He would burn the note and she'd never see it. But if she accepted his proposal, that would be another entirely different situation.

Although the hour was late, he wasn't shocked when Robbins came and announced Blackstone and Langford. Before Robbins could send them in, they burst through the door.

"What the hell, Hollingsworth?" Blackstone exclaimed as he helped himself to his brandy and handed out two more. "You broke Latham's nose without any provocation."

His two guests, who had never visited his home before, sat in chairs facing his desk. "Please help yourself to a drink and take a seat," he drawled through tight lips. "And by all means, come into my home and insult me." He downed his glass. "Have I ever hit anyone without provocation to your knowledge? Have you ever known me to lose my temper and take it out on anyone?" Nick was disappointed in his friends.

They shared a look between them that appeared contrite. "No," Langford replied.

"There has been a time or two in the ring at Gentleman Jackson's that I've feared you wanted to rearrange my face," Blackstone said with a shrug. "And then I think you're probably more afraid of my wife than me because she likes my looks just fine. Otherwise, you exemplify control."

"That's why I go to Jackson's several times a week. To keep control. What did Latham say?" Nick knew full well Latham wouldn't admit the truth.

Blackstone chimed in. "He said he was enjoying a drink with Mr. Stewart when you came over, hauled him up, and punched him, never giving him a reason."

"Some of what he said is true. He was having a drink with a man I didn't recognize—I assume this Mr. Stewart." He stood up, grabbed the decanter of brandy, and splashed some more into each glass. "I was sitting nearby, my back to them. Latham had no idea I was there. He had much to say about Lady Priscilla— very personal and insulting information. If what he said was overheard by other gentlemen in White's, her reputation would be in tatters. That man is no gentleman and has not changed his ways. He didn't come right out and say it, but it was clear he's pretending he has changed."

The three men sat in silence a moment, lost in thought.

"Sorry about the accusation," Blackstone said finally as he took another sip of his brandy. "I never believed Latham changed. The man hasn't a decent thought in his head. So that you know, Caldwell isn't fooled by his brother's newly acquired pristine behavior. He wanted us to tell you that he knew you must've had good reason if you hit him."

"I did."

"So, what will you do now?" Langford asked. "Challenge him to a duel?"

"No. I will not challenge him. I don't want to bring Lady Priscilla's name into it, and as long as Latham and Stewart keep their mouths shut, it won't be."

"Good," Blackstone remarked. "Dueling is illegal, and we

would hate to have to break you out of Newgate."

"Very funny. I don't mean to be rude, but I'd like to retire. It's been a trying night."

"There's one more thing," Blackstone glanced at Langford, who nodded. "We know why you were expelled from Eton."

"Everyone knows. I got into a fight with the son of an Austrian Prince."

"Fights happened at Eton all the time and don't result in expulsion," Blackstone added.

"Well, in my case, it did." Nick felt nauseous. The brandy churned in his stomach. "Just let it go. We fought. I got the better of him. End of story. Then I went to Harrow and liked it much better."

"Well, I won't hold it against you for attending Harrow," Blackstone said as he stood. "Come on, Langford, Emmeline is probably wondering where I am."

Langford chuckled. "Does she wear the breeches in your marriage?"

"No. But I would much rather be in bed with my wife than traipsing around London at this hour with you."

"As would I. Not your wife, but mine."

Nick listened to them with a twinge of envy.

CHAPTER FIFTEEN

THE DAY OF reckoning was upon Priscilla. First thing that morning, she had sent word to Latham, inviting him for afternoon tea. Even though his proposal had only come yesterday, she didn't need more time to give him her answer. She could never see herself married to him. Oh, she had fooled herself into thinking she could for a moment. But she couldn't. Even if it turned out this was to be her only offer, she would choose never to marry again rather than marry him.

The day dragged on as she waited for the appointed hour. She spent her time in the library pretending to read with Snowball curled up and purring on her lap. A fire blazed in the hearth on this rainy, windy, chilly day. The weather suited her mood perfectly.

After tossing and turning most of last night, Priscilla felt herself nodding off and was surprised when Eugenia entered the library.

"It is time to prepare for your visitor, my lady."

Priscilla went to pick up Snowball, but he jumped down and scurried out of the library. "Let us get ready then."

In the privacy of her chambers, Eugenia helped her change into a light-blue day dress with a matching shawl to ward off the day's chill. "Just comb out my hair and leave it loose—no need to impress the baron."

"Yes, my lady."

As she made her way to the drawing room, she heard her mother's and Latham's familiar voices, although the baron sounded like he had a cold. Thank goodness her mother was present—at least for now.

"Mother, Latham," she said as she swept into the room, feigning cheerfulness. Sitting on the settee beside her mother, she looked at Latham for the first time and gasped. "What happened to your face?" A hand flew to her chest. "Forgive me. That was rude." His nose was swollen and bruised—a ghastly sight. She was shocked he'd agreed to come for tea, looking as he did. For someone dressed in the finest clothes and impeccably groomed at all times, it must be damaging his self-esteem to be seen in public like this.

"Not at all. I explained to Her Grace that I had a set-to with Hollingsworth last evening."

"Oh," Priscilla said. She could see the damage but not the reason for it.

"I was minding my own business, enjoying a nightcap with an acquaintance, when Hollingsworth rudely approached me. Before I could defend myself or even know what he planned, he punched me in the nose. No warning. No words were exchanged between us. I was accosted for no reason at all. I have already started a petition to revoke his membership at White's. The man is unpredictable and a danger to others."

What the baron described didn't sound like Nick at all. Yes, he could be moody and standoffish, but to hit someone for no apparent reason didn't make sense. Nick admitted to being expelled from Eton for fighting, but he could have a reasonable explanation for it. After all, didn't schoolboys fight all the time? "I'm sorry for what Hollingsworth did, and I hope it had nothing to do with me." It was a silly thing to say because she knew it must. What else did the two men have to quarrel over? But why was Latham being so open about it? Was he trying to cause discord between her and Nick? Was he attempting to tarnish

Nick's reputation by portraying him as deranged and liable to punch anyone who aggravated him?

"He didn't say, but I believe it had everything to do with you and my marriage proposal from yesterday."

Priscilla turned to her mother and whispered, "Would you give us some privacy?"

Instead of answering, her mother squeezed her hand for support and left. Inhaling and exhaling several times, Priscilla prepared herself for what she must do. Knowing that Nick had hit him and broken his nose shouldn't make her feel bad for refusing his proposal, but somehow, it did.

Before she could speak, he moved beside her on the settee and grasped her hands. "I hope you have good news for me. When I received your note this morning, despite our horrible weather, I almost came right over in excitement and anticipation for your answer."

It took tremendous effort not to pull her hands away from his. Although he would surmise her answer if she did, and words would not be necessary. "David," she began, trying to find the right words to let him down gently. "I have enjoyed our time together, and I am flattered by your proposal, but sadly, I must decline."

He recoiled from her, staring at her in shock and something else that sent chills up her spine. It was a look she had never seen from him—or anyone else, for that matter. It looked like hatred. She stared as he opened his mouth to speak, closed it, and tried again to no avail. His complexion turned bright red like he had stuck his face close to a fire. But it wasn't from embarrassment. He was angry. With his swollen and bruised nose and his angry, distorted expression, the normally handsome Latham had transformed into something resembling a monster who frightened children in their sleep.

He stood and stomped out of the room without uttering a word. Priscilla released the air from her lungs, not even realizing she'd been holding her breath. She rested her head against the back of the settee, closed her eyes, and sighed with relief. Never did she ever want to go through anything like that again for the rest of her life. The look Latham gave her, the hatred pouring from his eyes, which came from deep inside him, would haunt her dreams. He had never felt anything for her, if it could turn so quickly to hate. His profession of caring for her was clearly a blatant lie. What other lies had he told her? Was anything he'd told her the truth?

"Are you feeling unwell?"

Nick.

She would need to speak to Berkely about letting Nick in without asking if she wanted to receive him. At the very least, he needed to announce the man to give her a warning.

"What are you doing here?" she mumbled as she didn't have the strength to speak correctly. All her energy had drained from her body after the brief, uncomfortable encounter with Latham.

"I came to speak to you."

"I don't want to talk. I'm tired. Just go away." She had yet to open her eyes. And she didn't plan on doing so. Not only did she not want to talk to Nick, she didn't want to look at his handsome face. A face that plagued her dreams at night for an entirely different reason.

"Too bad. I'm going to sit here until you talk to me. I'll stay all day and night if I have to." The settee cushion sank as he had the nerve to sit beside her. "I ordered a fresh tea tray. I refuse to share one that man touched."

Laughter bubbled up inside her throat, and she forced it down. Nick sounded like a petulant child. "The tray is un-touched."

"Still, the tea must be cold and the biscuits stale."

"Do you truly care?"

"I would kill right now for a hot cup of tea and your cook's sweet biscuits."

More laughter pooled in her throat that she refused to expel into the air. "You prefer coffee."

"Indeed," he huffed. "And that is what I ordered."

"No tea for me?"

"What do you take me for, an uncivilized wretch?" His voice was laced with humor.

Since her eyes were still closed, she could only picture his brown eyes warm with wit and his infuriatingly crooked grin.

"After witnessing your handiwork on Latham's face, I do think you are uncivilized."

"My carriage pulled up as he was pulling away. I had hoped to see my handiwork. The swelling and bruising are much more interesting a day later."

"You sound proud of yourself." Not that she condoned violence, but a part of her was thrilled that Nick had hit Latham. She was quite certain now that he deserved no less after witnessing the loathing in his eyes for her.

"Not proud."

"I've never known you to be violent."

"I'm not. I learned my lesson when I was expelled from Eton."

"One would think so."

"Are you ever going to open your eyes?"

She didn't want to. The sound of Nick's voice soothed her. "Do I have to?"

Footsteps approached from the doorway, and things rattled around. One tray was removed, and another was placed on the oval table before the settee.

"Tea has arrived."

"I heard." Sighing deeply, she turned her head toward Nick and opened her eyes. "Hello," she said with a sleepy smile, trying not to be blinded by his gorgeousness. "I was hoping to drift off to sleep before you rudely arrived. Next time, please ask if I'm receiving visitors."

His chuckle echoed throughout the room. "So you can say no and turn me away?" He poured tea from the teapot into a cup, adding sugar and cream as she liked. "I think not. You must sit up if you want to drink your tea. Otherwise, you will spill it down your lovely gown."

She wanted to remain as she was. Everything would become real if she sat up and focused on the room around her. Still, she did it anyway. Sitting up straight on the edge of the settee, she picked up her china cup and saucer and sipped. "Is this better?"

He continued chuckling, and her heart expanded. "Yes," he said as he drank his coffee, the pungent smell wafting her way. "Much."

"What are you doing here?"

"Just curious if you gave your answer to Latham."

"I did. He did not take my rejection of his proposal well. He stormed out without a word."

"He is no gentleman."

"So you have said before. Did you propose to Lady Grace?"

"No. Not yet. I'm debating on several things."

"Dare I ask what things?" She plucked a biscuit off the tray and took a small nibble. Her eyes were wide, anticipating his answer.

"No. I'm not in the mood for sharing."

"Then why are you here?"

"I already explained why," he said, holding up his cup. "Because your cook makes better coffee than mine." He picked up a biscuit and stuffed the entire thing into his mouth. "And biscuits," he said with his mouth full.

"You are incorrigible," she said, placing her empty teacup on the tray. Fifteen minutes ago, she thought she would never feel lighthearted or smile again that day, and she had Nick to thank for lifting her spirits. She wondered what had put him in such a light and teasing mood. She rather enjoyed spending time with him when he was like this. He was too severe and sour most of the time, but her heart loved him no matter his moods.

"Are you attending the theater tonight?" Nick queried.

"The Duke and Duchess of Blackstone invited me to their box along with Lord and Lady Langford."

"And me."

Warmth spread inside her. "I wondered."

He drained the last of the coffee from his cup and placed it on the tray beside hers. Standing, he bowed before her, taking her hand in his and placing his warm lips against the pulse point on her inner wrist. Heat traveled up her arm and turned her insides into an out-of-control inferno.

"Until later, my lady."

Her eyes were riveted on his back as he strolled out of the room. With her eyes closed again, she leaned against the back of the settee and visualized Nick as he had just been: smiling, teasing, laughing, and as light-hearted as she had ever seen him. She hardly dared hope it was because she'd refused Latham's proposal. Only time would tell, she supposed.

She must have dozed off because the next thing she heard Eugenia's voice saying, "Lady Priscilla, it's time to wake. Dinner will be served in an hour, and you must dress for the theater."

Lifting her arms over her head, she stretched and was surprised to find she had fallen asleep sitting up. Refusing marriage proposals was exhausting. As she and Eugenia ascended the stairs, she said, "I would like to wear the emerald-green-and-cream gown."

"That is a wonderful choice. It will make your eyes sparkle, my lady."

At the dinner table, she explained what happened with Latham to her parents. She even included how he'd looked at her with loathing. Her father was not pleased. After that, the conversation around the dinner table was quiet—at least on her part. Mother and Father discussed things that pertained to them alone, and she was glad the attention was off her.

At precisely eight, while Priscilla waited in the drawing room, Berkely announced the arrival of the Duke of Blackstone's carriage. She paused at the door, and Berkely helped her into her cloak and gloves. She followed the Blackstone footman, dressed in Blackstone livery, down the stairs and took his hand as he assisted her inside the carriage, where she sat opposite the duke and duchess.

"Good evening, Lady Priscilla," Blackstone said pleasantly.

"Good evening, Duke. I'm honored by your invitation this evening."

"We're friends, and you are welcome to join us anytime."

"Thank you. Good evening, Your Grace."

"And to you, Lady Priscilla," Emmeline said. "I must warn you that Hollingsworth is joining us this evening."

"Yes, he told me."

Emmeline leaned forward, took Priscilla's hands in hers, and queried, "Did you give Latham an answer?"

The duke cleared his throat. "Do you really want to have this conversation now?"

Emmeline looked apologetic. "I'm sorry. I should have waited until we were in private, but I'm dying to know."

"Fine. Go on," he said.

"Well?" Emmeline prompted.

"I turned him down."

"Thank goodness," Emmeline said as she sat back. "He may be the brother of our friend, but I never liked him. Now we need to work on finding you a husband worthy of you since Hollingsworth won't come up to snuff."

"Right," she huffed.

"Darling," Emmeline placed her hand on her husband's, "with all your connections, you must know someone worthy of our Priscilla."

"Please leave me out of it," he grumbled and then chuckled. "I will do anything for you, my darling, except matchmake."

The carriage arrived at the theater just in time to end this awkward conversation. Priscilla felt as if she might die of embarrassment. Emmeline meant well, but she didn't want to feel like a charity case. She could find her own damn husband—or not—if she so chose.

They entered the Theatre Royal, Covent Garden from Bow

Street into a large entrance hall and ascended the stone stairs to Blackstone's private box.

When they arrived, they found Lord and Lady Langford and Nick already there and seated. After they stood and exchanged greetings, they took their seats and Priscilla found herself sitting between Nick and Emmeline, with Lilly and her husband behind them.

"You look beautiful," Nick whispered in her ear, his warm breath making her shiver in a good way.

"Thank you." As she spoke, she looked across the theater and saw Lady Grace sitting with her younger sister, Lady Faith, and their parents, the Earl and Countess of Wilmington. Their eyes met, and Lady Grace blushed. Priscilla tilted her head slightly in acknowledgment. She felt sorry for Lady Grace having to watch her with Nick when she must wish to be sitting beside him. She hoped Lady Grace understood they were friends. "Lady Grace is looking at us. Why are you not in their box with her instead of here?"

"I was supposed to be, but I begged off. I said I couldn't refuse a duke's invitation."

"You are a fool."

"I beg your . . ."

"Be quiet, I'm not finished. If you still intend to propose, you should do so soon to spare the poor girl any more misery." When he proposed to Lady Grace, it would cause *Priscilla* misery, but it couldn't be helped. How unfair life could be.

"Honestly, I don't think she cares one way or another who she marries, only that she marries to get away from her unpleasant mother," he mumbled.

"Nick, I can't believe that."

"It's true. She confided in me that after her eldest sister died, her mother became unbearable to live with. The eldest was her mother's favorite."

"How sad. I didn't know there was a third sister."

"Yes, she came out the same year as Emmeline. The year

Emmeline married Mr. Fitzpatrick."

"I see."

"I'm not offended if Lady Grace marries me to escape her mother. I'm not seeking love—just a wife I can respect and tolerate enough to produce heirs. Other than that, she can do as she pleases, and I will do the same."

Who was this man sitting beside her? He wasn't the same Nick she had teased with that afternoon. What had happened between then and now for him to act so insensitively? She felt sorry for Lady Grace or anyone he married. She wanted to say something but couldn't find the words, so she stayed silent until the theater darkened and the curtain opened.

CHAPTER SIXTEEN

DURING THE PLAY, Nick thought his heart might leap from his chest. Whenever the inside of the theater was bathed in light, Lady Grace looked at him with pleading eyes, her face filled with sadness. The Countess of Wilmington glared at him. If looks could kill, he would have been dead ten times over. The countess made him want to tear his hair out, while Lady Grace made him want to run away. He hated disappointing anyone or making them sad. Over the past month, he had grown fond of Lady Grace. She was kind and easy to talk to, and she didn't judge him harshly for the things he had done. He wasn't fool enough to think she cared deeply for him—she didn't. She looked upon him as her savior. But any way one looked at it, she deserved a man better than him.

When the play ended, he thanked Blackstone, said his good-byes, and left. He wasn't in the right frame of mind to spend more time with Priscilla, nor did he want to speak to Lady Grace or Lady Wilmington. His joyful mood from earlier in the day had turned dark, and it wasn't fair to Priscilla or Grace to deal with him when he was like this.

He wandered the streets aimlessly until he found himself at the townhouse he had purchased for Anne, his former mistress. Candles still glowed, so he knew she must still be awake. He hadn't heard from her since the unfortunate encounter in the park with her father, nor had he heard from her father after the note he had sent. Well, there was no time like the present to find out what she and her father had decided.

He tapped his knuckles on the door. Six months ago, he would have walked right in, but the house now belonged to Anne, and it didn't feel right to barge in. The servants who cared for her were still under his employ, but they did not spy for him, per his request. He paid for their services but did not want to know what happened in the household or what Anne did.

After knocking several times without a response—where were the servants?—he sighed and turned the door handle. As he opened the door, he called out, "Hello? Is anyone home?" He stepped inside and closed the door behind him. "Anne, where are you?"

Still no answer. He climbed the stairs and checked the drawing room. Candles cast a soft light, but the room was empty. He hated intruding on Anne's privacy, but what if something was amiss? Perhaps she had given the servants the evening off and took to her bed sick, or worse, in early labor. She was with child, after all. He needed to know she was all right. With his heart pounding, he marched down the hall to the master bedroom and paused outside when he saw the door slightly ajar and voices coming from inside.

"Have you heard from Hollingsworth lately?" said a man's voice he knew all too well. It took all his self-control not to storm in there and strangle him. Nor could he bring himself to leave. What they discussed pertained to him.

"Not since my father and I saw him in the park," answered Anne.

"I thought you weren't speaking to your father."

"I'm not. Not since he tried to marry me off to his assistant. It was Hollingsworth's idea."

"Of course it was. The man insinuates himself into everyone's life."

"How is your nose?"

"Broken and hurts like bloody hell. I can't wait to find him alone some night and beat him senseless. I'll make sure I disfigure his face permanently so no lady will have him."

Nick's hands fisted by his side, and his entire body vibrated.

"Does he still believe this baby is his?"

"Yes. He will never learn the truth from me," Anne replied.

Red flashed in and out of his vision as he struggled to maintain control. Anne had deceived him. The child she carried belonged to Latham, and she had lied because she needed him to support her. After all, Latham was broke and unable to do so. How could she do this to him?

Soft footsteps echoed down the hallway, bringing him out of his shock. "My lord, what brings you here at this hour?" asked Mrs. Mullen, the housekeeper, her voice barely above a whisper.

"My apologies, Mrs. Mullen. I knocked, but no one answered, and I was afraid perhaps Anne had taken ill."

Mrs. Mullen shook her head, looking cross. "She isn't in bed because she is ill, my lord. Forgive me; I've wanted to send you a note, but you specifically asked us not to spy on Mistress Anne."

"I believe I understand what you wanted to tell me. Now that I know the truth, I can't keep paying your salary or anyone else's. I'm sorry. I will provide a month's pay and letters of recommendation."

Mrs. Mullen curtsied. "Thank you. That is very generous of you."

"Would you please inform the others?"

"Yes."

"Tell them to come to my residence tomorrow, and I will give them sealed letters and their pay."

"You are most kind, my lord."

"I thought you gave all the servants the night off?" Latham's voice traveled out to the hall, followed by footsteps across the room. The conversation with Mrs. Mullen had been quiet, but not quiet enough. The door swung open, and Nick came face to face with Latham, dressed only in breeches. The shock Nick witnessed on Latham's bruised, swollen face was almost laughable.

"Will you ever stop interfering in my life, Hollingsworth?" The man sneered with animosity.

"I believe it is you interfering in mine."

Latham hauled back his arm and threw a punch, but Nick stopped it quickly enough. He didn't spend several mornings a week at Gentleman Jackson's Club for nothing. It was how he managed his emotions. Perhaps Latham should consider joining the club. Although, if Nick ever found himself in the ring with him, only one person would be left standing on their feet.

"What the bloody hell?" he glared as Nick held onto his fist, squeezing as hard as he could.

"Let him go, Nicholas," Anne said as she came to the door wearing a night rail that did little to hide her figure or growing belly. "You left me. I had every right to find another protector."

Nick released Latham's hand and narrowed his eyes. "You lie. I heard everything. The child you are carrying is Latham's."

Anne and Latham looked at each other in alarm.

"The house is yours, but don't expect another pound from me. Your allowance is gone as of tonight, and so are your servants. Good luck paying the taxes and managing the upkeep on this property."

She reached out and grabbed his arm. He glanced down at her hand with disdain. "You promised to take care of me and the baby forever." She stomped her foot and yelled, "You promised!"

He brushed her hand off his arm like an unwanted bug and leaned close to her face. "I promised to take care of you if you chose *not* to take another protector, which you did. I promised to provide for the child when I believed it was mine." He paused, edged closer, and said, "You lied on both counts. I regret putting the deed to the house in your name." He paused. "You still have options. You can marry your father's assistant and give your child a name. You can sell this townhouse and buy something smaller and bank the rest to live on."

He moved his eyes to Latham. "Don't you ever speak to me or Lady Priscilla again. If you do, the dueling field it will be."

As he made haste to leave, he nodded to the housekeeper and practically ran down the stairs and out of the house. Several doors down, he bent over at the waist, gasping for air, and lost his dinner into someone's bushes. Every nerve in his body vibrated with anger at himself for not seeing Anne for what she was until tonight. Had she been entertaining Latham for years, making a fool of him? He wouldn't doubt it—not after what he knew now.

His only regret was the child she carried and not providing for it even though it wasn't his. The child, at least, was innocent. A conversation with her father was needed. Nick had to have confirmation the man would provide for them. And if Nick had to provide her father with funds, so be it. As long as it stayed between the two of them.

His mind raced along with his heart, and he knew he wouldn't settle down and sleep. He wandered the streets for the second time that night and found himself before Avery Manor. A single candle glowed in the entry hall. Nick knocked, hoping no one would answer the door. He did not want to explain his presence at this time of night. When no one opened the door, he walked to the side where the servants' entrance was. He turned the knob and frowned at finding it locked. He reached into his pocket and pulled out a small, black leather bifold. Ever since the day the viscountess, going by the name Esmeralda, led him astray, he kept tools with him. One never knew when a lock would need picking. That was one good thing that had come out of Eton. Holzer taught Nick how to pick locks.

Making quick work of the lock, he quietly stepped inside, closing and locking the servants' door behind him. He knew where to go. How many times had he been here, after all? Even drunk as he was the other night when he'd snuck in through this door, he'd remembered how to get to Priscilla's chambers. Though the door had been unlocked that night, which was a godsend, because in his inebriated state he didn't think his lock picking skills would have worked.

He tiptoed down the hallway, feeling his way along the wall, glad that he knew her parents' chambers were in the opposite wing. When he arrived at Pricilla's door, he paused, his hand covering his heart, which thumped fast. He tried to settle it down. After several breaths, he opened the door, snuck inside, closed, and locked it.

"Priscilla?"

"Nick. Why are you here? Can't a lady have privacy in her own chambers?"

He shrugged his shoulders, not that she could see him in the dark. "Obviously not. Can you please light a candle? I don't want to trip on something and make a loud noise."

"So demanding." He heard the rustling of the covers and the soft patter of her feet as she moved around. She proceeded to light several candles, and he found his eyes entranced by the shape of her body, perfectly silhouetted through the translucent pink nightgown by the glow from the candle. Before he could stop himself, he groaned.

"Don't make that sound. You are not an animal."

"Aren't I?"

"Nick, why are you here? I just saw you two hours ago at the theater," Priscilla said. She sat on her bed, her back against the headboard, and pulled the covers up to her chin.

Though it was a bit too late for modesty to be of much use. He had already seen every alluring part of her body thanks to the sheer night rail she wore, and he wanted nothing more than to peel it off her body.

He ran his hands through his hair. He hadn't come here to take her to bed; he had come to talk . . . again. But seeing her sitting like that had him suddenly feeling mischievous. He jumped onto the bed, sitting beside her, his legs stretched out and his booted feet crossed at the ankle.

"Get off my bed."

"I'd rather not. I have things to say and questions to ask you."

"I'm not in the mood for answering," she said with a challenge in her voice.

"What I have to say or ask cannot wait. I found out tonight that the child my former mistress carries is not mine."

She swung her head toward him and narrowed her eyes, likely trying to assess if he was telling the truth. "That is good news, is it not?"

He grinned. "Excellent news indeed."

"And whose baby is it?"

He grinned and snorted. "Take a guess."

Crossing her arms on her chest, she sighed. "I haven't the slightest idea."

He took pity on her. "None other than Baron Latham." He paused. His eyes studied her face. Her head lowered, her eyes closed, and she inhaled and exhaled deeply.

"I'm sorry. That man has turned out to be a menace to both of us."

"No truer words. I have a favor to ask." He had no right to ask this of her, but he was bone weary and didn't want to be alone with his thoughts.

"Yes?" Her eyes flicked to his and gave him a peek into her soul. A sweet, kind, patient soul.

"May I spend the night?"

"Nick, I don't think that is a good idea in so many ways."

"Just to sleep. I don't want to be alone." He knew it was much to ask, and he wouldn't have if he weren't so desperate. It wasn't just that he didn't want to be alone with his thoughts over the shock of what he learned from Anne and Latham, but also because—and he wasn't too prideful to admit it—his dignity was wounded. He'd always believed he was an intelligent man. How wrong he was. All his decisions lately proved that regarding Priscilla, Lady Grace, and Anne.

He also didn't want to be alone physically. He needed to be with someone he trusted. And he trusted Priscilla with his life. The sound of her breathing, the jasmine scent of her hair, the knowledge that she lay beside him would go a long way in easing the turmoil inside him and help him get the rest he needed. If he slept soundly, perhaps he would see things clearly tomorrow.

"What if someone sees you in the morning?"

"Did anyone see me leave the other morning?"

Sighing deeply, she looked at him again, her hazel eyes showing the soft gold color from within. "Fine. Just stay on your side of the bed." She pointed at his feet. "And get those filthy boots off."

"Yes, my lady," he said with a relieved laugh. He slid to the side of the bed and struggled to pull off his boots. The little minx didn't offer to help. Once he got them off, he stood, removed several articles of clothing until he was left in his shirt, breeches, and socks, and climbed beneath the covers of Priscilla's bed. A bed he never thought he would be in. And up until recently, never wanted to be.

CHAPTER SEVENTEEN

S HE HAD NO idea what to make of Nick in her bed and beneath the covers. Part of her, the part that made her heart race and her woman parts tingle, was ecstatic. Her levelheaded side felt nervous about being discovered. And still another part of her wanted to reach out and take what she had desired for a long time. Then even if he never married her, she would have this one night to remember.

She moved her pillow down so she lay flat on her back. She was afraid to make a sound, move, or even breathe. She feared he would change his mind and leave if she drew attention to herself.

"Priscilla?" he said, as he turned and looked at her with eyes bright with desire and his memorable crooked grin on his face. "I find myself suddenly wide awake." He reached out and brushed his fingers down her cheek.

"Nick. I don't think this is a good idea." She knew without a doubt what he wanted.

"Why not? We are both free. You are a widow, and I'm single. There's nothing wrong with us enjoying the pleasure of our bodies." Her eyes widened as he sat up, tugged her toward him and guided her until she straddled his lap. The fabric of her night rail gathered up around her thighs and she refused to look down to see how exposed she was to him. The evidence of his arousal pushed against her core and she swallowed a moan. Curling one hand around the back of her neck, he pulled her face close to his. Instinct had her running her tongue across the top of her lip. Nick groaned. "There is nothing wrong with giving and receiving pleasure between two people who care about each other."

Whatever she was about to say was swallowed up by Nick's mouth as he kissed her with a passion belonging to him and him alone. His kiss, in its raw intensity and need, captured her within its power, and she willingly gave herself over to him. To her surprise, the kiss transformed and he gave himself over to her.

Finding herself in a complete fog, but needing air, she wrapped her hand in his hair and gently tugged his head back. "Nick." She broke the kiss and gasped for air.

"Breathe, but please don't think. Just feel. Let me make you feel good." Nick's large, warm hands brushed the hem of her nightgown and she shivered. "Can I remove this?"

Not trusting herself to speak or even to look at him, she closed her eyes, nodded her head. The soft linen of her night-gown teased her sensitive nipples as he pulled it over her head, exposing her completely to him. Even her legs were open since she remained straddling his hips. Her entire body quivered with excitement and desire. She had only experienced lovemaking twice on the night of her wedding to Jasper, and she'd been self-conscious and nervous.

Neither of those things existed right now with Nick.

"You are so beautiful," he said in a tone she'd only heard from him a few times. His hands cupped her breasts, causing her to arch her back and her head to fall back. "Your breasts fit perfectly in my hands." He leaned forward and down, taking one nipple into his mouth and sucking it hard and deep. Priscilla moaned as she felt the connection down to her very core. "Your nipples taste so sweet and they're so sensitive and responsive." He moved to the other nipple and did the same thing, and heat scalded her between her thighs.

Without warning, he flipped her onto her back. She opened her eyes to see Nick's grinning face as he now straddled her waist.

"Now I have you just where I want you." He reached up and behind his back, pulled off his shirt, and tossed it onto the floor. Her eyes widened at the sight of his muscular chest sprinkled with dark hair that tapered down and disappeared into his breeches.

"You are making me amorous with those seeking eyes of yours," he chuckled as he moved down her body, his warm lips placing featherlight kisses down her neck and across to the other side. Every inch of her skin tingled with greed wanting to feel his sinful lips.

He kissed down her chest, between her breasts, and downward still. She gasped and held her breath as heat and wetness pooled between her thighs. And lower he went. "Nick," she whispered. Was he going to . . .? She had never experienced this but had seen pictures of it in a gentleman's manual she once found hidden behind other books in their library. He eased her legs open with his hands. "Oh my God," she breathed as he licked her between her thighs, causing her body to tremble. His fingers opened her folds, his mouth sucked on her nub, and he inserted a finger inside her channel. He kept doing this pleasurable form of torture, and she never wanted it to end. Except it was overwhelming—too much and not enough simultaneously. Needing an anchor before she lost herself in what was happening, she reached down and fisted Nick's hair in her hand and exploded. She tried to speak, to ask for mercy, but the words wouldn't come. She was incapable of anything but feeling. Her entire body shook as something she'd never experienced before battered her from the inside out. And she meant battered in an exceptionally good way. "Nick," she gasped, her hand now pushing at his head. "I can't. Too much."

He chuckled—the audacity of him. He kissed his way up her body, taking her mouth in a deep, languid kiss, and she tasted something earthy.

"Stay right here." He jumped off the bed.

Where did he think she would go? She couldn't move even if

she wanted to. Her body still pulsed from the pleasure he had given her. And yet, she desired more. Wanted to feel the fullness of him deep inside her as he sought his pleasure.

After he removed his breeches and undergarments, he climbed back on top of her and grinned. "Miss me?" He kissed her, then frowned. "You're quiet."

"I can't speak," she giggled. "Or rather, I couldn't speak. Not after . . ."

He shook his head. "I don't know what I was thinking. I don't have a French letter on me. We can't . . ."

"Yes, we can." French letter or not, she wanted this. Wanted him regardless of the risk. "We can."

He took her lips, his lips sipping and tasting her. His tongue danced with hers. One hand touched her, his thumb circling her nub, setting her nerves on fire. His manhood nudged against her opening, and she spread her legs, wanting him. All of him.

"Priscilla," he groaned as he entered her in one push until he was seated deep inside her. A place she always knew he belonged. She wrapped her legs around his waist. "You are so warm and tight," he murmured against her neck as his hips retreated, then returned, tantalizing her and making her legs tremble and weaken. He kissed her again, his tongue mimicking his manhood. In and out. In and out. Faster and faster. Her back arched, taking him as deep as her body would allow. Shooting stars flashed across the room as her body trembled. She hugged Nick as his body coiled up tight and he groaned through his clenched teeth. He collapsed on top of her, then rolled to the side, his arms wrapped around her waist, pulling her back to his front. "Thank you," he murmured as he kissed her neck. "That was amazing."

Tears silently trickled down her cheeks onto her pillow and she hoped Nick didn't see them. Her emotions were overwhelming her senses. She was happy, sad, in love, and frightened. What had happened between her and Nick just now? Was it normal?

"You are quiet again," Nick said, his breath warm against her neck. "Did I hurt you?"

"No," she whispered as she placed her arms over his. "It was wonderful. I'm half-asleep."

"Go to sleep then. I'll bid you goodbye now, as you'll be asleep when I leave."

"All right." It was true that she was half-asleep, but she didn't want to sleep. She wanted to enjoy this night with Nick, as it might be their only one. She fought to stay awake and enjoy being cradled in his arms. His breathing slowed and he began to snore, she sighed with relief. His snoring wasn't loud enough to rattle the floorboards, but it wasn't soft either. She turned around, facing him and studied him by candlelight having kept two candles lit. When relaxed in sleep, Nick looked younger and more at ease. Usually, he was wound tight and ready to pounce, which made her wonder what caused the tension that had been a companion to him ever since she could remember.

How exhausting it must be for him to deal with it day in and day out. He needed to find a way to tame it. After tonight, he had one less thing to contend with. Her stomach fluttered. He wasn't going to be a father to his ex-mistress's baby. The shock when Nick spoke Latham's name and the relief she felt knowing he was out of her life pleased her.

She cupped his cheek with her hand, and pulled it back immediately when she witnessed his brows draw tight, his mouth frown, and his body tense. And when he yelled, "Stay away from me!" Priscilla froze.

"Come near me again and I'll kill you." Nick's head thrashed from side to side. "No. Get out!"

Priscilla held her breath, wondering if she should wake him. He appeared distressed and frightened, and his voice sounded like a young boy's. She placed her hand on his chest, shocked at how fast his heart beat against her palm. "Nick. It's Priscilla. You're having a nightmare."

He swatted her hand off his chest. "Get away from me, you bloody arse!" he cried out.

She tried again. Her hand rested on his chest again. "Nick,

wake up," she whispered in her most soothing tone. "You're dreaming."

His arms flailed around and he yelled, "No!"

"Easy. It's Priscilla. You are safe."

"Priscilla?" His eyes focused on her. "What are you doing in my bed?"

Her heart eased at hearing his voice almost back to normal. What was he dreaming about? He sounded like a terrified boy. Had something happened to him when he was young?

"You are in *my* bed."

"Your bed. What am I doing in your bed?"

"You don't remember?"

He sighed deeply and scrubbed his hands down his face. "Give me a minute."

And so she waited, her hand still resting on his warm chest. It rose and fell with his breaths. The beat of his heart thumped against it in perfect rhythm.

"I'm sorry. Was I dreaming?"

"Yes. Did someone do something to you?"

"It's not something I talk about."

"Can't or won't?"

"Priscilla. Let it go. It's nothing. It happened a long time ago. I hardly dream about it anymore."

"I don't believe you."

"Well, it's the truth," he huffed.

"Tell me about it?" She rubbed her hand up and down his arm.

He closed his eyes tight and shook his head. "I can't. It's awful and embarrassing. I've never told anyone."

"You can trust me," she said as she touched his cheek, and his hand clasped hers.

"I know I can. It's not a matter of trust. It's a matter of pride and humiliation. It's also about anger and feeling inadequate and damaged."

"Does that even make sense?" she questioned.

"To me, it does."

"Perhaps if you unburden yourself, it will help. And I'll understand you better."

He choked and cleared his throat. "I highly doubt it."

"Please? The thought of you having these nightmares when you are alone saddens me. I want to help you."

"Nobody can help me," he groaned.

"How do you know?"

"Because I do." His chest rose and fell in a deep sigh. One of acquiescence. "You will be the death of me."

She took their pillows, fluffed them, and placed them against the back of the headboard. "Sit."

Her hands rummaged around the bed. Finding her nightgown, she pulled it on over her head. She felt this was not a conversation requiring nakedness—quite the opposite. They both rested against the pillows, and beneath the covers, they held hands. She squeezed his, giving him the courage to tell his story.

"You know I was expelled from Eton for fighting."

"Yes."

"He was the son of an Austrian Prince. The day my father dropped me off at Eton, I was thirteen and eager to make friends and earn good grades—anything to make my father proud." He paused, and Priscilla could sense the difficulty in his voice; he had to force the words out. "Holzer was two grades ahead of me and befriended me immediately. He was popular with his classmates, so I didn't understand why he wanted to befriend me—until I found out why."

She squeezed his hand, giving him the courage to continue his story.

"My roommate became ill and went home. I don't know what happened, but he never returned, nor did I get a new roommate. One night, I awoke to find Holtzer standing over me. I jumped right up still groggy from sleep but when he threw the first punch."

She wrapped an arm across his chest and leaned her head on

his shoulder, hoping she could ease his burden somehow. "I'm so sorry."

"I fought him off. I may have been smaller, but I had much to lose." He gulped. "I locked my door every night, but he picked the lock. I could never sleep, I had to stay awake prepared to fight him when he arrived. Which he always did. I don't know why he chose me, but I think he craved the battle of wills and strength. It lasted most of my first year at Eton. The crazy thing was, I knew that if he was coming to my room at night, then he wasn't doing it to anyone else. I spent that year sticking to him like ticks to a dog."

Her throat burned from her tears. How had he survived the sleep deprivation, the fighting, and the strain of knowing this boy would come for him night after night? Every sound in the room ceased to exist. All she heard was Nick's ragged breathing. Her heart ached for the boy of thirteen and the man of thirty-six. He'd been living with these memories for years.

"When I returned for my second year, I'd grown a foot and put on two stone. This time the physical odds were in my favor. So I knew fighting him off would be much easier. But after several nights went by and he didn't show up, I began prowling the halls looking for him. One night I finally saw him enter a room, I burst in after him." He paused, inhaled and exhaled. "Holzer confided in me that day that he had come to me nightly the year before hoping I would beat that part of him, the part that liked to see pain in others, out of him. I felt sorry for him. Until he said it couldn't be beaten out of him, and that was why he'd sought out someone else. I'm ashamed to say I beat him badly that night, which brought on my expulsion. The only good thing about me getting thrown out of Eton was that Holzer returned to Austria and never came back to Eton."

"Oh, Nick."

She snuggled closer. "You should be proud of yourself for standing up to that bully. You following him and fighting him saved other boys from what you went through and possibly worse."

"The boy whose room I followed Holzer into appeared shocked to find us there. He had no idea who Holzer was which gave me much relief. He is now an earl and I often wonder if he thinks about that night. Or wonders what the hell it was all about."

"Do you see this earl now?"

"Yes. He attends most of the same functions we do. He is unmarried and, as far as I know, is not courting anyone. The earl is affable and well-liked by the ladies. He also belongs to my pugilism club."

"Hmmm. I didn't know you boxed. Will tell me about that later? Because right now, I'd like to ask you something, if I may?"

"You may, and I'll try to answer."

"Several times, you told me I deserve someone better than you. Or that you can't be the man I want you to be. What did you mean?"

His body stilled. She didn't think he breathed or his heart beat, though that was impossible.

"It's because it's true. I'm damaged. Some days, I wake up and don't want to get out of bed. Other times, I have excessive energy, or my demons plague me, or I hate myself, and I visit my pugilism club. I fight to control my emotions when they are too much to bear."

"How often do you box?" There were so many questions she wanted to ask him about the things he just told her, but she went with the least intrusive. Perhaps there would come at time when she got the answers to the rest.

"Several times per week at Gentleman Jackson's Club. I box with the earl I told you about and Blackstone. Blackstone joined shortly before he married Emmeline."

"Does it truly help?"

He tightened his arms around her. "It does. Though it's clearly not a miracle cure if I'm still battling Holzer in my dreams."

Tears leaked from her eyes, landing on Nick's chest. And they still flowed from her eyes as she closed them and succumbed to sleep.

CHAPTER EIGHTEEN

WITH PRISCILLA WRAPPED around his body, he knew the instant she fell asleep. Her breathing evened out, and her body relaxed on his. And her tears stopped. When her tears dropped one by one on his bare chest, it stole the very air from his lungs. He hated and felt honored, which was a contradiction he knew, that she cried for him. And still he didn't feel worthy of her.

When she'd woken him up from his nightmare, he'd had no intention of telling her about Holzer and his time at Eton. He had never wanted anyone to know how terrified he had been and how he had to fight for his life every damn night. And how that had caused a residual effect that he battled daily. It had altered his brain. It didn't work right. As he confided in Priscilla, *he was damaged*.

That was really why he'd never asked for Priscilla's hand in marriage back when she was eighteen. It's why he hadn't asked anyone. Oh, he convinced himself he was going to propose to Lady Grace, but he knew he would never ask her. Certainly not after tonight.

He had never wanted to drag anyone else into his life—a life he sometimes had trouble controlling. But after tonight with Priscilla, he wanted to become the man she deserved, the man he knew was hiding somewhere deep inside him.

He still sat against the headboard, holding her while she slept. He had never admitted to himself that she was the most precious person in his life. Regardless of what the future held, she always would be. He would always look out for her, but not the way a brother would. He used to refer to her as a sister, but that was a lie. He had realized that when she was eighteen and had her first Season.

He still didn't know if he was ready to marry or if he ever would be, but he was making progress toward it. And just in case he was never ready, he would have to tell Priscilla. She had the right to know. He would never ask her to wait for him; that would be unfair to her, even if it broke his heart to see her married to another man.

For an hour, he held her, not letting himself fall asleep. He'd had enough nightmares for one night. Tonight, with her, would forever remain etched in his heart and mind as the best and most important night of his life. He'd kissed her before, and those kisses had transcended time. Tonight, it was more. He was alive and present and felt everything deep inside his soul. She had become his everything: every kiss, every caress, every heated glance. The joining of their bodies meant more. He had never experienced feelings, love, and emotions like this.

The world around them had vanished. They were the only two people who existed. His touch became hers, her kiss became his, and her body became his until they indeed became one. Priscilla became his entire world.

He kissed the top of her head as tears pooled in his eyes. What they shared—was it enough to base a lifetime together on? He never wanted to cause her pain or regret *if* they married. He'd managed to hide it well over the years, but he could act irrationally, and he didn't want the burden of his actions to fall on her shoulders. He looked up at the ceiling and whispered, "Please let me heal, so we can become each other's world."

It was close to sunrise. As much as he hated to leave her, he had to. He gently extricated himself from her embrace, tucked her in, and kissed her forehead. She stirred, curled up on her side, and hugged her pillow closely, which brought a smile to his lips. "Good night, my love," he whispered as he dressed, slipped out, and went home.

He slept for four hours in his own bed before leaving his house again in his carriage to go to his pugilism club on Bond Street. He sparred with whoever was available; this morning, it was the earl he'd mentioned to Priscilla. After last night, Nick didn't feel the usual angst vibrating inside him, but since he planned to visit Viscountess Norton afterward, he needed to tire himself out. He wouldn't leave her home until she'd explained what was going on with Latham. He hadn't forgotten what he'd heard Latham say at White's. What was all that talk about going into business with the viscountess? Nick had a bad feeling nothing good would come of those two joining forces.

"That's going to bruise, you know," the Earl of Middlebury said after he landed a series of punches that Nick was too preoccupied to protect himself from. "You are usually focused, and fight me like you want to hurt me mortally, but not today." He jabbed several more times, but Nick blocked these and got in a few punches himself. "What's on your mind?"

"Christ," Nick said, moving around. "You must have hated getting in the ring with me, until today." The earl moved with him. Nick backed out of the way and counterpunched.

"Only if I drank too much the night before. I got really good at dodging and blocking as I just showed you."

"Damn, that was some blocking."

"I heard you're courting Lady Grace. Is that true?"

Lady Grace? Middlebury hit him with a solid punch which rattled from one side of his chest to the other. If that were for Lady Grace, he deserved it for being such a reprobate. More importantly, why was Middlebury asking? Hell, Nick didn't know up from down this morning. He needed to call off the courtship with Lady Grace. Truly, he didn't believe she would be surprised or disappointed. He would feel terrible if she had feelings for him, but the one and only time he'd ventured to kiss her, they both knew there was no spark. She just enjoyed his company and was relieved at the chance to be away from her mother. "Ah, possibly."

Disappointment flashed in Middlebury's eyes as he prepared to hit him again. Fortunately, Nick saw it coming, ducked, spun around, hit Middlebury with a punch of his own, and took him down.

Nick took off his glove and held out his hand. "Sorry."

Middlebury took his hand, shaking his head. "Don't be. We are here to box, after all. Though I think I'm done for today."

"Me too. Before you go, are you interested in Lady Grace?" Nick couldn't think of a better gentleman to court her than Middlebury.

Middlebury shrugged his shoulders. "Does it matter?"

"It does, and you may be surprised to find her free from any suitors by the day's end."

"Thanks." The wide smile Middlebury gave him was all the thanks he needed.

He entered Gentleman Jackson's bathing facilities and prepared to face the day ahead no matter what was in store for him. Once dressed and looking presentable, he left the club, waved to his driver, Fitzroy, and readied himself to face the viscountess.

When he arrived at her townhouse, her butler answered the door and let him in. Nick went to hand him his calling card, but the servant waved him off. "I remember who you are, my lord. I will inform the viscountess that you are here." He disappeared up the stairs and came back down moments later. "She will see you now. Follow me."

He was led to the drawing room he had visited the first time, when Norton still lived. Emma sat on a settee with a book in her hands. "What a surprise to see you so soon," she said with a wide smile. "Have you changed your mind about me?"

Bloody hell, he had completely forgotten about her proposition to become his marchioness. "I'm afraid I haven't." He sat down before she could offer and stretched out his tired legs. "I've heard some interesting news."

Her blue eyes widened. "And what news is that?"

"I have overheard Baron Latham speak of a business arrangement involving you."

She glanced down at the book in her hands and shook her head. "I would deny any involvement with him if my dear, departed husband hadn't struck a deal with him." She paused and stared at him with her cold blue eyes. "My husband chose unwisely if Latham openly discusses it."

When Nick had first heard Latham at White's, he ignored the comment, as the man's words about Priscilla had been his main concern. But Nick could no longer dismiss it. He had a bad feeling in the pit of his stomach about this business between Latham and Emma. If their business dealings were legal, he couldn't care less about it. But due to both their pasts, illegal dealings were most likely what they were involved in. And Nick had a huge problem with that. "What is the nature of this business? If you don't tell me, I'll dig until I find the answer. If you do tell me, it goes no further than this room and a conversation with Latham." He motioned to his surroundings. "It looks as though Norton did well, I can't believe you need the money from any business venture that Latham would be involved in."

She put the book down beside her and glared at him with angry eyes. "If I tell you, it stays between you, me, and Latham. No matter what I confide in you."

"Agreed." He hoped agreeing wouldn't come back to haunt him.

"Here's goes nothing," she huffed. "I told you I was a barmaid when I came to London and was offered a better job by two tavern customers. What I left out was that they worked for Norton. Norton married me eventually, and I retired from an active role. However, the business continued scamming gullible people out of their money. My dear husband had been doing it for years before I met him, and yes, he amassed a fortune. But just before he died, Norton decided to retire from his active role, as well."

"What about you? When exactly did you retire?" Nick was stunned to find out about Norton's criminal side. He had never heard any rumors or gossip about the man. He had hidden his nefarious activities well.

"You were my last. He didn't want me soiled by the business any longer."

"Where does Latham fit into the equation?"

"Norton offered him the chance to take over the business—while still giving us a cut, of course."

Nick cleared his throat. "Of course."

"Since my husband's death, I've been training him."

"You're doing a terrible job since you neglected to tell him to keep his mouth shut."

"He's obviously an idiot who fooled Norton," she snapped.

"What will you do?" Nick asked.

"I don't know."

Nick stood and paced the room. "If I were you, I'd shut the business down. Let your two hired men do what they want. And warn Latham to keep his mouth shut before his tongue gets him in trouble." He paused right in front of her. "If you want to marry again within the *ton*, distance yourself from Norton's past activities. You said that you have money. Reenter Society after your mourning period. As a wealthy widow, you shouldn't have difficulty finding a husband."

"In the meantime, how will I occupy my time?" she pouted.

"Don't you have any friends or acquaintances?"

"No."

"Join a club or something. Work with a charity. Make friends, be useful, make yourself known so when you are out of mourning, single gentlemen will already be taking notice."

"Why are you telling me all this?"

He sighed and ran his hands through his hair. "Because I believe, deep down, that you are a good person who has lost sight of that." It was a lie. He didn't believe she was ever a good person, but he needed all this to come to an end.

"I hope you are right. I've been pretending to be someone else for so long I've forgotten who I am."

"I'll be watching both you and Latham. Distance yourself from him, or he will ruin you. As for him, he'll ruin himself on his own." He bowed. "Good day, Viscountess."

Well, that had gone better than he expected, he mused as he entered his carriage. It was time for a much-needed drink, and he told Fitzroy to hurry to White's.

About an hour into his visit, sitting and minding his business, Latham approached and said, "You cad, how could you tell her?"

That was fast. He'd only left Norton Hall a little over an hour ago. "I'm not sure what you mean."

"Don't play dumb with me. You know exactly what I'm talking about. Are you trying to ruin me?"

Nick indicated the chair across from him. "Take a seat. You and I have much to discuss."

Latham took a seat and signaled for an attendant. "Whisky, please." After he had his drink in hand, he glanced at Nick. "What could we possibly have to discuss?"

Nick raised an eyebrow. "Is your stupidity an act, or are you really ignorant about what's happening around you?"

"I can visit my brother if I want to be insulted."

"Fine. The first thing I want to discuss is Anne. How long?"

"How long what?"

"How long have you been bedding her?"

Latham counted on his fingers. "Almost nine months now."

Nick fought to stay still. His answer meant that both of them were bedding Anne for several months. "Did you use a French letter?"

"Why would I? Anne understood the risks."

"Are you going to marry her?"

"You didn't marry her, so why should I?"

Nick closed his eyes briefly, took a deep breath, and then

exhaled. "Forget I asked. Will you take care of the child?"

"I have no money. I thought I would acquire some, but you ruined that for me now, too. So the answer is no. But there is good news for her: Anne agreed to marry her father's assistant."

"I'm glad to hear that. That's one problem solved, and I won't bring it up again. Your brother need not know." Nick sipped his brandy. "I had to talk to the viscountess. I overheard you bragging about your new moneymaking venture. It would only be a matter of time before you got into trouble you couldn't get out of. Marry some unfortunate girl for her money and act like a gentleman."

Latham groaned and gulped his whisky. "I tried to do that with Priscilla, but once again, you interfered."

"Fortunately for *Lady* Priscilla, I did. Whether you know it or not, you have a good life. Caldwell and his wife live with you; from what I understand, they manage your household and holdings. With your brother at the helm, your estates should become profitable. Have patience and learn from him."

Latham stood up and left without saying a word. When Latham had first approached, Nick anticipated they might come to blows. Considering his nose was still broken, however, Latham was wise not to instigate an altercation that could turn into fisticuffs.

CHAPTER NINETEEN

WHEN PRISCILLA AWOKE, she rolled over and reached for Nick's body. She knew he wouldn't be there but did it anyway. She hoped they would wake up in the same bed one day. Cradling his pillow, she inhaled the woodsy scent that still lingered on it and tears welled in her eyes.

When he'd asked to spend the night with her, Priscilla believed Nick had no ulterior motive for staying. But things had happened, and she was just as much to blame as Nick for the turn of events. Though she would never regret a single moment of last night. Except for his nightmares and what caused them.

When he shared his experiences at Eton, she had hardly been able to imagine something like that happening. And then to know that she was the only one he trusted to tell . . .

He'd always appeared larger than life to her ever since she was a small girl. Seeing that side of him last night had broken something inside her. She understood him much better now and realized why he never had real friends.

It must have taken him a tremendous amount of faith and trust to become friends with Blackstone, Langford, and Caldwell. Thank goodness they saw something in him worthy of friendship. She couldn't think of better, more honorable gentlemen to be friends with.

"My lady," Eugenia knocked and entered her chambers with

a breakfast tray, as lately, Priscilla had been having breakfast in her room. She placed the tray on the bed beside her. "Is there anything else, my lady?"

"I would like a bath."

"I'll see to it immediately."

Since Priscilla had no plans for the day, she enjoyed her bath, the warm water soothing her sore muscles from being intimate with Nick. When the water cooled, Eugenia helped her dry off, dress, and comb out her hair. She left it loose so it could dry. She scooped up Snowball and went to the library, where she curled up on the sofa for several hours reading the latest gothic novel.

"You have a visitor, my lady," Berkley announced as he entered the library, startling Snowball, who scurried away.

"Who is it?"

"Baron Latham."

She frowned, wondering what he could possibly want with her. "Send him in Berkely, and leave the door wide open."

"Yes, my lady."

The footsteps sounding on the rug made her aware of his arrival. "Please have a seat, Latham."

He took a chair beside the sofa. "Thank you for seeing me."

"To what do I owe the pleasure of your company?"

"I was hoping to persuade you to rethink my marriage proposal." His eyes did not meet hers, but his cheeks flushed, making her believe he felt embarrassed.

"I . . ."

"May I plead my cause?"

"Yes. If you'd like."

He moved to the seat beside her but refrained from touching her, which relieved her. "I must apologize for my actions when we last met. I was so shocked and heartbroken by your rejection that I needed privacy. Anyway," he said as he adjusted his neckcloth, "we get along well, enjoy each other's company. We could have a good marriage."

"I would prefer you speak the truth rather than lies."

His head swung her way, his expression one of shock. "I . . . suppose I can do that." He exhaled loudly. "The truth is that I haven't met any other lady I could see myself married to except you."

"Thank you."

"For what?"

"Your honesty. I enjoy your company, but not enough to marry you. You see, I'm in love with someone else, and as long as there's even the slightest chance of being with him, I cannot marry anyone else."

"I had to try. Good luck with Hollingsworth, and thank you for seeing me." He stood, bowed, and left, and Priscilla breathed a sigh of relief. Hopefully, he wouldn't come back asking for a third time.

That evening, she was set to attend a small dinner gathering at Blackstone Manor—a cozy assembly of thirty guests. She was perfectly capable of going alone, but at the last minute she sent a missive to Emmeline asking if she could bring her mother. Of course, Emmeline agreed, and her mother was happy to oblige. So at the appointed time the two of them were riding in their carriage on the way to Blackstone Manor.

A family of butterflies fluttered around inside Priscilla's stomach in anticipation of seeing Nick that night. Would he treat her differently after what they'd shared the night before? Would he finally acknowledge that they belonged together, that he loved her? Oh dear, the butterflies transformed into birds with enormous wings.

The Avery coach arrived at Blackstone Manor alongside numerous other carriages disembarking their passengers. Sitting in the queue, Priscilla gripped and released her reticule with her fingers. Her nerves were stretched tighter than she had ever experienced before. To impress Nick, she had worn her favorite evening gown in medium blue with deep-blue embroidery. She also wore a blue cloak that matched the embroidery and complemented her gown. Her blue slippers also matched, as did her reticule. Though none of that would matter if she cast up her accounts all over herself.

"I'm nervous," she burst out.

"And why is that, my daughter?"

"I can't say."

"Could it have anything to do with Nicholas spending the night?"

Her mouth opened and formed words, but no sound came forth.

"Close your mouth. You resemble a fish."

"How did you know?"

"I couldn't sleep, so I went to the library. It was still dark outside, but morning approached. I saw him sneak out of your room. He never noticed me, which was fortunate. The last thing I wanted was a conversation with him about why he'd spent the night in my daughter's room."

"Are you shocked? Do you think less of me? Does Father know?" The questions flew from her lips before she could stop them.

Mother leaned forward and patted her hands. "Perhaps if you hadn't already been married, I would be, and then again, perhaps not. You've loved that man for so long only a saint could stay away from him. And goodness, no, your father doesn't know and never will. Not by my lips. Dare I ask if he has any plans to propose?"

Tears pooled in her eyes as she quickly took out her handkerchief and dabbed them away before they left watermarks on her cloak. "Not that I know of."

"Oh, my dear child, I might need to talk to that foolish man."

"Please don't."

"I won't unless he has gotten you with child. We will talk then, and he will marry you."

Priscilla's hand covered her belly. Of all the things to discuss right before she faced him and more than two dozen other people for an intimate dinner. "He would marry me then without protest. He is too honorable not to." The carriage stopped. "Wonderful, it is our turn." A footman opened the door, lowered the steps, helped the duchess exit the coach first, then Priscilla. They now stood before a large stone manor aglow with hundreds of candles. The guests' voices traveled out the door as they ascended the stairs.

Just before they entered the mansion, her mother squeezed her hand. "Hold your head high and flirt with every eligible gentleman in attendance until Hollingsworth's head spins and he proposes."

A footman took their cloaks. Regarding her mother's words, Priscilla didn't know whether to laugh, cry, or do both. Her mother was revealing a side of herself Priscilla had never seen before. Flirt with all the eligible gentlemen? Perhaps it was something her mother had done, but Priscilla could never do it. Flirting was an art, one she never developed, like painting—she was terrible at that as well.

Because it was a small gathering, there was no receiving line, but they approached the duke and duchess immediately, which was proper etiquette. "Your Graces," her mother curtsied. "I'm always in awe of your beautiful home."

"Thank you, Your Grace," Emmeline said with a curtsy and a welcoming smile.

"You are too kind, Duchess," Blackstone bowed over her mother's hand.

Emmeline kissed Priscilla's cheek. "I'm so glad you are here. I feel it's been ages since we've seen each other."

"It's only been a few days." She turned to Emmeline's handsome husband and curtsied. "Blackstone, thank you for inviting me."

He bowed over her hand and grinned. "That is what friends do."

When she turned to speak to her mother, she had vanished. Undoubtedly, to find Lady Hollingsworth, who Emmeline had added to the guest list so her mother would have someone her age to converse with. Priscilla's cheeks flushed. Would her mother tell the marchioness about her and Nick? Oh dear, she hoped not. It would be mortifying.

"What has you blushing so becomingly, my dear?" said Nick in his smooth, deep voice as he walked up, seemingly out of nowhere.

"Who says I'm blushing?"

"I do. And you are. Blackstone, Emmeline, do you mind if I steal Priscilla away?"

Emmeline's eyes widened, and she smiled. "Not at all. We have other guests to welcome."

Nick wrapped her arm through his and led her out onto the veranda. The large drawing room felt warm, and the night air was refreshing against her skin.

"Please accept my apologies for leaving without saying good-bye."

She smiled, and her heart eased. "You said goodbye before I fell asleep."

"I did, but I didn't know if it would count."

"It did." His chuckle eased her riotous belly. "I had an interesting day," she said and went on to tell him of her visit from Latham.

"That's odd. I spoke with him at White's and instructed him to leave you be. I thought he would."

As they discussed Latham, Priscilla saw him stroll arm in arm with Lady Faith, Lady Grace's younger sister, onto the veranda. Poor Lady Faith. As a wallflower, she was probably happy to receive Latham's attention. Since Priscilla knew him better than most, she frowned, contemplating whether to warn Faith. Ultimately, she decided against it. He wasn't a terrible person; he just made questionable choices. Perhaps his experience with her had helped him turn a corner.

"That's an unusual couple," Nick remarked, tilting his head toward them. "Perhaps Lady Wilmington can turn Latham into an honorable man. Courting Lady Wilmington's daughter is challenging and could do him good."

"Since you brought it up," she said with a faltering smile, "what about Lady Grace?"

He ran his fingers through his hair. "I intend to speak to her tonight."

"Are you pro . . . pro . . ." She swallowed the words before she screamed them, avoiding making a fool of herself.

He took her hands in his, his thumbs rubbing gently over her wrists. "Do you think so little of me that after what we shared last night, I would propose to Lady Grace?"

The hurt in his voice, more than his words, spoke to her heart. "Forgive me. My mind has been playing tricks on me all day."

"There's nothing to forgive. Considering my past behavior, you have every right to feel that way. And the answer is no, I'm not going to propose to her. But I need to find a gentle way to end our courtship. I believe after dinner would be the perfect time."

Just as the words left his mouth, Lady Grace and her mother stepped onto the veranda and strolled their way.

"Or perhaps now would be better," he mumbled.

Priscilla didn't like the look she received from the Countess of Wilmington, but she imagined the expression would worsen tenfold when Nick broke off his courtship with Lady Grace. Poor Grace. Just when she was finally escaping wallflower status, she was destined to return to it after tonight. She was such a dear; there had to be some worthy gentleman for her. As mother and daughter approached, Priscilla curtsied. "Forgive me. I must attend to my mother."

NICK'S EYES FOLLOWED Priscilla as she strolled away from him and into the drawing room, which was a crush of bodies. Would it be too much to hope for the dinner bell to ring so he could delay what he needed to say to Lady Grace? Even though he believed she would be relieved, it was the mother he worried over.

"Marquess," Lady Wilmington said as she curtsied. "What a lovely evening we're having."

Nick bowed. "Yes, the weather is perfect."

She tugged at her daughter's hand, urging her to move closer to him. "Doesn't Grace look beautiful? The cream gown highlights the softness in her brown eyes."

He bowed to Lady Grace. "You look lovely this evening, Lady Grace. Your eyes do have a certain warmth to them."

"Thank you, Lord Hollingsworth," she said, curtsying stiffly.

"Lady Wilmington, may I show Lady Grace the gardens? They are rather unique in their design."

The countess smiled, clearly pleased by his request. "Why, yes, Hollingsworth. My daughter would be delighted to go with you."

Lady Grace rested her hand on Nick's arm as they descended the stairs and stepped onto the path. The crunch of stones beneath their feet sounded louder in Nick's ears than they should. He felt nervous, which was unlike him.

"Did you have something you wanted to discuss with me?" Grace asked, her eyes filled with curiosity. She was quiet, likely because her mother never stopped talking or let Grace speak for herself. Her features were striking, and she had dark hair and eyes. Her figure was slim yet feminine. He knew she was twenty-one years old. Hopefully, Middlebury would sweep in and steal her away.

"I'm sorry," he said with a smile. "My mind wandered. But yes, I wanted to talk." He stopped walking and turned to her, taking her hands in his. "I find myself in a dilemma. I care for you, Lady Grace. I'd like to believe we have become friends. I've enjoyed your company; you are charming, witty, kind, and considerate. However, I think you know I feelings for someone else."

"It's Lady Priscilla, isn't it?"

"Yes."

"I see how you look at each other." She tugged her hands from his and patted her hair. "Honestly, I'm glad our courtship is over."

One brow arched. "You are?"

"Yes, there's a gentleman I admire." She sighed, her eyes sparkling in the moonlight, and she smiled dreamily. Not a smile he'd ever witnessed her bestow on him, and he hoped the gentleman who had her favor was worthy of her.

"Has he called on you? Made his intentions known?"

Her smile faltered. "No. I've never spoken to the man except when we were introduced several years ago. Sometimes, though, I see him watching me. I'm sure I'm not mistaking the yearning in his eyes."

"May I be of service? If you tell me his name, perhaps I can mention you in passing conversation."

Her cheeks flushed, giving her a youthful and carefree appearance. "It's the Earl of Middlebury."

"Ahhh. He is a fine, upstanding, and likable fellow. And I know him well. We both belong to Gentleman Jackson's Club. Just this morning, he asked if I was courting you. Perhaps you are correct in your assumptions regarding his feelings toward you."

"Oh, do you think so?" She looked so wistful; he hoped not to disappoint her regarding Middlebury.

"I do. And I believe he's here. I'll talk to him tonight."

"Thank you. I want to return to my mother now." She paused. "Thank you for spending time with me and putting up with my mother. I hope we can continue to be friends. And I wish you and Lady Priscilla all the best."

Nick returned Lady Grace to her mother in the parlor and sought out Middlebury. "May I have a word?"

"Yes."

Nick relaxed once they were in a quiet corner of the drawing room, far from prying ears. "I want you to know that Lady Grace and I are no longer courting." Nick waited, watching Middlebury closely to gauge his thoughts.

The man exhaled and ran his fingers through his hair. "This is good to know. Do you think if I call on her, she will be receptive?"

"I would talk to her tonight during this small gathering, no sense waiting for tomorrow. But to answer your question, I believe she would. Send her flowers in the morning and pay a visit during receiving hours. But be careful with her heart. She is sensitive and overly kind. However, I believe you two would suit perfectly."

Middlebury took his hand and shook it with much enthusiasm. "Thank you. You have no idea how much this means to me."

"I wish you all the best." He paused. "One word of advice. Don't let Lady Wilmington scare you away. She is a forceful woman, but she is all talk and wants the best for her daughters. I believe she will approve of you and your pursuit of Lady Grace."

"I thank you again, Hollingsworth," he said as he dipped his head and walked off.

The heavy weight Nick had been carrying around in his chest since the morning eased. Perhaps he would get the future he hoped for. He headed in Priscilla's direction just as the dinner bell rang. "May I escort you to dinner, my dear?" he asked, holding out his arm in invitation.

"Thank you," she said, resting her hand on his forearm. She looked over her shoulder. "Mother?"

"Go on." She waved them off with her hand. "I am perfectly capable of finding my way into dinner."

Nick wasn't surprised to find Middlebury and Lady Grace sitting side by side near the end of the table by Blackstone.

Thank goodness Latham was at the other end, flirting with Lady Grace's younger sister, Lady Faith. He didn't begrudge the man his attendance. He was, after all, Caldwell's brother. But if he developed a courtship with Lady Faith, he would try to ensure he treated her with the utmost respect she deserved. Beneath his wastrel exterior, perhaps a gentleman lurked and struggled to escape. Of course all that also hinged on whether he disassociated himself from Viscountess Norton. If he didn't, Nick would have to interfere with Latham and convince him Lady Faith wasn't for him.

"What are you thinking about?" Priscilla asked, placing her hand on his thigh beneath the table, hidden by the tablecloth so no one could see. With her gloves off so she could eat, her bare hand warmed his leg and his heart.

"Latham," he replied, covering her hand with his. "From his flirtatious behavior it appears he has set his sights on Lady Faith. And she seems to welcome his attentions."

"Perhaps she will be good for him."

The dinner courses came and went, and Nick listened to the conversations going around the table. Most pertained to who was courting whom, who was seen with whom, Parliament, and the latest on-dits. Nothing remotely interesting to Nick. So, as the conversations went around the long rectangular table, with no one the wiser, he and Priscilla shared intimate touches and caresses beneath the table. And he wondered if he could sneak into her house again that night.

CHAPTER TWENTY

NO MATTER HOW she tried not to, sharing caresses beneath the table with Nick had her cheeks heating. Her eyes moved around the table hoping nobody noticed. Especially her mother. Thankfully, she was engrossed in conversation with Nick's mother as usual.

Eventually, the ladies retired to the drawing room, and the men stayed for port and cigars or cheroots, whatever struck their fancy.

"Excuse me, Lady Priscilla," Lady Grace said softly, a blush staining her cheeks. "I want to apologize if my actions while courting Hollingsworth caused you any undue discomfort."

Touched by Grace's words, she smiled. "Not at all, but thank you for saying so. Now that you and he are no longer courting, is there a gentleman you are sweet on?" By the added color to her cheeks, Priscilla had her answer.

"There is." She went on to relate her conversation with Nick about Middlebury.

"I was introduced to him during my first Season, but I don't really know anything about him," Priscilla said. "However, according to Hollingsworth, he is an amiable gentleman. I wish you both well."

"Thank you," she said nodding her head.

"You are most welcome. Can I ask you a question, Lady

Grace?"

"By all means," Lady Grace replied with a friendly smile. "But please call me Grace."

"I will if you call me Priscilla?"

"I hope we can become friends, Priscilla."

"I would like that. Meanwhile, what do you suppose the men talk about when we ladies leave them to their own devices? They are always mysterious about the goings on."

Grace giggled. "Mother says they discuss Parliament, investments, and their mistresses." She frowned. "Do you really think they talk about their mistresses?" Her pretty light-brown eyes widened. "Do you think Middlebury has one?"

Priscilla couldn't imagine Nick ever discussing anything about Anne when she was his mistress. What a mistress shared with her protector should always remain private. Though she knew better than to think all men were loyal and considerate. Latham came to mind. She hoped she was wrong about his character for Lady Faith's sake if anything was to come from their flirting. "I do not know. I do believe they talk about Parliament, perhaps business investments, and what ails the citizens of England. Here they come."

Nick and Middlebury joined them. "Lady Priscilla, Lady Grace," Middlebury said as he bowed. "How wonderful to see you both."

One glance at Grace and the panicked look on her face had Priscilla stepping forward with a curtsy. "Lord Middlebury, I'm pleased to see you. Do you know His Grace well?" What a silly thing to say. Of course he knew Blackstone, or he wouldn't be here.

"Yes. He belongs to Gentleman Jackson's Club, as do I."

"I see." She stared at Grace with her eyes wide open in a prompting look, hoping to untie her tongue for her. She knew they'd sat beside each other at dinner. Had there been no conversation between them?

Finally, Grace curtsied. "Lord Middlebury," she said so softly that Priscilla had a hard time hearing her.

Middlebury's face softened, and he smiled genuinely at Grace. "I hope it wouldn't be forward of me if I asked you to join me in a stroll through the gardens?"

The transformation in Grace was amazing. The mouse, afraid to speak, became a lioness. "I would like that." She took his offered arm. As they walked away, she looked over her shoulder and smiled shyly at Priscilla.

"Well," Nick said as he watched them stroll away arm in arm, "that went well. I declare there will be a marriage contract and proposal within the month."

Priscilla giggled. "Three weeks and not a day longer."

"Ahhh, you may be right. Lady Wilmington will not allow Middlebury to get away. He is perfect for Lady Grace in every way. Would you care to visit the gardens, as well?" Nick suggested with a sly grin and a twinkle in his eyes.

"What do you have in mind besides admiring the flora?" she teased.

"Perhaps I can steal a kiss or two?"

"From the flowers?" She couldn't help herself, and she burst into giggles. "I hope you aren't allergic because if you are, you will sneeze, and your eyes and nose will get runny."

He wrapped her arm around his elbow and chuckled, making her head tingle. He was in a good mood this evening, and she loved him that way. She loved him in any mood, but lighthearted and flirtatious was her favorite.

"No, silly. Not the flowers. There is a young lady who has lips as soft as rose petals and tastes as sweet as dew drops. Her skin smells like the air after a rainstorm. All clean and fresh. Her hair is as soft as snow and smells of a wildflower field that's never been disturbed."

"Nick?" she murmured.

"Yes, my dear?"

"Will you kiss me now?"

Nick, relinquished her arm, took her hand in his instead and hurried down a garden path. When they stopped, Priscilla realized they were alone in a dimly lit section and she could no longer hear any voices.

Nick pulled her into his arms, and right before he kissed her, he whispered, "To answer your question, I thought you'd never ask."

He kissed her delicately as if she were a rose petal that could bruise easily. His lips were full and soft and tasted of port. Her arms circled his neck, and she flattened her body against his, causing a moan to escape his mouth. The delicate kiss suddenly vanished, and in its place was a kiss full of need and desire that ran out of control until they were clinging to each other and gasping for air.

"Your lips fit mine perfectly. I will never tire of kissing you," he said as he nuzzled the sensitive spot behind her ear, causing her to melt in his arms.

"Me either," she sighed as he nipped her neck with his teeth, and her knees threatened to buckle. She gripped his shoulders to keep from falling to the ground. "Nick. Will you come to me tonight?"

He stopped cherishing her skin, cupped her cheeks, and looked deeply into her eyes. "Nothing would please me more."

"But?" she murmured when she witnessed the concern in his eyes.

"For two nights this week, I was lucky. We were lucky. I'd hate to be seen and the household gossip about you. Or for your mother and father find out."

She took one of his hands, placed her lips on his palm, and felt his body quiver. "I don't care what the household sees or says or does. And Mother knows. She saw you leaving this morning. She promised she wouldn't tell my father."

"Your mother knows?" he chocked a brow.

"Yes. But don't worry. She isn't shocked or upset." She smiled up at him. "Forget about Mother and let's go back to talking about us." She placed a hand on his cheek, feeling a little bit of stubble. "After last night, I crave you. Did you slip something in my wine so you are the only man I desire?"

"Never. You desire me as I desire you."

His words made her heart pound. For he admitted he desired her. He cared for her and perhaps even more. He knew she loved him, and she didn't want to say too much or do too much to scare him away from her. She honestly didn't know if she could ever get over another rejection from him.

"Do you think your mother will mind if I escort you home? And perhaps she could give my mother a ride?" He took her hand in his, entwining their fingers. "Since your mother knows about us, she won't be shocked by the request, and I believe my mother will be beside herself with excitement." He tugged on her hand. "Come. The sooner we are inside my carriage, the sooner I can kiss you again." As he led the way through the gardens, her pulse soared with how happy and enthusiastic he sounded.

It would take some time to convince herself that Nick wanted to be with her—not as friends but as a couple courting and in love. Her foot caught on a rock, but with Nick's help, she quickly recovered her footing.

"Did you hurt yourself?" he asked with concern.

"No. You caught me before I could fall forward and land on my face." She glanced at him sideways, and her face heated. "Thank you, by the way."

He brought their joined hands to his mouth and placed his lips on her knuckles, and she melted on the spot. "You are very welcome. I'll save you always."

ONCE THEY ENTERED the drawing room, Nick eyes moved around until he found their mothers sitting on a settee with Emmeline's mother, Baroness Connolly. Bowing, he said, "Your Grace, Mother, Baroness." He was surprised to find he had bowed while still holding Priscilla's hand. "If acceptable, I would like to escort Lady Priscilla home. Your Grace, would you mind bringing Mother home?"

"Not at all, Nicholas. We are ready to leave as well."

They bid goodnight to all their friends and thanked the Duke and Duchess of Blackstone for a wonderful evening. Nick couldn't wait to get Priscilla alone. The taste of her lips remained on his, and he wanted to taste them again. Their mothers joined them at the door. Nick and Priscilla escorted them to the Duke of Avery's carriage and once Nick was assured they were settled in, he signaled the driver to be on their way.

His carriage was close by, and after he assisted Priscilla into the carriage and joined her on the seat, his arm went around her back, holding her close. "This is nice." The palm of her hand rested on this thigh and the warmth from it radiated through the fabric of his breeches.

"It is nice." Her head dropped onto his shoulder. "What do you suppose our mothers are talking about right now?"

Laughter echoed inside the coach, and Nick was surprised at how joyous he sounded, especially for what he would say next. "After your mother confides in mine that I snuck out of your bedchamber this morning, no doubt they are planning our wedding." Whenever he'd thought about marrying Priscilla before, he would break out in a sweat, and his body would tremble out of control. Tonight? There was no sweat dripping down his back. If his body trembled, it was with desire. His heart raced, not in fear, but in excitement. For once in his life, the idea of marrying Priscilla didn't terrify him. If anything, it filled him with joy and tenderness.

He found it odd that just last night he believed he wasn't ready to marry Priscilla and give himself to her completely, nor did he want to burden her with his issues. But he'd been mistaken. There was still work to be done on himself, but with her by his side he was convinced anything was possible. He would declare himself to her soon. The time wasn't perfect, and it had to be perfect. She deserved no less for waiting so long for him to stop being stupid and admit what he'd always known.

He pivoted on the bench, cradled her face, and kissed her lips. Never in all his life had he felt the things he did when he kissed her. His needs, desires, and wants were strong, screaming at him to be fulfilled, but he pushed them back. All of Priscilla's desires, needs, and fulfillment came first. That was how much he cared for her. He would take whatever scraps she had to give and be happy.

The kiss went on, and he tried to convey his feelings for her within the kiss. Her fingers combed through his hair, then he tilted his head as she took over, devouring him. Her tongue demanded that his dance with hers. *Always and forever*. He was never letting her go.

Her mouth disappeared and moved to his neck with a soft kiss. "If I'm not mistaken, the carriage stopped a short time ago."

"It did?" He chuckled, then groaned as her teeth nipped his earlobe.

"Did I hurt you?"

"No."

"Humm, perhaps I should try again."

Before she could, he had her beneath him on the bench, his body over hers. He grinned down at her, showing his teeth, then licked his lips. "Perhaps I'll flip up your skirts and have a late supper."

Giggling and wiggling her hips, she said, "Don't you dare."

As he snaked his hand up the inside of her skirts, there was a knock on the carriage door. They both froze and looked wide-eyed at each other. "Let my daughter out, or I'll come in there and get her."

Priscilla's mouth opened into a wide *O*.

Nick buried his head in her bosom, his body shaking with laughter.

"What's so funny?" she asked, sounding nervous.

"Your mother. I'm laughing because she *would* come in." He

sat back on the bench and helped Priscilla up. "Where are your hairpins? I don't remember plucking them out."

"You didn't—I did. They were stabbing my skull. Forget about them. I'll get them another time." She kissed him quickly. "You'd best let me out."

Nick rapped on the roof, and footman opened the door. Nick alighted first and then helped Priscilla. Taking her hand, he walked her up the stairs and to the door, which popped open to Berkley standing there. The duchess was nowhere to be seen. "Good night, my love. I think it's best if I don't visit you tonight. I have a feeling your mother will be standing guard outside your chambers." He kissed her cheek, turned, and she was behind the closed door by the time he climbed inside his carriage.

Sighing, he leaned back against the squabs and closed his eyes. What a strange night—first breaking off his courtship with Lady Grace, then Middlebury and Lady Grace hopefully forming one, then him and Priscilla. He did not have the urge to run away and hide from her, which shocked him. He would sleep well tonight. He had too many happy memories to let the horrific ones inside his head tonight.

CHAPTER TWENTY-ONE

SOMETHING AWOKE PRISCILLA. A noise, a smell, the wind, she didn't know. All she knew was she lay in bed, on her back with the coverlet up to her chin. She tried not to breathe. The sound came again. Footsteps outside her room. Was it Nick, even though he said he wouldn't come tonight? No, no. It couldn't be Nick. There was more than one set of footsteps, and when Nick came before, he was silent. More shallow breathing as she waited, only this time, her heart pounded, causing her to hear it inside her ears. Who could it be? It was like she was a little girl again, and the monsters living in the forest were coming for her.

Frozen in fear, she heard the creak of her door opening slowly and closing again. Two sets of footsteps shuffled on the thick Aubusson rug. If she didn't make a sound, would they leave believing the room was empty? *No, Priscilla, they will not. Get up and run and scream! Now, do it now!* Before she had the chance, a shadowed figure pinned her to the bed. Another person forced her mouth open and poured something vile tasting down her throat. She tried not to swallow it, but her mouth was held shut.

As the liquid slid down her throat, she recognized it as laudanum. But why? Who would do that? One of the assailants stuffed her mouth with a foul-tasting cloth, flipped her face down on the bed, forcing the air from her lungs to disperse out her nose. Large hands held her tightly as the other tied her arms behind her back and her feet together at the ankles with rough rope. Strong arms reached out, and she tried to move away, but all she managed was to move her head away from him. Her skin crawled in disgust and her heart beat so fast, she thought it would burst and she would die. Perhaps dying would be preferable to what these blackguards had planned for her.

Nick's face flashed in her mind and she fought back tears. She took a deep breath in through her nose and fought to get up on her knees. She sagged back down, exhausted and defeated. Without the use of her arms it was pointless. She was at their mercy.

Deep rumbles of laughter reached her ears. "Are ye done fightin', girly?"

Suddenly, she found herself in the air and then dropped back on the bed on her back none too gently, which forced a strangled cry from her, though it was muffled by the cloth in her mouth. The arms came for her again. She was hauled up and slung her over a shoulder so her head hung down her assailant's back and her feet dangled down his chest and her mind screamed, "Nick!"

Her head tingled from being upside down. Or from the laudanum. Or both. They made their way through Avery Manor and out the servants' entrance as if they'd been there before. They ran down the street, her body bouncing and jarring against unforgivable bone and muscle. She fought not to cast up her accounts every time her stomach made contact with shoulder bone. Dear God, would her agony ever end?

They stopped abruptly, and her body sagged in relief, then she was dumped inside a small hackney. The door closed, leaving her alone in the dark, on the floor at an odd angle. The carriage lurched forward and settled at a fast clip sending pain lancing throughout her entire body as she was jostled around repeatedly. Dressed only in a night rail, which was bunched around her knees, the top draped off one shoulder, had her shivering and wishing she could bring her arms and knees together to hug herself and ward off the chilly night air. She exhaled through her nose and suddenly didn't care anymore. Ah, the laudanum.

The pain ceased troubling her.

The muscles in her body liquified.

Her heart slowed, and her eyelids became so heavy she had to close her eyes as the effort to keep them open became too much.

And then nothing.

THE FIRST THING Priscilla noticed when she came to was that her tongue was stuck to the roof of her mouth. Dry. Her mouth was dry as sand and tasted foul. The second thing she noticed was that she lay on a bed in a cold, dark, and stale-smelling room. When she tried to lift her head, dizziness and nausea hit her.

"Ahhh, she is awake," a voice belonging to a female spoke from across the room. Priscilla turned her head to the side gently so as not to disrupt her equilibrium and saw a lady, small in stature, draped in a black cloak with a hood. Her face was hidden, so she didn't know if she knew the person.

Moving her tongue around the inside of her mouth, she prepared to speak. "Wh . . . who are you?"

"You may call me Esmeralda."

She had heard that name before, but where? The throbbing inside her head was relentless, making it difficult to focus. "Why am I here?"

Esmeralda paced the room in small strides. "You have interfered in my plans."

"H-how?"

"You need not concern yourself with the particulars. Just be quiet and do as I say, and everything will be fine."

How could the woman say that? She had been drugged and taken in the dead of night, and everything would be *fine*? What world did she live in? Nothing good happened when someone was kidnapped. Priscilla had led a modestly dull life compared to most young ladies of the aristocracy. What could she possibly have done to thwart this person's plans?

"I will return soon. If I were you, I would sleep off the laudanum, so your head and stomach will feel normal when you awaken next time."

A door opened and closed somewhere in the room, and the sound of a lock clicking resonated loudly in the dark room. Priscilla didn't want to sleep. She was too frightened to sleep. But her drugged body and mind had other ideas, and she drifted off into a sleep full of distorted faces and figures that chased her through London's dark, deserted streets.

HUGHES, ACCOMPANIED BY a footman, knocked and entered Nick's chambers the following morning as they did every morning to open the curtains, bring fresh water and towels for washing, bring a breakfast tray with coffee, and assist him in dressing. Last night wasn't the satisfying sleep he had hoped for. His head was foggy, and his body was fatigued. He'd had strange dreams involving Priscilla last night.

"A note arrived for you just now, my lord. It's on the breakfast tray," Hughes said.

"Thank you. That'll be all for now." He reached over to the night table and picked the cup of coffee off the tray. Finding it warm, he drank every drop. Then he stared at the folded paper resting on the tray. It was addressed to him in an unfamiliar handwriting. Inhaling, he climbed out of the warm bed, put on his trousers from last night, picked up the note, turned it over and frowned at the Avery seal. It meant one of only three people could have sent it. Breaking the seal and unfolding the paper, he read:

Nicholas,

What have you done with my daughter? Where is she? No one

in this household has seen her since she retired to her chambers after you returned her home last night. I pray she is with you and not among the missing. I have sent word to the Duchess of Blackstone, the Duchess of Greenville, and Lady Langford. She is not off at one of her meetings. His Grace and I are worried and are awaiting your reply.

The Duchess of Avery

Eyes wide, heart pounding, he quickly scanned the note a second time, not believing what he read. It slipped from his hands as he hurried to his wardrobe, dressed in riding clothes as fast as he could, and bellowing for Hughes, who never strayed far when he was in his chambers.

"My lord?"

"Help me with my boots and have Bandit brought around." Once presentable—or at least dressed—he ran down the stairs, taking two at a time, and paced the entry hall while awaiting his horse. The coffee he had drunk sloshed around inside his stomach, and every muscle in his body constricted. Where the bloody hell was Priscilla? Had she ever disappeared without telling anyone her whereabouts before? Perhaps she had gone for a ride in the park? No. She would have needed a groom's help to prepare her horse and to accompany her, and the duchess said no one had seen her.

"Your horse is ready, my lord," Robbins said, opening the door.

Nick hurried down the steps, mounted his horse, and took off for Avery Manor. When he arrived, he jumped out of the saddle before his horse had fully stopped and threw the reins to a footman standing sentinel at the bottom of the stairs. "I don't know how long I'll be. Keep my horse ready."

He jumped the stairs, skipping half of them, and almost fell into the house when the butler opened the door as he was about to knock.

"This way, my lord."

Nick followed the butler, whose name slipped his mind because, bloody hell, his mind refused to think of anything but Priscilla, and followed him to the duke's study. The duke sat behind his desk, a worried look on his face, and the duchess stood shrunk into herself, looking out a window.

"I came as soon as I read your note."

A loud moan escaped the duchess, and her head fell forward. "So she is not with you then?"

"I haven't seen or heard from her since I returned her home after the Blackstone dinner."

His Grace stood and joined his wife at the window, his hand resting on her shoulder. "We will find her. And if God forbid, someone took her, and they want a ransom, we will give them anything they want."

"Do you think she was kidnapped?" Nick asked as he fought down the coffee trying to reappear. Kidnapping wealthy children of the *ton* for ransom did happen. However, they were usually young children or babies.

His mind went to Latham and Viscountess Norton. And then there were Anne and her father. Although now that he knew the baby she carried wasn't his, he couldn't imagine them doing this.

"I'm going to visit Blackstone, Langford, and Caldwell," Nick said. "They have connections with a Bow Street Runner. With any luck, Lady Priscilla will be home before afternoon tea." He wanted to believe it, but he said it mostly to alleviate some of the misery he witnessed on Priscilla's parents' faces.

Back out the door and mounted on his horse once again, he sped off toward Latham House to speak with Latham and Caldwell.

He left his horse in the mews behind Latham House, walked briskly to the front door, and knocked. Once inside the entry, Nick handed over his calling card. "Please tell the baron and Mr. Caldwell that it is of the utmost importance that I speak with them immediately."

"Yes, my lord."

A few moments later, he was let into a drawing room. "Please make yourself comfortable. They will be with you shortly."

The furnishings, though pleasant and comfortable, didn't interest him. His feet ate up the distance back and forth from one side of the room to the other. His mind and body were too jittery to be still. Where was Priscilla? Was she hurt or even worse . . .? He couldn't let himself think that way, or he would break down and be no help finding her. He needed to keep his wits about him. If he couldn't, it was another reason to bring his friends and a Runner into Priscilla's disappearance.

"Hollingsworth," Caldwell said as he hurried into the room dressed in his trousers, boots, and a white shirt, the sleeves rolled up. "What has happened? You look like hell."

"Priscilla is missing. No one has seen her since last night."

Caldwell walked to the open door and spoke to someone outside the room, then turned back to Nick. "My brother will be right down." Caldwell frowned with a thoughtful look on his face. "If you think Latham is involved, I can tell you he is not. He returned home with us last night and hasn't left since."

Nick couldn't lie to Caldwell. "It crossed my mind."

"What crossed your mind?" Latham asked as he entered the room, dressed better than his brother, with a footman carrying a tray.

"Lady Priscilla has been missing since last night," Caldwell said as he took the liberty of pouring three cups of coffee.

Latham frowned as he said, "Missing? You don't think I have anything to do with it, do you?"

Hell if Nick knew what he thought at this point. It was all so unbelievable. "I might have."

"Well, think again. I had nothing to do with it," Latham paced the room, running his hands through his hair. "I asked her to marry me twice, and she turned me down twice. That was humiliating enough for me to stay away from her."

"I keep thinking about Emmeline and Lilly and what happened to them," Nick said as he ignored the coffee in favor of toast with butter and jam. His stomach needed something to soak up the coffee already eating a hole in his stomach.

"Have you spoken to Blackstone or Langford yet?" Caldwell asked.

Nick snorted. "I came here right after I met with Priscilla's parents. Avery said he did send word to Emmeline and Lilly asking if she was with them, though. And he heard back that she wasn't."

Caldwell left the room for several moments and then returned. "I've sent word to have them come here as soon as possible, explaining that you were here."

"Thank you," Nick said as he finished another piece of toast before he finally picked up a cup of coffee. "Would you mind sending word to your Bow Street Runner?"

"Already done. Hopefully, all three of them will arrive within the hour. In the meantime, do Lady Priscilla or her parents have any enemies that you know of?"

"I can't think of anyone who would dislike Priscilla. As you know, she mostly keeps to herself. She's a member of the Ladies' Society of Mayfair, but I don't think it has to do with that." He finally collapsed into an overstuffed chair and sipped his coffee while it was still hot. "I don't believe the duke and duchess have enemies, either." He exhaled loudly. "Any ideas?"

Nick was surprised when Latham spoke up. "Well, now that you mention it, Viscountess Norton isn't feeling favorable toward *you* right now. She didn't take the news of you interfering with the business Norton ran for the better part of fifteen years very well."

"What?" Caldwell bellowed. "What are you talking about? What business?"

Nick explained all about the business the Viscount and Viscountess Norton were involved in, including what had happened to him. "According to the viscountess, Norton was retiring from his role in criminal activities and chose Latham to fill his shoes."

"What?" Caldwell bellowed again.

"Relax, brother. Thanks to Hollingsworth, I never got a chance to partake in anything. What I did get were copies of Norton's records of who he schemed and blackmailed and the amounts paid to him." Damn, the cad, if he didn't look right at Nick and grin. "Imagine my shock at finding your name on the list. Now I understand where the gossip came from." He frowned. "The list is quite shocking in its entirety. The well-known and prominent names and the amounts Norton collected are staggering. If anyone knew such a list existed and that I had it in my possession, my life would be in danger. What I don't understand is why Norton didn't continue blackmailing them, or why the viscountess doesn't do it now. Most would pay dearly to have their secret remain hidden."

"Get the list," both Caldwell and Nick demanded simultaneously.

"Then both your lives will also be in danger."

"We will risk it," Nick said, pausing. "Still, the names on the list have nothing to do with Priscilla."

"Actually," Latham began, "the Duke of Avery was one of the first swindles nearly fifteen years ago. However, I don't believe this concerns her father." He paused. "You do realize the viscountess wants you for herself, don't you? Not only is she a social climber, but she's also money hungry. A marchioness is quite high in the rankings compared to a viscountess. You also come from one of the oldest and wealthiest families. All things she desires."

"How do you know her so well?" Caldwell barked out.

Latham exhaled and turned to Nick. "She won't take no for an answer. She doesn't care that you threatened to ruin both of us if we proceeded with the business. She believes that you are bluffing, that you would never ruin her or the brother of a friend. Perhaps she took Lady Priscilla to force your hand or to ensure you keep your mouth shut. Or maybe she's ransoming her off to the duke for money."

Nick's fingers went to his temples, and he massaged them,

trying to ease the stabbing pain. The day had barely begun, and he wanted it to end. To end with Priscilla in his arms in her bed, safe and sound. "I need quiet to think."

"Done." Caldwell sank into the chair beside his.

Latham stood at the window staring at God knew what. All Nick knew was it was silent. This business with Priscilla—it must have something to do with him. Priscilla had no enemies. At least Nick didn't believe so.

He dozed off for a few minutes, then voices and footsteps aroused him.

"What is this I hear about Lady Priscilla being missing?" asked Lady Langford. Wonderful. The ladies had come, too. Not that he had anything against Lady Langford and the Duchess of Blackstone, but the pounding in his head was growing, and the more people were here, the louder the room became. He pushed the pain aside. He needed to concentrate, and they needed to all work together to figure out Priscilla's disappearance.

"Do we know anything?" Blackstone asked as both he and his wife sat on the settee.

"Forgive me a moment," Caldwell said, then ducked out of the room. When he returned, he came with several footmen, each carrying a chair which they placed around the low table where the breakfast tray sat. "Please have a seat."

Once everyone was seated, the Runner, Mr. Whitcomb, arrived, joined the conversation, and listened intently.

They reviewed everything and anything they could think of regarding Priscilla, Nick, and her parents. It always came back to the viscountess. Mr. Whitcomb left to assemble a team of men he trusted to start surveillance on the viscountess and any known associates of Norton's business.

Langford placed his hand on Nick's shoulder. "Trust Whitcomb. He will find her."

"Yes," Blackstone chimed in, "he will."

After Langford and Blackstone left with their wives and it was just the original three of them, Caldwell said, "What about that list?"

Latham groaned. "I hate for anyone else to see it. Believe me, it is dangerous knowledge. If half of the men on the list knew it existed, the viscountess and I would be dead, and the list burned or used for other despicable reasons. Someone could make a fortune off these men. Those who are living anyway."

"David," Caldwell groaned. "You wouldn't dare."

Latham looked affronted that his brother would even think such a thing about him. However, Nick had no problem believing it.

"Never mind," Caldwell continued before Latham could answer. "I don't want to see it. If I were you, I'd burn it. But know this, brother: If you have a sudden influx of coin, you will answer to me."

Nick stood and stretched out his sore muscles. "I'll leave you two to argue. I'm going to inform Priscilla's parents of what we know then I'll go to Norton Hall to visit the viscountess. I know the Runner's looking into her, but I'd feel better meeting with her myself." He wanted to see her face when she denied or admitted to having anything to do with Priscilla's disappearance.

CHAPTER TWENTY-TWO

WHEN PRISCILLA OPENED her eyes this time, her head was clear, but her stomach was upset from the lingering effects of the laudanum. Or she was hungry. Which made her wonder how long it had been since she'd last eaten. Feeling much better overall than when she'd awoken the first time, she rolled over and sat up slowly, not wanting the dizziness to return. When it didn't, she stood barefoot and shivered when she looked down to find herself only dressed in her night rail and nothing more. She hugged herself to ward off the chill, and when that didn't work, she removed the surprisingly soft blanket from the bed and wrapped it around herself like a huge shawl.

The room was small and sparsely furnished. It had a slopping ceiling with boarded-up windows at each end. The room resembled servant's quarters in an attic, and it was cold and dark, with no fresh air. The wooden floors were bare, and she was careful as she paced the room not to get a splinter. It was hard to judge the time of day without being able to see outside. And it was hard to tell how long she'd been asleep with the laudanum in her system. It could have been an hour, several hours, or even longer, perhaps an entire day.

Stopping her pacing, she sat on the edge of the mattress and listened for any sounds that might give her clues as to why that woman had taken her. Priscilla vaguely remembered the lady telling her what name Priscilla could call her, but her mind didn't remember. She listened some more for any sounds and sighed when she heard nothing. It was as though she were the only one there.

The shaking started slowly. First her fingers, then her hands, then it climbed up her arms and spread throughout her entire body until her insides and outsides shook so hard it hurt. Even her teeth chattered. But it wasn't because of the chill—the blanket was keeping her warm. Her body was reacting to her panic. It was a living, breathing entity, one she couldn't stop. Then the tears started, and she wanted to scream. They dripped down her face like a never-ending gargoyle downspout on Notre Dame Cathedral during a rainstorm. She hated feeling weak and threatened.

What bothered her the most was how worried her parents must be. Did they believe she was dead and would never see her again? Then there was Nick. Did he think the same? Or was he riding around London yelling her name over and over again? Was he looking down every alleyway and inside every tavern?

What were Emmeline and Lilly thinking? Were their husbands with Nick? She hated to think she was causing them anguish and worry. Not that she wouldn't be worried if the roles were reversed.

The banging of a door and footsteps climbing stairs resonated through the room. The lock on her door clicked, the door swung open, and in walked the lady from before, dressed much the same. Dark strands of hair hung outside her hood. It was the only feature Priscilla could see properly to describe her. Also with her were two burly men who looked quite frightening.

"I brought you dinner. You must be hungry. Don't move as I place it on the foot of the bed. As you can see, I brought some bodyguards. I'd hate to have to tell them to tie you up."

Priscilla would hate that, too. Not a muscle in her body so much as twitched until after the tray sat beside her on the bed. One quick glance at it, and she saw roasted chicken, potatoes, and carrots, as well as tea with several biscuits. "Thank you."

"We can talk while you eat."

Seeing no utensils on the tray, she picked up the chicken leg and bit into the juicy piece. Whoever this person was, she had a good cook. And as the woman remained silent through Priscilla's first couple bites, she thought she might as well start the conversation. "I don't remember much about our earlier conversation except you said something about me getting in the way of your plans. But I don't understand how. Why am I here?" She placed a small potato into her mouth.

"Without giving my identity away, let us just say there is a certain gentleman threatening to ruin me if I do something. He has to pay for his threats. I will not allow anyone to dictate what I do or don't do with my life. He has also warned my associate that he will do the same to him."

"I'm sorry. I can't imagine what it has to do with me. I have a very—and I mean very—tiny circle of friends. Other than them, I have my parents. No brothers or sisters."

"Trust me, you know who I'm talking about."

Priscilla thought for a moment. It couldn't be Blackstone, Langford, or Caldwell, as they were married and this woman would have kidnapped their wives if she wanted to hurt them. The only other men she knew were Nick and Latham. Honestly, she could be punishing either one of them. Except she no longer had an attachment to Latham.

"So Hollingsworth is trying to ruin you?" she guessed.

"You are a smart one. Perhaps you would like to join me in my business. Between the two of us, we could make a fortune."

Perhaps if she played at being interested, the woman would let her guard down, and she could escape. "What is your name?"

"As I said before, you may call me Esmeralda."

"Please call me Priscilla." Now she remembered the name and how she knew it. Esmeralda was Viscountess Norton. She had previously gone by the name Esmeralda back when she had blackmailed Nick.

"Very well, Priscilla. Do you like money? Nice things? Jewelry?"

She shrugged her shoulders. "What lady doesn't?"

"Do you know anything about Hollingsworth and what caused the rumors?"

She answered truthfully. "Yes. He told me.

"He was so handsome, so approaching him at the masquerade ball was no hardship. After flirting with him for a spell, I almost felt sorry for drugging his drink, but I had a job to do. You see, that is what I used to do—drug men's drinks. Now, I have two ladies who work for me doing the task. That way, no one recognizes me." She paused, then paced the room. "The ladies drug the gentlemen's drinks and take them to a private residence. Mind you, we do nothing to them, except divest them of their coats, waistcoats, and shirts to make them believe they participated in the debauchery going on around them. They wake up surrounded by naked or partially naked men, and we persuade them to pay for their secrets. That is what happened to Hollingsworth."

Priscilla thought she might cast up her accounts and sighed with relief when she saw a chamber pot across the room. Nick must have died a thousand deaths when this happened to him. Believing he was leaving with a lady and waking up in a fog from being drugged to find himself surrounded by unclothed men. Closing her eyes, she breathed to steady her heart. She needed to stay calm and feign interest if her plan would work.

"This works? You make money doing this?"

More giggles from Esmeralda. "Yes and yes. We plan who we target ahead of time, learn all we can about them. It's easy if you set your sights on wealthy rakes—gentlemen who pride themselves on their masculinity. They fall the easiest and hardest when they find themselves in a gentlemen's den of iniquity."

"I imagine so." Priscilla paused, studying the food left on her plate. "What would I have to do?"

Vile laughter ricocheted around the room. "Do you honestly

think that I would invite another woman to share my spoils? You are a stupid chit. I'm well aware you only hoped to pretend to join me so you could escape." She indicated one of the men. "Take her tray and stand guard outside the door. Oh, and one last tidbit. Long before I meet Norton, your father, the esteemed Duke of Avery, fell to the same scheme." Her laughter reverberated around the room making Priscilla flinch. "He was one of Norton's first targets."

Left alone with her runaway thoughts, Priscilla lay on the mattress with the blanket wrapped tight around her as tears flowed from her eyes. Her father? She couldn't believe it. How long ago had it happened? Her father would be horrified if he ever found out she knew.

⊰⊱

Sitting across from the Duke of Avery in his study, Nick accepted a glass of brandy from him.

"My wife is resting. I didn't tell her of your arrival. She is already on the verge of a nervous collapse." He downed the entire contents of his glass. "What do you have to tell me?"

"Mr. Whitcomb, the Runner, is investigating Viscountess Norton and her known associates," Nick stated. He explained her business and admitted his own involvement with her while watching the duke for any signs of recognition. Nick would eventually admit to knowing of His Grace's involvement, but it would be less awkward if the duke would relate his experience of being duped himself.

As Nick spoke, Avery became very still, poured himself a fresh brandy, and downed that one as well. In all the years he'd known the duke, Nick had never seen him overindulge. He supposed having one's daughter go missing was as good a reason as any, not to mention the possibility that one's past secrets might be exposed.

"What I'm about to say is in the strictest of confidence and doesn't leave this room," Avery said as he toyed with the empty glass in his hands. "Many years ago, I was at a gaming club, and I was approached by a young lady named Genevieve."

"What did she look like?" Nick asked.

"She had red hair and green eyes. I will never forget what she looked like. Nor have I ever seen her since then. I was drugged and woke up in a rather seedy establishment that catered to men. Exactly what happened to you." He brought his fist down on his desk with a resounding thud, and red tinged his face. "I paid dearly to keep it quiet. But I have always expected them to return and demand more money for their silence. It was the worst night and morning of my life. That is why I rarely socialize."

"Please forgive me for not saying so right away, but I recently discovered you had been targeted as well, and I'll explain how I came by that knowledge in a moment." Nick drained his glass. "The night I was drugged, the woman who approached me was called Esmeralda, and she had dark hair and blue eyes. I looked for her everywhere since that night. I finally found her. She is the Viscountess Norton."

Sitting forward, His Grace eyed him with curiosity.

Before he spoke, Nick continued. "Norton was behind it for fifteen years, so I've been told. You were one of his first targets."

"Norton . . . Christ, the blackguard."

"The viscountess claims he needed money. And there is more. Baron Latham and Norton's widow each possess a copy of the list of all the targeted gentlemen and the sums they extorted. I haven't seen the list myself, but Latham assured me the list is long, and the money Norton collected was exorbitant."

"I'm afraid to ask how Latham got his hands on this list."

"Norton, before he died, approached Latham regarding taking over the day-to-day activities of his so-called business for him. I believe Latham agreed. Thus, he came into possession of this list, and he informed me this morning that your name is on it."

"Bloody blackguard," the duke said as he pounded his desk

again. "If this list falls into the wrong hands . . ."

"Being in the possession of the baron and the viscountess, I believe it already has. I threatened both the viscountess and Latham, saying that I would see them ruined if they continued the scheme. I told her I would help her marry well if she let it go. As for Latham, he is easy to ruin. But all this happened before I knew of the list's existence. Had I known of it, I would have chosen a different method of shutting them down. Latham thinks he could be killed if anyone finds out about the list. Can you imagine what would happen if it became public?"

"You need to get the list and destroy it—both copies. We must hope there are *only* two copies."

"Latham's list won't be difficult. I can have Caldwell get it. The viscountess . . ." He shrugged his shoulders. "She is another matter."

"This is all good knowledge to have, but what does this have to do with Priscilla?"

"The viscountess most likely has her. She is punishing me for refusing her offer of marriage and for threatening to see her ruined."

The duke huffed, "Has she no shame or conscience?"

"No." Nick stood and placed his glass on the duke's desktop. "When I leave here, I'm going to visit her. Perhaps I can convince her that I've changed my mind or that I want to join her in business. I need to do whatever it takes to get me close to the list or to finding out where Priscilla is. Wish me well."

"Good luck. Find my daughter and bring her home safe to us."

"I will."

Nick mounted his horse with shoulders weighed down as though with invisible sacks of grain. He hoped like hell Mr. Whitcomb would have something soon, because he didn't know if he was capable of the subterfuge needed to convince Emma, the viscountess, that he had changed his mind and now wished to marry her and take over from Norton.

It didn't take him long to arrive at her townhouse. Leaving his horse in the mews nearby, he walked up to her door and knocked, and the butler let him in. "Please wait here. I will see if the viscountess is receiving visitors."

With his hat and gloves in his hands, Nick waited in the entry hall. Several minutes later, the butler returned. "She has agreed to see you, my lord. Come with me." Nick was led up the stairs and into a parlor he'd never been in. The room was empty. "The viscountess will be with you soon."

Nick didn't know which would ease his nerves, sitting down or standing up. He decided to pace as every nerve ending in his body pulsed, making it impossible to be still. When he'd decided to pay Emma a visit, his plan was to seduce her, without actually going through with the seduction. With any luck, with a few touches and some kissing, she would reveal her secrets if she had any more to tell.

"Hollingsworth," said Emma as she swept into the room, her silk dress clinging to her, making him think she'd skipped her undergarments and dampened her legs and breasts, hoping to entice him.

"Viscountess," he said with a perfectly cut bow. "Thank you for receiving me."

She curtsied deeply, giving him a view down her low-cut gown. If she were anyone else—if she were Priscilla—perhaps he could have enjoyed the peek, but this woman made his skin crawl. *Pretend to be enthralled, Nick, or you will never find Priscilla.* He forced his eyes to drink her in and grin.

"Please call me Emma and join me on the settee," she said with a sly smile.

He would have to observe her closely. She had been deceiving people for years and was an expert. "Thank you." He sat beside her, close enough that their thighs touched.

"What can I do for you?" she said, her tone seductive.

"I have been thinking about our conversation from the other day." He paused to get her interest piqued.

"Yes?"

"Perhaps I was hasty in refusing your advances." He rested his hand on her thigh and gently squeezed, relaxing his hand, and keeping it there.

She brushed his hand off. "What if I'm no longer interested? Perhaps I've found someone else."

He turned toward her, placed a finger beneath her chin, and arched a brow. "I don't believe that to be true. Not with that display during your greeting and the fact that you wear nothing beneath that thin, silky gown." He leaned close and whispered into her ear. "Did you put it on just for me? Dampen your skin just for me?"

"Perhaps. You found me enticing once before. The very first night we met."

He placed his lips close to her ear and whispered, "I still find you enticing."

She sighed. "Come upstairs with me."

"Half of the fun and appeal of seduction is taking one's time." He kissed her neck. "A little bit here." More kisses. "And a little bit here." He kissed the swell of her breasts and moaned. "And here."

"You are teasing me," she said with a throaty laugh.

"Is it working?" He hoped so because he didn't know how long he could continue kissing and flirting with her.

"You know it is," she purred as her hand went to the front of his buff riding breeches. He grabbed her hand just in time. If she found him soft, his deception would be over.

He chucked loudly. "I'm afraid if you touch me, I'll embarrass myself. I do not carry extra breeches with me."

"Perhaps you should the next time you come."

Of course, she intended the double entendre. "Oh, my dear, next time I come, it will be inside your sweet body." He hoped he was flirting correctly and that people truly said such things. He had never been one for dirty bedroom talk or flirting.

"Nicholas," she whined. "Why not now? I'm so wet." She

tugged her skirt over her knees and took his hand, placing it on her bare leg. "Go ahead. Feel for yourself."

His hand slid up the top of her leg. Emma gasped and held her breath. His fingers carefully crossed her mound over to her other leg. Her thighs parted, and she moaned long and low. She turned to him and purred, "Will you join me in my bed?"

Sitting on the edge of the settee, he took her hand in his and kissed her fingers, trying not to gag. "After our conversation the other day, I was thinking you should be rid of Latham and I will be your partner in crime." Bloody hell, he had not planned on saying that. It could work in his favor, though. If she had anything to do with Priscilla's disappearance and she believed they were becoming business associates—and more—perhaps she would share all her secrets with him. And if she didn't know anything about Priscilla, he would simply back away.

Her lips curved up into a wide smile. "You have no idea how that pleases me. Latham is an idiot. He will never do." She sighed. "But I must think on it."

Nick didn't like her hesitation. Perhaps she was an actress worthy of the stage, and she was using him. It was something to consider. He leaned over and brushed his lips across hers. "I will leave you to ponder."

"Stop by tomorrow for afternoon tea."

He rose to his full height, bowed, pivoted around, and forced himself to stroll out of the room at a normal pace, but he couldn't get out of there fast enough. His stomach churned, and his head hurt from the tension of it all. Hurrying to the mews, he retrieved Bandit and returned home for the first time since leaving early that morning.

He made haste in ordering a bath hoping to wash the vile scent of Emma off his body. It didn't take long for him be sitting in hot water with half a crystal decanter of whisky and glass resting on a stool beside him, since he planned to get good and drunk. He hoped to fall asleep and make the time go by and numb his mind from all the terrifying visions of what might be happening to Priscilla. Where was she? Was she hungry? Cold? Frightened? Of course, she was frightened. How could she not be?

"Damn it all to hell," he mumbled as he leaned forward in the tub, grasping his head in his hands. It was going to be a long, torturous night. Both for him and, worse, for Priscilla.

"Hughes," he bellowed, "my robe, please. And have cook send up a tray. Nothing heavy. My stomach won't handle it."

When his valet left to request a dinner tray, Nick stepped out of the tub, dried off and threw on his robe, tying the sash around his waist. Grabbing the glass and the whisky he'd yet to touch, he moved to his favorite over-stuffed chair and filled his glass almost to the top. No sense pretending he wasn't going to finish every drop of liquid in the decanter.

When his dinner tray arrived, chicken stew and a sweet roll, he forced himself to eat as he didn't remember the last time he'd had a sustenance. The stew and roll went down without incident and would help soak up the whisky. Hughes returned, turned down his bed, and removed the tray without a word. Hughes knew when not to bother him and Nick was forever grateful for his service.

An hour went by with Nick staring into the unlit fireplace. The wall clock ticked in perfect rhythm reminding him time was moving, but at a slow pace. Not a drop of whisky remained in the decanter or his glass which had both been discarded onto the carpet with a soft thud. He inhaled and exhaled as he readied himself to move from the chair to his bed across the room. Using the arms of the chair he pushed himself to his feet, swayed, and landed back in the chair. He tried again and this time he managed to weave his way to his bed, where he plopped face down and welcomed the oblivion that descended down around him, and he knew nothing more until Hughes came back.

"Good morning, my lord. Or should I say good afternoon?" Hughes's voice, although spoken quietly, made Nick feel as though the man had yelled directly in his ears. He shuddered at the pounding ache in his head. His stomach didn't feel well and his tongue stuck to the roof of his mouth. The taste was dreadful.

"There is nothing good about it," Nick groaned as he struggled to sit up. "What time is it?"

"It is nearly two."

He blinked several times trying to clear his vision and was thankful the curtains were closed blocking out most of the sunlight. "Any messages for me?"

"Unfortunately, no. I would've woken you immediately if there had been any word." Hughes placed a tray on the nightstand closest to him and the aroma of coffee had him almost smiling. "Mrs. Meadows made you her special concoction. You should feel better once you drink it and have something to eat. I will be back to help you wash up and dress shortly, my lord."

Nick pulled his body closer to the night table and his breakfast tray. His hand hovered over the black coffee for a moment, but sighing, he picked up the disgusting tasting remedy from Mrs. Meadows instead and guzzled it down at once. It shocked his insides, and he let it settle for a few minutes, in case it came back up. When it didn't, he ate a piece of toast with jam. And when that didn't turn his stomach, he picked up his coffee, stood and went to the window, and slowly opened the curtains hoping the light wouldn't pierce his eyeballs. A dull gray day lay outside the window. It matched his mood, as concern and fear for Priscilla, always a constant worry, increased immensely. He tried like hell not to dwell on it. How petrified she must be at the mercy of her kidnappers and wondering what they would do to her.

The drink and toast in his stomach churned around and around but stayed down as he swallowed and breathed repeatedly. He reached out and placed the palm of his hand on the cool glass and whispered, "Please, don't let them hurt her."

CHAPTER TWENTY-THREE

THE DAY CREPT on. Nick forced himself to sit in his study and go over the accounts to his properties and reread several messages from his estate manager, but his eyes and mind didn't comprehend a thing. No matter how he tried to distract himself, he failed. Several times during the course of the late afternoon, he thought about taking to the streets of London on horseback, yelling Priscilla's name over and over like a town crier.

Around six in the evening a short, scribbled message came from Whitcomb, stating he had nothing new to report yet but hoped to later. Anger and despair tore through him, he ripped the note to shreds. He scribbled several notes of his own and rang for a footman to deliver them immediately. One was to Emma begging his forgiveness for missing afternoon tea and stating he would stop by that night.

When darkness finally descended upon the streets of London, Nick's body vibrated with the need to escape the confines of his study and his townhouse. Fortunately for him, he had someplace to be. He hurried down the hallway to his front door and mumbled, "Send for the carriage. I'm going out," to Bradley.

When the carriage came around, he donned his jacket, flew through the door, and nearly tumbled down the stairs in his haste to be on his way. As his coach pulled up to Blackstone Manor at half past nine, he hoped Langford, Caldwell, and Whitcomb had already arrived. The three men hadn't replied to his message, so he took that as an indication they were able to attend. The only person he had heard back from, confirming having the meeting at Blackstone Manor, was Blackstone. If everything went according to his plan, he would arrive at Norton Hall at half past ten and know something about Priscilla shortly after.

Before he could knock, the door opened, and the butler greeted him. "His Grace is expecting you. Come this way." Blackstone was standing looking out a window in the drawing room Nick was led into. A room he'd been in many times before.

"See anything interesting outside?"

"Your carriage." He turned briefly to his butler. "Send everyone else in when they arrive, Winters."

"Yes, Your Grace."

"How are you faring?" Blackstone asked Nick as Winters left.

"Not good."

"What did you do all day?"

"Why don't we wait for the others? That way I only have to explain once." Nick went to the sideboard. "Can I help myself to your fine brandy?"

"Go ahead and pour me one as well," Blackstone said as he pivoted to face him, his arms across his chest. "Do you have good news or bad?"

Not knowing how to answer, Nick handed Blackstone his drink and shrugged his shoulders.

The duke held up his glass and said, "Well, that sums up things, doesn't it?"

"Winters said to see ourselves in," Langford said as he arrived with Caldwell and Latham.

Christ, he wasn't in the mood for Latham. But it seemed he couldn't get away from the scoundrel. And he *was* a scoundrel no matter how he pretended otherwise.

"Help yourselves to a drink, and let's hope Whitcomb arrives soon."

"I'm here, Your Grace," Whitcomb said as he went to the

sideboard and took the glass Langford held out. "Thank you."

"Please, everyone, sit," Blackstone said.

"Thank you for coming on such short notice," Nick said. "I was hoping you had good news to share, Whitcomb?"

The Runner sat, sipped his drink, and cleared his throat. "Excuse me. I have a tickle in my throat today. This brandy should help nicely. And yes, I have much to share. My men have watched Viscountess Norton's home for twenty-four hours, and she hasn't left. Although several people have come and gone." He paused and cleared his throat again. "We have witnessed two large men who appear quite out of place come and go. Besides them, Lords Hollingsworth and Latham each made appearances."

All eyes turned to Latham, but he remained quiet. Nick spoke up, "Why did you go there, Latham?"

"I told her I was joining her business venture and your threats of ruination be damned. I tried to get her to open up." He downed the contents of his glass. "She doesn't trust me. Her trust doesn't come easily. She mentioned your visit, and how you want to replace me as her partner. She suspects your motives behind it." Standing, he went to the sideboard and helped himself to another brandy. After he returned to his seat, he said, "Like I said, she has trust issues. It may take time to gain it."

"We don't have time," Nick bellowed. "We don't even know if she has Priscilla." Nick turned to Whitcomb, his brows raised. "Do we?"

"Not for a fact, no."

"Where does that leave us?" Blackstone asked.

Nick groaned. "She may not trust me completely, but it doesn't matter. I'm visiting her tonight. I'll tie her up if I have to, but I'm scouring that house one room at a time until I find Priscilla. And if I come up empty, we start over tomorrow with a new plan, new ideas."

"I have something to add," Whitcomb said. "My men and I will be outside by the servants' entrance. When the viscountess is asleep, let us in. Those men who visited her are armed, and so are we. You can't go alone in your search for Lady Priscilla. You are likely to become a liability."

"I doubt that," Nick shrugged. "But I'll let you in. I need all the help I can get. On another topic, Latham, we need your list. It has to be destroyed. Whitcomb and I will find and destroy the viscountess's list tonight. Let us hope there are only two. If that list lands in the wrong hands, that person has the means to ruin or blackmail many members of the *ton*."

Latham glanced at Caldwell and shook his head. "Caldwell burned it."

"Good."

"Can I add something?" Caldwell asked. "I admit I scanned the list, and was stunned by the prominent names I read. Shocked, really, at how well Norton ran his scheme and how many well-known and connected gentlemen were bilked out of money." He looked at Hollingsworth and winced. "Apologies if what I said insulted you."

"Not at all. Glad I was in good company." He grimaced. "Not really. I'd rather it hadn't happened to me or any of them."

"The Duke of Avery," Caldwell added, "was one of the first to fall for Norton's scheme. Could that be why Lady Priscilla was taken? To collect a ransom?"

Nick hurried to speak. "I don't think that is the most likely scenario. Otherwise, why not just blackmail Avery? Why take Priscilla at all? Not to mention there has been no demand for ransom, which doesn't coincide with that logic." He took the last sip of his brandy. "Which comes back to the likelihood that she's punishing me by taking Priscilla."

"I'm confused," Langford interjected. "Why have no demands been made for Lady Priscilla's return?"

"Right," Blackstone added.

Nick threw up his hands. "Bloody hell, I don't know. All I do know is I have a gut feeling that Viscountess Norton took Priscilla to get me under her thumb. She wants us to marry and continue what she and Norton had." He groaned. "That is why I'm heading there to seduce her, restrain her, and find Lady Priscilla." He stood and looked right at Whitcomb. "Are you coming?"

"Yes," Whitcomb replied.

"Is there anything you need us to do?" Caldwell asked.

"If it all goes to bloody hell, and I die, promise me you won't give up until you find Lady Priscilla," Nick said with a shudder.

THE DARKNESS AND airlessness of the room closed in on Priscilla. She had never been afraid of the dark. Until now. There was a significant difference between the darkness within the safety of one's bedroom and the darkness of the unknown. Yes, she knew what the room looked like, but it felt unfamiliar. And the sounds and movements from beyond the closed door in the hall were unsettling. Knowing that one of the giant men had access to her left her trembling and worried for her safety. He could do anything to her anytime, and Esmeralda, Viscountess Norton, would be none the wiser.

"Stop it," she moaned. "Don't think such things." It was far easier said than done. She had nothing but time for her mind to play all sorts of tricks on her. She'd always had a vivid imagination, and it plagued her like a curse right now.

To keep herself sane, she decided to play a game. For every sound, creak, or noise she heard, she would name what it was. She may be up in the attic but could hear many sounds from the corridor beyond her door as well as below.

Numerous footsteps creaked outside her door. Easy—her guards were exchanging roles.

The sound of his heavy footfalls descending the stairs came next.

Priscilla closed her eyes and concentrated on the flow of movement and sound unique to this house. Muffled voices traveled upstairs, along with very soft footsteps and a door opening and closing. Her captor had a visitor. So it couldn't be as late as she'd originally thought. More muffled voices mixed with female laughter. Footsteps on the second floor traveled to the third, right below her. She sat up, her stomach fluttering with excitement. Perhaps if she banged the floor repeatedly, her guest would demand to know . . . something . . . anything. She blew out her breath—stupid idea. Whoever was here probably worked with the lady and knew all about her.

She lay back down, thinking about tomorrow. She would inspect the windows which were nailed shut with boards and see if she could pry them off somehow. She couldn't spend another day here without trying to escape.

"MY DEAR, NICHOLAS," Emma, said as she moved into the entry hall. "It is late. I was going to retire."

His lips curved into an enticing smile. "That is what I hoped for." He leaned close to her ear. "You invited me into your bed yesterday. And I couldn't think of anything all day but being with you. I'm hoping the offer still stands. You can have me for the entire night if you so wish." He blew gently against her neck.

Without saying anything, she entwined her hand with his and led him up two flights of stairs to the first door on the right and straight into her chambers. She sashayed around the room, extinguishing several candles, leaving the room in a soft glow from two remaining ones. "Would you care for a nightcap?"

"If you'll join me," he said, wondering how many drinks she needed to consume before she would be drunk.

"But of course," she replied, pouring two glasses from a decanter sitting on a night table, and held one out to him. *How convenient having it beside the bed.*

Nick forced his feet forward, took the glass from her and downed the liquid and returned the glass to the night table. He watched silently as she did the same. Moving close behind her, he buried his head in her hair, inhaling. "You smell divine. Good enough to eat."

"I certainly hope so," she giggled.

He kissed his way down the side of her neck. A moan escaped her lips as her head tilted to one side. "That feels wonderful."

As he continued to kiss and nip his way down her neck, he slid her robe off her shoulders, his hands continued down her arms until he held her hands behind her back. His free hand pulled several neck cloths from his jacket pocket. All the while his mouth stayed on her skin to distract her. With his heart pounding inside his chest, he quickly tied her hands together.

"What are you doing?" she queried, her voice high pitched.

"Just having a little fun, my dear," he replied. "You will enjoy yourself, I promise." Before she could react, he stuffed a cloth in her mouth, and she knew this wasn't just about fun. He struggled to pick her up with her legs thrashing about wildly. Her feet and knees connected with his body and he shook off the pain. Finally, he made it to the side of her bed, where he tossed her as gently as he could on top of the covers. He had no intention of hurting her, only subduing her. Her legs were flailing as moans tried to escape her cloth-filled mouth. Her eyes, wide with fear and hatred, never looked away from him.

"I'm sorry. I have to do this." Every time he had her ankles together she showed renewed strength until finally he succeeded in tying them together. When this idea had come to him, he'd almost decided to bring strong rope for the job, but he didn't want to burn or mar her skin. Not that she deserved gentleness, if she had Priscilla. But the gentleman in him wouldn't allow it.

He moved her body so she was on her side and checked the knots—secure but not too tight. Leaving her side he rummaged around in her dressing room, found several useful sashes and used one to wrap around her mouth so the cloth wouldn't fall out and knot it behind her head. Bending her knees back, he tied her hands to her ankles.

"Once again, please accept my apologies if you have nothing

to do with Lady Priscilla's disappearance." Then, without another thought to her, he carefully snuck out of the room and down two flights of stairs. Fortunately, Norton Hall had candelabras lining the halls, so he could see where he was going. Also, many of the townhomes in London had similar floor plans, making it easy to find the servants' entrance. Opening the door, he let in Whitcomb and one other Runner. Whitcomb ordered the two other Runners to stay outside standing guard.

"The main stairs are this way." Nick pointed. "We must be careful."

"I want to check the cellar first," Whitcomb stated. "You two stay here while I go to the kitchen."

By the time Whitcomb returned, every nerve in Nick's body quivered, ready to do anything to rescue Priscilla.

"She's not down there," Whitcomb said. "Follow me to the stairs, we're going to start at the attic. I don't think she would be held anywhere on main floors." He removed a pistol from his jacket pocket as they made their way silently toward the main staircase.

Nick didn't want to say anything, but he thought it odd that they ran into no servants. He knew the butler was here somewhere. Though even when he was with Emma, he hadn't encountered anyone but him. Had she given the rest of the servants the night off? It certainly worked to their advantage.

When they reached the stairs to the attic, Nick sighed with relief. The stairs were not elaborate but closed on both sides, affording them some cover as they ascended.

Whitcomb paused halfway up and put a finger to his lips. "Stay here," he whispered. "I'm going to take a look. I'll signal when it's safe to proceed."

Every nerve in Nick's body tingled, and his mind screamed to move forward. Instead, he took a deep breath and waited, his eyes narrowed on Whitcomb for any sign. The Runner reached the top step, looked around the wall, and snapped back, his body tight against the wall, his finger went to his lips again. He waited for several seconds before slowly moving to where Nick and the other runner anxiously waited.

"One large man," Whitcomb whispered softer than Nick had ever heard anyone whisper before, yet he understood every word. "Sitting on a chair outside the last door on the left. There's a pistol resting on his lap. He may have another I can't see." Whitcomb wiped the sweat from his brow. "He'll see us coming. We need a diversion to draw him away from the door."

"I'll go," Nick whispered back. Priscilla must be there. What else could the man be guarding? "I'll come up with something to send him down the stairs. Be ready."

Nick, his heart beating like a drum inside his chest, climbed the rest of the stairs. When he entered the hallway, he said, "You there, I'm Hollingsworth—" Before he could finish, the thug stood and pointed his pistol at his chest. "Easy there. Viscountess Norton sent me. She wants a word with you."

"Where is she?"

"I'll take you to her." The man remained still. "Would I be here if she didn't trust me?" Nick said, trying to look annoyed instead of nervous as hell. "We'd better hurry. She appeared anxious to speak with you." Nick waived his arm. "After you."

The man's beady eyes narrowed, but he began to move. However, he kept the pistol in his hand. Nick hoped like hell Whitcomb was prepared.

As they approached the stairs, Whitcomb and the other Runner rushed the burly man from the front, knocking him on his back. The arm holding the pistol rose, and Nick kicked it out of his hands, sending it sliding across the corridor.

"Good work," Whitcomb said as he and the Runner stuffed something in the man's mouth and tied his hands and feet together. Whitcomb checked the man's pockets and held up a key.

Nick almost fell to his knees in gratitude. Instead, he grabbed the key, ran down the hall to the door the man had been sitting in front of, shoved the key in the lock, and turned it. The sound of it clicking was the greatest sound he'd ever heard. With shaking hands and a pounding heart, he turned the door handle. He took a deep breath to prepare him for whatever he found on the other side. For all he knew, Priscilla could be elsewhere. Or she could be . . .

"Hurry," Whitcomb said. "We can't waste time."

That was all Nick needed to snap him out of his fear. He opened the door and squinted into the darkness. The only light filtering into the room came from the hall, making it hard to see. "Priscilla?"

"Nick? Oh my God, Nick, is that you?"

"Easy there, my lord," Whitcomb said as Nick staggered when Priscilla slammed into him, her arms wrapped tightly around his neck.

"Priscilla," he breathed as he took a moment to hug her close. "We must go."

"Follow close behind me and Burton and do what I say," Whitcomb said. "We'll get both of you to safety and return for the list."

Nick held Priscilla's hand tightly. Nothing would separate them. All was well until they neared the servants' entrance and encountered another large man blocking the exit door with a pistol in each hand aimed at them. "Stop, or I shoot."

Whitcomb and Burton stood close together directly in front of the man. They were protecting Nick and Priscilla with their bodies. Both Runners aimed their pistols at the man. Whitcomb said in a demanding voice, "Move aside and let us go, and nobody gets hurt. If not, you have two choices. The first one is I arrest you, and you rot to death in Newgate, or better still, hang at the gallows. The second: I shoot you, and you die."

The man's hands held steady, and his features were in shadow, making it impossible for Nick to judge his thoughts, but after a moment he spoke. "If you're looking for help from your men who were outside, forget it. They're out cold. If I let you go, Viscountess Norton will kill me."

"Not if I tie you up as I did your cohort."

The sound of hurried footsteps coming up behind them from the front of the house, had Nick reacting. He stepped in front of Priscilla so she was now between him and the Runners. He reached behind his back and gripped her waist so she wouldn't move. Latham approached with a pistol in one hand while Emma came up beside him.

"What is this, Hollingsworth?" Latham demanded.

Nick hadn't felt the urge to pummel someone into a bloody mess since Eton. Until now. And Latham would deserve each and every punch he landed. "I should be asking you that question, Latham."

"I would've been here sooner to warn Emma if my brother hadn't detained me with all this nonsense about the viscountess and Priscilla. The two of you—no, make that the four of you, as Blackstone and Langford are no better—make me sick with your goodness."

Nick should have trusted his instincts, knowing Latham hadn't changed.

"Kill them," Viscountess Norton said with a hateful sneer Nick could see even in the dim lighting.

Nick's hands tightened on Priscilla's waist when he heard her gasp. He needed to protect her. She was too precious to die. Whitcomb moved, ever so slowly. He came forward to stand beside Nick, his pistol aimed at Latham's chest. Nick assumed Burton still faced the man behind them. Three guns to two. They were not the best odds. Just then, Nick felt the cold steel of a gun brush up against his hand. He gripped it but didn't let Latham see he was armed. They needed an advantage here.

"Kill them," she said again.

"If Latham so much as twitches," Whitcomb said with his gun aimed at the viscountess now. "I'll shoot you."

Latham's hand dropped slightly, not a sure grip on the pistol. Nick took the opportunity. He whispered to Whitcomb, "Take care of Lady Priscilla." Then he pushed his gun into Priscilla's hand right before he rushed Latham. Both men crashed into the wall from the force of Nick's attack and struggled over control of Latham's weapon.

Nick didn't dare look at Priscilla. He had to trust Whitcomb to keep her safe. All he knew was he heard other struggles as well and Emma yelling over and over, "Kill them!"

Latham was stronger than Nick had believed. The fight to control the pistol took everything Nick had as he worked to keep it from aiming at anyone and going off.

"You will not win," Latham growled, his face red and his neck muscles bulging.

Not bothering to answer, which would take too much energy, Nick finally seized the gun from Latham's hand. He spun around. The sound of a gunshot rang out. A burning pain sliced his upper arm. Even with his ears ringing, he heard the heavy thud of a body falling behind him. Nick aimed the gun he had taken from Latham to where Emma had stood, but she had vanished. Another shot echoed inside the hallway, the stench of gunpowder strong and repugnant. Smoke filled the air.

"Priscilla!" Nick bellowed, swatting at the cloud of smoke.

"I'm fine." She took several hurried steps, wrapped her arms around his waist, and held tight. "I believe Latham is dead."

Nick turned around. Latham lay on his back, his eyes open and sightless. A large hole in his chest oozed blood. He didn't know what to think. He had never cared for the man, but he'd never wanted him dead.

"You're bleeding," Priscilla said with concern as she touched his left upper arm just below his shoulder. He sucked in air to prevent him from screaming out in pain. The bullet that grazed his arm must have killed Latham. But who had fired? "A fine time to not wear a cravat." She bent down, tore a piece of cloth from the hem of her night rail, and wrapped it tightly around his arm. "This should do until your physician can look at it."

"Whitcomb," Nick called out as he pulled Priscilla alongside him. She was surprisingly calm, considering the dead body close by. Not to mention his bleeding arm. Perhaps she was in shock. However, she didn't appear so. "What happened while I struggled with Latham?"

Before Whitcomb answered, he opened the door, and Nick saw the two Runners they left outside, crumpled on the ground. Whitcomb approached them, placing his hands on each of their chests and came back. "Burton, ride off for the constable." Then he turned to Nick. "Burton protected Priscilla while I engaged the giant of a man. Bloody hell, he was strong. His gun went off in the struggle and hit Latham. Then I shot him." His eyes widened. "Is that blood seeping through that bandage?"

"Yes. The bullet that killed Latham grazed me. I'll be fine."

"Thank goodness. I wasn't sure we were going to survive."

"Me either," Nick said as he hugged Priscilla close with his good arm. "If you don't need us, I'd like to take Lady Priscilla home. We can meet with the constable tomorrow if he has any questions."

"Go. I'll take it from here." His eyes traveled out the door, "Good, my men are stirring. Hopefully they can help me find the viscountess, and get that list of hers. Meanwhile, who will inform Caldwell about his brother?"

"Christ, I hadn't thought about that."

"Go. I'll visit him when I leave here. You need that arm looked at."

"Thank you," Nick said, making eye contact with Whitcomb. "I owe you a debt of gratitude."

CHAPTER TWENTY-FOUR

SITTING INSIDE NICK'S carriage, her body resting against his, Priscilla began to shake, and tears rained down her cheeks. While she had been held inside that room, she had been scared. But nothing had prepared her for how terrified she had been while Nick and Latham had struggled for control of the pistol. She didn't think she blinked once while the fight took place. Poor Burton had been trying to keep her safe and out of firing range, and all she did was try to get free and go to Nick's aid. Which, of course, would have been a stupid thing to do. It would have put both Nick and her in danger.

When the gun exploded from close behind her, and she witnessed Latham go down, she had almost fallen to her knees with relief. Until she saw the blood staining Nick's upper arm. She had needed to go to him, touch him, feel his heartbeat beneath her palm, and see the rise and fall of his chest.

In fact, *terrified* didn't begin to describe the emotional onslaught that had taken over her mind and body. She was proud of herself for remaining calm in the moment, though. It wasn't every day a lady saw two dead bodies. If ever.

But now that they were safe, it was a different story. Her chest heaved with silent sobs trying to escape, and she didn't know how long she could hold them back.

Giving up, she wrapped her arms around Nick's waist, mindful of his injured arm. She leaned her head on his good shoulder and let the big gulping sobs escape. This was Nick; she didn't need to be embarrassed if she cried all over him.

He rubbed his head against the top of hers. "There, there. Let it out. You deserve a good cry after all you've been through." He cleared his throat, and she thought he might also be crying. "I have never been so petrified in all my life as when you were taken. I thought I would die if I never saw you again. I was ready to tear apart anyone, limb from limb, if they did anything to prevent me from finding you. I was crazed with worry."

"I thought about you constantly, but I didn't want you worrying about me. I didn't want to cause you pain if the worst happened. I hated that someone had kidnapped me, hurting the people I love most." She sniffled. "I was afraid I'd never get to tell you again that I love you."

He kissed the top of her head. "I was afraid of the same thing. I was a bloody arse for not telling you what I felt for you when you were eighteen. And then again, when you came out of mourning. Which, to be fair, was only recently."

"Yes?" she prompted him.

"I love you. My heart, my soul, my life belongs to you."

"As mine does to you." Her heart was ready to burst.

"Will you do me the honor of marrying me and becoming my marchioness?"

She couldn't help herself. She started to giggle.

"What's so funny?"

Was she a terrible person for enjoying hearing the touch of panic in Nick's voice? "My answer is yes." She tipped her face up and kissed him. "I was laughing because I was taken back to when I was ten and stated that I would be your marchioness."

"I'm glad you can pronounce it now."

"Can we get married right away? I don't think I can wait."

This time, he kissed her. "Eager to have me back in your bed, are we?"

"There is that. I want to spend the entire night in your

arms—every night. Is it selfish of me not to want to wait for the banns to be posted?" She rubbed her head against his shoulder. "But mostly, I'm worried something may suddenly materialize and keep our wedding from happening."

He turned on the seat and cupped her cheek with his good hand. He looked into her eyes with love in his. "I'll go tomorrow for the special license." He kissed her, and she felt his love for her resonate through the kiss. It transcended time and place. "I love you so much." He kissed her quickly. "Your parents have probably been beside themselves since we arrived ten minutes ago."

"We must hurry."

Nick tapped the roof, and the driver opened the door and lowered the steps. Nick struggled to exit the coach, but he waved off any assistance. He held his hand out to Priscilla, and she took it. No sooner was she standing outside the carriage than her parents engulfed her, all three crying, while Nick stood nearby, grinning as tears slid down his cheeks.

"Thank God you are home safe," her father said as he stepped back. Her mother placed her arm around her waist, keeping her close.

"Yes. Thank God," her mother said, wiping her tears with her free hand. "Nicholas, we can't thank you enough for bringing our daughter home to us."

"Yes," her father added. "Anything you want, just name it."

Nick met her eyes, winked, and then looked at her father. "As a matter of fact, Your Grace, I want to marry your daughter as soon as next week. Assuming I have your permission?"

Her father slapped Nick on the back, and Nick clenched his teeth. Priscilla could only imagine how the jarring made his arm ache. "Of course, my boy, you have our blessing." He paused and frowned, squinting at Nick's arm. "Were you injured? Why didn't you say anything? Let's get you inside and send for our physician right away."

Her father ordered a footman to ride for the doctor and not

return without him. Once in the drawing room, Priscilla and Nick sat on the settee while her mother ordered refreshments and her father poured drinks at the sideboard. He handed all four of them brandy. "I think we could all use a drink."

"I most certainly could," Nick said as he downed his. "Do you mind sending word to my mother? Tell her Priscilla is safe, and I'll return home shortly."

"Yes," her father said as he left the room. He soon returned and filled Nick's glass again.

"About this wedding," her mother said with a smile and tears in her eyes. "We are beyond thrilled. But in a week? Planning a wedding takes time."

"Mother, Father," she said as she held Nick's hand. "We have waited a long time already. *I* have waited a lifetime to marry Nick. We don't want to wait any longer. There is no need for a fussy ceremony. And we only want our closest friends and family in attendance."

"If that is what you both want, then that is how it shall be," her mother said.

"I will procure a special license tomorrow," Nick said.

After the physician came, cleaned, stitched, and bandaged Nick's arm, they found themselves alone at last. "How does your arm feel?" Priscilla asked, her head resting on his good shoulder.

"Good, now that I've had several drinks."

Her hand rested on his chest right over his beating heart. "Do you think anyone will miss us if we sneak up to my chambers?"

Not only did she hear him laugh, but her hand felt the vibration from inside his chest. "I believe they will."

"A week is a long time to wait."

He placed his hand over hers. "Patience, my love. Once we are wed, we have a lifetime to spend together."

CHAPTER TWENTY-FIVE

The Wedding

PRISCILLA AWOKE ON her wedding day feeling jittery and anxious for the ceremony. She had dreamed of this day for so long that she had trouble believing it was finally here. The day she would marry her best friend—the gentleman she had loved for most of her life. Even as a young girl, she had felt that puppy love. Then that had blossomed into a young lady's love as she grew older. But when she prepared for her first Season, her hopes of being his marchioness died a slow, torturous death. She had married Jasper and truly hoped for a long life with him. But now it seemed fate had other plans.

She stretched her arms over her head, then hugged herself and smiled. She wondered if Nick was as anxious as she was.

There was a knock on the door, and Eugenia's voice called out, "I have your breakfast tray." Eugenia let herself in and placed the tray on the nightstand. "After you eat, we'll prepare for your wedding, my lady." Her maid walked to the windows and swung open the curtains. "Such a lovely day for a ceremony. I'll return shortly."

Priscilla nibbled on her toast with jam and drank her tea. When her maid returned, she helped her dress in the beautiful gown Madame Serena had made in the most exquisite cream silk with intricate seed pearl flowers sewn across the hemline and waist.

Now that she was dressed, Priscilla sat at her dressing table while Eugenia fixed her hair into an elaborate coiffure adorned with pearl pins. As her maid put in the last pin, her mother entered, looking splendid in a deep-blue gown and wearing the family's sapphires.

"You look beautiful, Mother."

Last night at dinner, her father had gifted Priscilla with his mother's pearl choker, bracelet, and earrings, and Priscilla wore them now. Standing before the looking glass, her hand flew to her chest. She could hardly recognize herself. She looked beautiful. Was this how Nick saw her?

"It is time, my dear. The guests are assembled, and your father is waiting out in the corridor," her mother said, wiping tears from her eyes. "You look like a princess." Her mother kissed her cheek. "I am so happy for you. I pray for a long and prosperous marriage. Eugenia, could you excuse us?"

As the maid left, her mother took Priscilla's hands into hers and smiled. "I know you will think I'm crazy, but I have the strangest feeling in my heart that you conceived a child the night I saw Nicholas sneaking from your room."

Priscilla couldn't find the words to reply to her mother's instincts. She also had the feeling as well. It wasn't something she could explain. It was just an intuition and an awareness that something was changing inside her body. "I love you, Mother."

"Oh, my dear girl, I love you. I wish to hug you but don't want to wrinkle your dress. We will hug later after your nuptials."

On her father's arm, Priscilla descended two sets of stairs to the parlor entrance adjoining the dining room, where they paused outside the closed double doors. Her legs trembled, and her heart beat a fast staccato. It wasn't nerves but excitement at finally marrying the man of her heart.

"Are you ready, my dear?" her father said with a suspicious catch in his voice.

She understood. Her emotions were getting to her as well. "I am more than ready."

Her father signaled a footman. The double doors swung open, and the room hushed as all eyes turned to them. Priscilla's eyes went to Nick, dressed formally, standing beside the officiant, and her heart calmed. One glance at his smiling face and his loving brown eyes had all her jitters from earlier disappearing. They never broke eye contact as she walked down the aisle created by three rows of chairs that were full of their friends and family.

When they stood before Nick, her father kissed her cheek and joined her mother in the front row.

Nick whispered, "You look beautiful."

Her cheeks heated, and she suddenly felt shy. "You look handsome as ever."

He mouthed, "I love you."

And she blushed deeper as she mouthed, "I love you."

They were so captivated by one another that they didn't notice the officiant had started the ceremony until he asked Priscilla to repeat her vows. Several chuckles could be heard from their guests. When Nick said his vows, he placed a stunning emerald and diamond ring on her finger, which her mother told her had belonged to Nick's grandmother. It brought tears to her eyes.

Soon everyone was cheering and wishing them well as they entered the dining room for the wedding breakfast.

They sat beside each other at the center of the table, surrounded by everyone they cared about: the Duke and Duchess of Blackstone, Nick's mother, Lord and Lady Langford, and Mr. and Mrs. James Caldwell, and of course her parents, who sat at either end of the table as the hosts.

Priscilla could hardly keep up with the conversation going around the table. Her mind was on leaving for Hollingsworth House. Her new home. She was the Marchioness of Hollingsworth. Her hands shook as she realized her life would never be the same. She would never live with her parents ever again.

She expected to feel sad, and she was, but the excitement of starting her life with Nick took precedence over anything else. She loved him with everything she had and couldn't wait to share that love.

WHEN NICK HAD first seen Priscilla enter the parlor, all the air escaped his lungs. He became breathless from her beauty, and knowing she would soon be his had only added to the intensity in the most extraordinary way possible.

She had glided up the aisle, her smile only for him as his grin was for her. The beat of his heart had accelerated, making him wonder if all the guests could hear it. He'd held her hands during their vows, knowing they would anchor each other for all eternity. The past week had been torturous, as his arm began to heal and they prepared for this day. The waiting and the anticipation had nearly undone him, but their moment had finally arrived.

Thankfully, Priscilla had never completely stopped loving him, and he would cherish her and prove his love for her for as long as he lived. He silently vowed to himself that he would be a better man, that he would be the man Priscilla deserved. He would no longer be a damaged person with a defective heart.

Sitting beside her at the center of the table now, his hand resting on her thigh, he wondered how long they needed to stay. He didn't want to disrespect his new mother- and father-in-law, but he needed to get his bride alone.

He leaned close and whispered, "How long before we can leave?"

Her hand moved beneath the table, covering his and squeezing. "There's only one course left. I think we can leave."

Nick didn't wait another second. He stood, almost knocking his chair over in his haste, then helped Priscilla up from her chair. "I want to thank the Duke and Duchess of Avery for hosting our wedding and this wonderful breakfast. My wife and I want to thank you for celebrating this special day with us. We bid you good day." He took Priscilla's hand in his, brought it up to his mouth, and kissed it. "I'm taking my bride home."

They left to cheers, clinking glasses, and well wishes.

They held hands, laughing their way through the house, out the door, and into their carriage. "Home, Fitzroy," Nick said as the driver shut the door. "Come here, dear wife."

Priscilla giggled as she sat on his lap, her arms wrapped around his neck. One of his hands circled her waist, keeping her secure, while the other ran up and down her arm and he ignored the little sting of pain from his wound. "Have I thanked you for never giving up on me?

"You thanked me, but I'm not opposed to you thanking me again," she whispered with a coquettish look as she rubbed her bottom against the bulge in his trousers. That was something he'd been fighting since he'd woken up that morning, knowing they would spend the entire night in each other's arms.

"You little minx," he moaned as he slipped the hand of his good arm up the inside of her skirts to the opening in her pantaloons.

She gasped, "There isn't time."

Chuckling, Nick said, "There is." He crushed his lips to hers, tasting her, leaving no part of her mouth or lips untouched or unexplored. He familiarized himself with the taste of his new wife. And to his surprise, she tasted better than ever. She made little purring sounds as his fingers spread her folds and his thumb teased her nub. Over and over, he brought her close, then eased until she broke their kiss and buried her head in his neck, gasping and moaning.

"Nicholas," she breathed.

He gave her what she wanted. Her entire body vibrated as she climaxed. Nick held her tight to his heart as she finally relaxed in his arms. This exquisite woman that he would do anything for. If she asked for the stars, he would find a way to give them to her.

EPILOGUE

"DO YOU REMEMBER the day of our wedding?" Priscilla asked her husband of four years. It was their anniversary, and they were picnicking near a wildflower field on their country estate. Their two children, Thomas, the heir, age three, and Scarlett, ten months, were napping in the nursery.

Nick leaned across the blanket and kissed her cheek. "Best day of my life."

Her cheeks heated. "Mine as well. We never had a honeymoon."

Nick lay on the blanket on his back and held out his arms. "Come here."

She snuggled up against him. His arms immediately held her tight, and she sighed with contentment.

"Would you like to go on one now? We could tour the continent?" His lips found the sensitive spot beneath her ear that always made her melt.

"Not really. I was making a statement. I didn't and don't need a honeymoon. I feel as though we've been on one for the past four years. Besides, I don't want to leave the children. Hmmm, keep doing that, and you might get to have your way with me."

More kisses. "Do you promise?"

"Always. Why do you think I prepared our picnic so far from the estate where no one would see us?"

"My wife—always thinking of everything." His arms dropped to the blanket. "Climb on up, my love, I'm all yours."

Priscilla straddled his lap, her favorite place to be, and took them on a blissful journey filled with contentment, serenity, and pure, pure love.

THE END

About the Author

Christine Donovan is an International Bestselling Author who writes romance that touches the heart, soothes the soul and feeds the mind. In addition to writing historical romance set in the Regency era, she also writes contemporary romance.

When she landed her first job at sixteen as a cashier at a supermarket, the first thing she did each week on payday was stop at the local bookstore and buy the latest historical romance. It was a dream of hers back then to become a romance author.

She lives on the Southeast Coast of Massachusetts with her husband. She has four grown sons, two granddaughters, two cats, and a black lab named Luna. In her spare time, she can be found at the beach, reading, painting, or gardening. She loves to tackle DIY projects.

Website: authorchristinedonovan.com
Newletter: www.authorchristinedonovan.com/newsletter
Amazon: amazon.com/Christine-Donovan/e/B00APR743Y
Facebook: authorchristinedonovan
Instagram: christinedonovan6

9 781969 349164